A MURDER FOR THE B

The door to Don't Dilly-Dahlia was cl I knocked, not wanting to startle Bethany ing unannounced.

No one answered this door either. I tried knob, expecting it to be locked like the front, but the knob turned easily in my hand. I pushed the door open and stepped inside. The overhead light was off. The only sources of light were from the opened door and the tiny window over the sink.

"Bethany?"

Silence.

Where on earth was she? Why hadn't she called if she needed to reschedule? Since I was already inside, I'd wait a few minutes to see if she came back.

I strode across the room, hit the light switch, and turned around. My breath caught.

Bethany lay face-up on the floor near a work table. The front of her ivory-colored blouse had turned a violent shade of dark red. What appeared to be blood pooled around her body. Her eyes were wide open, staring at nothing.

My breath started coming in hitches. I felt like my insides had turned to ice.

Now I knew why Bethany had missed our appointment.

She was dead . . .

Books by Staci McLaughlin

GOING ORGANIC CAN KILL YOU

ALL NATURAL MURDER

GREEN LIVING CAN BE DEADLY

A HEALTHY HOMICIDE

MURDER MOST WHOLESOME

MARRIAGE IS PURE MURDER

Published by Kensington Publishing Corporation

Marriage Is Pure Murder

Staci McLaughlin

KENSINGTON PUBLISHING CORP.
http://www.kensingtonbooks.com

KENSINGTON BOOKS are published by

Kensington Publishing Corp.
119 West 40th Street
New York, NY 10018

ISBN-13: 978-0-7582-9492-0
ISBN-10: 0-7582-9492-1
First Kensington Mass Market Edition: June 2017

eISBN-13: 978-0-7582-9493-7
eISBN-10: 0-7582-9493-X
First Kensington Electronic Edition: June 2017

10 9 8 7 6 5 4 3 2 1

Printed in the United States of America

Chapter 1

I woke before my alarm rang, and practically hopped out of bed. With the workday looming before me and my wedding day approaching, my mind was already racing. After a quick shower, I donned a pair of blue jeans and a long-sleeved work shirt with *O'Connell Organic Farm and Spa* embroidered on the front pocket. I stuck my phone in my pocket, grabbed my sunglasses, and glanced around my bedroom to make sure I wasn't forgetting anything.

Satisfied, I headed to the kitchen for coffee. My younger sister, Ashlee, was already sitting at the table, clutching her cup of coffee with both hands. Her blond hair, three shades lighter than mine, was piled on top of her head in a frizzled mess.

She looked at me with bloodshot eyes. "Why is six-thirty so early in the morning?" she asked with a groan.

She wasn't an early riser on her best day, and I couldn't help needling her. "It's only early if you go to bed too late," I said in a loud voice. She winced at the noise. "Why are you up anyway?" I asked.

"My boss's cousin has a dog that needs an operation. Since he's doing it for free, my boss wanted to squeeze it in before our regular appointments and insisted the entire staff be there, too."

I poured myself a cup of coffee, added a spoonful of sugar, and took a sip. "Getting up early for work just this once won't kill you. I do it every day." I picked up one of my sneakers off the floor and slid my foot inside. "You could have gone to bed at a reasonable hour, you know."

She glowered at me. "I was on a date."

No surprise there. Ashlee was always dating guys she met at the vet's office where she worked, or that she met at the grocery store, or waiting in line at the coffee shop, or when friends set her up. Her main criteria for any guy seemed to be their hotness, as Ashlee herself would say.

"I had to stop by Brittany's on my way home," she said. "Logan and I met up with a bunch of his friends, and one of them is totally perfect for her. By the time I finished describing him, one of our favorite shows came on. Next thing I knew, it was after midnight."

"Just think," I said, tying my other shoe, "in another week and a half, you and Brittany will be sharing this place. You can tell her all about your dates the second you get home."

Ashlee shook her head, letting loose a cascade of hair on one side. "I still can't believe you and Jason are getting hitched. My sister, old and married already." She let out a pretend sob.

"Hey, I'm not even thirty."

"You will be in a few months. That means I only have three more years before my life is over, too."

I couldn't help but laugh. "Stop being so melodramatic. Being almost thirty isn't bad, even if I did yank out a gray hair the other day."

Ashlee's hand flew to her head. "Tell me you're joking. Am I going to start getting gray hairs, too?"

"You never know. Don't forget Uncle Fred's hair turned white at thirty-five. One of us could have gotten stuck with his genes."

"I bet it's because he got married so young. Weren't he and Aunt Lucy teenagers?" She grimaced, as if marrying that young was a death sentence. "And you're getting married at the farm. Where's the grand ballroom with the chandelier? The chocolate fountain? The swan ice sculpture?"

"I don't need a big shindig. The highlight of the day is that I'm marrying the guy I love. And let's not forget Jason and I are trying to keep this whole affair on a budget."

She made a face. "Budget, schmudget. Just wait until I get married. My wedding will be so awesome people will be tweeting about it for weeks. Facebook and Instagram will explode from all the pictures my friends will be posting." She held up a hand. "Not that I'm planning on getting stuck with the same guy anytime soon. I'll leave that to you."

"Thank you." I rose from my chair, placed my coffee cup in the sink, and pulled my jacket from the hall closet. "Make sure you don't sneak back to bed once I'm out the door."

Her eyes lit up, as if considering the suggestion.

If she did go back to bed, she'd better not count on me to stick around and wake her up. I had to get to work.

With a last good-bye, I stepped out of the apartment. The early-November morning brought a chill to my skin, and I stopped to pull on my jacket before I headed down the stairs to my Civic. It started without too much protest, and I soon found myself cruising down Main Street, Blossom Valley's major artery through the downtown. The town would never be as trendy or artsy as Mendocino, the seaside tourist destination just over the hill, but Blossom Valley had a homey, small-town vibe that I loved. Having only five thousand residents probably helped.

On my way past the Don't Dilly-Dahlia Flower Shop, I checked to see if anyone was there, but the place was closed at this early hour. I had an appointment during my lunch break with the owner, Bethany Lancaster, to go over final decisions about my wedding bouquet. With the big event only days away, I was getting down to the last-minute details.

I almost slammed on my brakes at the thought. While I'd had five months to savor Jason's proposal, the idea of my actually being married still seemed more like a hypothetical situation. The reality probably wouldn't sink in until I was walking down the aisle and saying, "I do."

I had met my fiancé, Jason Forrester, at the O'Connell farm after a guest was murdered there. It wasn't the most auspicious beginning to a relationship. As lead reporter for the *Blossom Valley Herald*, Jason had been so focused on the story that I'd found him pushy and overbearing when we'd first started talking, and I'd wanted nothing to do with him. Now, I couldn't picture my life without him.

Turning my attention to my driving, I merged onto the highway that led out to the farm. A few miles and three turns later, I pulled into the far corner of the farm's parking lot.

Esther O'Connell and her husband had always wanted to turn their modest farm into a bed-and-breakfast someday, but her husband had died before they could finish their plans. Esther had no experience in the hospitality business, but she'd decided to carry on their dream by adding a row of guest cabins, further developing the trails that wound through the back of the property, and making sure any meals served in the dining room used vegetables from her own garden. More recently, she'd added a spa, where guests could be pampered with facials and massages. I'd worked here as the marketing guru from the first day and practically considered the farm a second home.

I got out of my car and followed the side path past the vegetable garden and to the guest cabins. With the spa off to my right, I turned left and crossed the patio. I caught a whiff of the fragrant rosemary in the herb garden as I entered the farmhouse through the back door.

In the kitchen, Zennia Patrakio, the farm's healthy and organic-centric cook, sat at the kitchen table with a tray full of stuffed mushrooms near her elbow. Her long dark hair, with hints of gray, hung in a braid down her back, and Birkenstocks peeked out from under a long cotton skirt.

As a fast-food enthusiast from a young age, I'd been repulsed and slightly terrified by Zennia's tofu fish sticks and wheatgrass shots when I'd first started sampling her inventive cuisine. Lately, though, I often found her dishes downright tasty, even if she did use a ridiculous amount of vegetables.

I studied the contents of the cookie sheet. "You're serving stuffed mushrooms for breakfast?" I asked.

Zennia laughed. Her light, twinkly laugh always made me smile in return. "Of course not. My egg-white and broccoli casserole is in the oven. While I have a few minutes, I thought I'd experiment with a new appetizer." She picked up a mushroom. "Here, try one."

I stuffed the mushroom into my mouth and raised my eyebrows as the flavors of goat cheese and roasted red pepper exploded over my tongue. "Wow, this is really good, Zennia."

"I'm glad to hear you say that. If you think the mushrooms are delicious, then I'm sure your wedding guests will, too."

Zennia had witnessed Jason's marriage proposal and been absolutely thrilled when I'd said yes. Once she found out I'd be holding the reception here at the farm, she'd offered to cater the event.

I bent down and gave her a hug. "I can't thank you enough for everything you're doing for me."

She patted my back. "You're more than welcome. And I even promise to use plenty of butter and cheese, just this once. One day of eating all that saturated fat won't damage your arteries too much."

"And let's not forget the luscious cake with buttercream frosting from the Hand in the Cookie Jar bakery." I licked my lips as I remembered the cakes I'd sampled there.

Zennia cringed. "Maybe I'll add a vegetable platter to the menu." She checked the rooster clock on the wall and stood up. "But right now, I'd better finish getting breakfast ready for the guests."

"Need any help?" I asked.

She shook her head as she slipped on a pair of oven mitts. "I've got it covered, thanks."

I left Zennia to her preparations and headed out of the kitchen. Voices drifted toward me from the dining room, but I went straight into the office across the hall and sat down at the desk. While I waited for the computer to boot up, I hung my jacket on the back of the chair, put my purse in the bottom desk drawer, and checked my cell phone for messages.

I had a text from Jason, inviting me over tonight for home-cooked beef stroganoff. We spent almost every Friday night together, but we usually went to the Breaking Bread Diner for a burger or fish and chips. I felt a warm glow in my chest as I thought about how lucky I was to be marrying a man who made me homemade meals. I quickly texted back my acceptance; then I set the phone on the desk and started my workday.

As the sole marketing person, I performed a variety of tasks, including creating and placing ads in local publications, designing brochures and pamphlets, maintaining the Web site, and coming up with different ways to attract new customers and keep the old ones coming back. So far, our loyalty programs, coupons, and two-for-one manicure and lunch deals had proved the most popular.

When I wasn't working on marketing-related tasks, I helped with odd jobs around the farm. Some days I filled in for Gordon Stewart, the farm's focused and money-conscious manager, at the front desk when he had to run errands, helped Zennia serve meals to the guests, or restocked towels and other supplies for Gretchen Levitt, the young masseuse and facial expert who spent her days running the spa that Esther had built. When there were no other pressing matters, I occasionally resorted to cleaning out the pigsty.

By now, I was almost as familiar with the farm as Esther. While uploading pictures of the duck pond and flower garden to the farm's Web site one day, I'd realized what a perfect location the farm would be for our wedding ceremony. When I'd suggested the idea to Esther, she'd been downright tickled. And as I'd started nailing down the specifics, I'd realized that Esther's farm would be a fantastic place for anyone to get hitched, not just Jason and me.

If everything went according to plan, my first order of business after returning from my Hawaiian honeymoon would be to start advertising the farm as the perfect getaway destination for a wedding in the country. Though we'd had a steady rise in business since first opening, too many people still didn't know we existed. This little venture might finally put Esther's place on the map.

As if on cue, Esther walked into the office. "Morning, Dana," she said as she ran a hand through her curly gray hair.

"Hi, Esther. Did you need to use the computer?" I asked.

"No, I'm just here to look for some papers I misplaced. Don't let me interrupt your work." She pulled open the bottom drawer of the small file cabinet in the corner and started digging through the folders.

I turned back to the computer and opened a pamphlet I'd been designing. As I moved the images around on the screen, Esther muttered behind me, "I'd swear I left it in here." I continued to work while she mumbled to herself.

After a few minutes, I heard an "Aha!" and spun around in the chair. Esther held a small stack of papers aloft as if it was the National Dairy Championship trophy and she'd just won a year's supply of ice cream. When she caught me looking, she gave me a sheepish grin. "I'll get out of your hair."

I held up my hand. "Hang on. As long as you're here, let me get your input on this pamphlet."

Esther stepped up and leaned over my shoulder. "What a lovely photo of the vegetable garden," she said as she read through the material. "And I like how you mention how close we are to Mendocino. Everyone loves the cute little shops and the beach."

"Considering it's less than an hour away, it seems like a waste not to capitalize on it."

Esther nodded and patted her curls. "I wouldn't change a thing. After all, a bird in the hand is worth two hands in the bush."

Esther's version of the proverb was a little off, but I knew what she meant. "I'm glad you like it." She left the office, while I continued my work.

I spent the rest of the morning printing out samples and fine-tuning the pictures and text. Around eleven, I went into the kitchen and washed my hands so I could help Zennia with lunch prep, watching the rooster clock as I did so. I didn't want to be late for my appointment at the flower shop.

At a quarter to twelve, I stopped in the bathroom to freshen up and then grabbed my purse from the office before heading to my car. Bethany and I had already met on two previous occasions to decide on the flowers for my bouquet, as well as Ashlee's, who was maid of honor, and in the boutonnieres for Jason and his best man.

Bethany had insisted on one final meeting after telling me about all the brides she'd dealt with who had last-minute changes. I knew I wouldn't be switching my selection from the tiny roses and delphiniums I'd picked out from the samples she'd shown me, but another meeting to verify my order couldn't hurt.

I exited the freeway, drove partway down Main Street, and pulled into a space in front of the Don't Dilly-Dahlia Flower Shop. The electric Open sign flickered in the window, the only change from when I'd driven by on my way to work this morning.

Grabbing my purse off the passenger seat, I got out of the car, locked it, and stepped up onto the sidewalk. Next door, the Get the Scoop ice cream parlor had its front doors propped open, but I didn't see any customers inside. I guessed ice cream didn't sound as appetizing on a cool November day as it might in the middle of summer. A teenaged girl mopping the floor under the round tables smiled at me on my way by.

Smiling in return, I grabbed the doorknob to the flower shop and twisted it.

Locked.

I frowned and glanced at the Open sign merrily flickering away.

I turned the knob again but got the same result. I pulled my phone from my pocket and checked the time.

Noon on the dot.

Had Bethany forgotten about our appointment? But why was the door locked in the middle of the day?

Perhaps she'd been called away on a flower-related emergency, though I couldn't imagine what would be considered a flower emergency. Maybe a couple had decided to elope and needed a bouquet right away. Maybe a woman had broken up with her boyfriend and he'd ordered five dozen roses to try to woo her back. I looked at my phone again to see if she'd called or texted, but she hadn't.

Cupping my hands against the glass door, I peered inside. The cool fall air made my hot breath fog the window, and I shifted to the side for a better look.

The lights were on, and I could see the displays of flowers and plants that filled the small space. What I couldn't see were any people. I knocked on the glass, just in case Bethany was in a corner of the shop out of my line of vision.

Unease started to grow in the pit of my stomach as I waited for a response. For our first two meetings,

Bethany had been prepared and waiting. She'd had binders full of photos set up on the counter and a pot of coffee brewing in the back. Her sudden absence seemed out of character.

What if she'd somehow injured herself and was lying inside? What if she'd been robbed and was tied up in the back?

I knocked again, but no one came to the door. After waiting a few more seconds, I took a step back and glanced around. My eyes settled on the side alley just past the ice cream shop. I knew it led to a small parking lot in back, where there were rear exits to all the businesses. If I couldn't get in through the front door, maybe I could get in through the back.

I just hoped Bethany was all right.

Chapter 2

The door to the flower shop burst open before I had a chance to walk around to the back. Bethany poked her head out and waved. Since our last meeting, she'd gotten her red hair cut in a flattering pageboy style that framed her thin, oval face. She wore a canvas apron with large pockets over an ivory blouse and black slacks.

"I thought I heard someone knocking." She beckoned me inside. "Come on in. I hope you weren't waiting long."

I entered, relieved that nothing sinister had befallen her and annoyed with myself that I'd let my imagination get the better of me. I crossed to the far side of the store, took a seat on the metal stool she kept available for customers, and set my purse on the counter. "Did you know your door was locked?"

Bethany tilted her head. "I noticed that. I guess I forgot to unlock it when I opened up this morning. My daughter is normally here working with me, but she has the day off, and I've been busy in the back creating several funeral arrangements."

I looked around the shop, with its selection of bouquets and flowering plants. Had no walk-in customers stopped by the entire morning, or had she simply not heard anyone knocking? I wasn't sure how precarious the flower business might be, especially in a town as small as Blossom Valley, but I couldn't imagine she'd want to miss out on any potential customers.

"Now then," Bethany said. She opened a three-ring binder with a series of alphabetized tabs and flipped to the *L*'s. She ran her finger down a column. "Lewis, Lewis, Lewis." Her finger stopped. "Here you are. Have you made any changes to your bouquet request?"

"No, I'm happy with the roses and delphiniums."

She placed a checkmark on the paper. "And the colors are still fall colors with mostly oranges and dark yellows?"

"That's right."

Bethany nodded. "Excellent. I'll be calling my supplier this afternoon to make sure everything is lined up on his end." She jotted notes on the sheet. "Did you tell the lucky groom about your choices? I only ask because every now and again a bride will find out at the last minute that the groom hates a particular color or is allergic to certain flowers."

"Jason gave me the go-ahead to pick whatever flowers I'd like." I smiled to myself as I remembered how he'd practically begged me not to make him help pick out flowers. "This is one area where he didn't think he'd have much to offer. Of course, I didn't hear him say that when it came time to sample the cakes."

Bethany laughed. "Sounds like a lot of men I know. They have no interest in flowers, but food is another story altogether." She peered at me over the top of her glasses. "Jason's a reporter for the *Blossom Valley Herald*, isn't he?"

"Yes, the lead reporter," I said, knowing Jason would be the first to point out that his position wasn't nearly as thrilling as it sounded. Crime in Blossom Valley tended to involve shoplifting, the occasional burglary, and nuisance calls. Unfortunately, murders occasionally happened, too, but they were few and far between.

"People don't realize how much power a reporter has, especially in a small town. He must know everything that goes on around here, and plenty of secrets, too."

Her voice had taken on an almost dreamy quality that made me squirm a little on the stool. "I don't know about that. But if he does uncover any secrets, he keeps the information to himself."

Bethany leaned closer. "He never tells you anything? Not even a little hint?"

I leaned back, not sure why she was making me so uncomfortable. "Like I said, he keeps his mouth shut."

When I didn't offer anything more, she straightened up. "I'm sure he does," she said stiffly. She closed the binder. "I almost forgot. I received a shipment this morning that contained fern fronds, and I immediately thought how lovely they would look in your bouquet. Would you like to see them?"

"Sure."

"They're in the workroom. As a rule, I don't let customers back there, but it'll be too much trouble to bring everything up front. Follow me."

While I hopped down from the stool, she came around the counter and plucked a handful of flowers from various tall vases on display. She led the way behind the counter and brushed aside the curtain that was hanging across a doorway. I followed her in.

Two large worktables filled most of the floor space in the back room. A folding chair sat in the corner. Shelves lined the two side walls, full of empty pots, gardening tools, and piles of ribbons and bows. A large, deep sink and a short counter, along with a small window, took up the back wall next to a door that I assumed led out to the parking lot in back. A large refrigerator with double glass doors sat next to the doorway we'd come in through. A fluorescent light hummed overhead, and a small radio on the counter emitted jazz music.

Next to one of the tables, a large wreath of red and white flowers hung on a wooden stand, while a collection of flowers in fall colors spilled out from two baskets on the table. These must be the funeral arrangements Bethany had been working on.

She bypassed the tables and stepped over to the counter. She turned off the radio and picked up a small gathering of fern fronds from next to the sink. Unlike the thick, sturdy ferns I was used to seeing in bouquets or even the occasional yard, these ferns were wispy and thin. Bethany expertly added the fronds to the flowers she already held in her hands. "Of course, your arrangement will look slightly different, but this should give you an idea. These ferns won't overpower your bouquet and will add a pop of green for extra depth." She lifted the bouquet, as if she were a bride about to walk down the aisle. "What do you think?"

I fingered the delicate fronds. "I love them."

She smiled. "I had a feeling you would."

My gaze shifted to the glass doors of the refrigerator. The right-hand side was full of various greenery and floral arrangements, while the top shelf on the left side held a lone flower in a vase. I stepped closer for a better look.

I'd never seen such an unusual flower. Instead of the petals surrounding the center of the flower, as with most types, five large, jagged-looking petals arched away from the middle. The edges of the petals reached so far back that they almost formed a ball on the other side. Six or seven filaments stuck out from the center of the flower. The base of each petal was pale yellow, but the rest was a deep and vibrant red. "What kind of flower is that?" I asked.

"It's called gloriosa, more commonly referred to as a flame lily or fire lily."

"I've never seen anything quite like it before."

Bethany came over, slid open the refrigerator door, and took out the vase. Up close, I could see the tiny stamens with their individual grains of pollen and the smooth texture of the petals.

"I usually don't carry gloriosa in the store, since they live for such a short amount of time, but a woman wanted one specifically for an anniversary corsage. I had to special order it from San Francisco.

It came in this morning, and I'm keeping it back here so a customer won't touch it and damage it." As if afraid I might suddenly reach out a hand, she put the vase back and shut the refrigerator door. "I hope you don't want to add the gloriosa to your bouquet at this late date. Since it's a special order, I couldn't guarantee the shipment would arrive in time."

"Considering how fancy the flower looks, I can't imagine it would fit into my budget anyway," I said.

Bethany scowled. "Some brides don't know what that word means. They think nothing of the value of these flowers. Why, I had a client a couple of years ago who ordered dozens of roses in peach and then changed her mind at the last minute. She literally threw the flowers in the Dumpster and insisted I find replacement flowers in coral."

I frowned. "That's ridiculous. Think of the waste."

"Then there was the bride who ordered white roses and wanted me to spray-paint gold accents on each one to match her bridesmaids' dresses. I was up half the night and she never even said thank you."

"How rude." I found myself drawn into Bethany's tales of her over-the-top clients. My voice rose in volume. "It's more than rude. It's outrageous!"

Bethany lifted one shoulder in a half shrug. "As the saying goes, the customer's always right."

"Still, I find it completely unacceptable." Good thing I wasn't in the flower business. I'd tell those brides exactly where they could stuff their bouquets, thorns and all.

"That's why I find these final meetings invaluable. I'd hate for you to be unhappy in some way on your wedding day." She pulled the fronds out of the bouquet and dropped them in their original place on the counter.

Behind me, I heard someone clear their throat twice in a row. "Excuse me?"

I turned to find a mousy, middle-aged woman standing in the doorway. Her hands were clasped in front of her, and her face was turning a bright shade of red. "I'm sorry to interrupt, Bethany. I just wanted to pick up my order."

"Yes, of course. It's ready to go." Bethany set the rest of the bouquet on the counter and brushed past the woman into the main part of the store.

The woman glanced at me, then down at her feet. "I didn't mean to bother you," she said. "Please don't be upset with Bethany." She darted past the curtain and toward the front.

Well, that was weird.

I took one last look at the fire lily in the refrigerator before making my way through the doorway. The woman was signing a credit card slip. She handed it back to Bethany. When she saw me, she hastily picked up her potted plant and clutched it to her chest. "Hang in there," she said to Bethany before hurrying out the door.

This woman's behavior was becoming curiouser and curiouser.

Bethany frowned after the woman, then tucked the sales slip away and flipped open her binder. "Let me jot down a note about the ferns. It'll only take a second," she said.

While she was busy, I took a closer look around the room. The walls were covered with photographs and artwork of the area, especially the redwood forest and the beaches of nearby Mendocino. Several shelves held potted plants, many of them ivy, their long tendrils cascading down. Bethany had strung half a dozen small, fake birds from the ceiling, and for a second, I almost felt like I was out in the woods. "You have a wonderful shop here. How long have you been in business?"

Bethany looked up from her writing. "Twenty years. I opened the place after my divorce. I'd never run a business before, as my ex-husband was quick to point out when I told him my plans, but I've managed to muddle along. Some years are better than others, of course."

"It's so neat that your daughter works here with you. She must have inherited your love of flowers."

Bethany started writing again. "I wouldn't say that, necessarily. She was in between jobs a couple of years back, when the economy was struggling. I basically created a position here for her, handling deliveries and the simpler orders. It seems to really suit her, though. She always had a creative mind." She set down her pen. "Isn't that how you ended up here in Blossom Valley? You lost your job due to downsizing?"

I pulled my head back. How did Bethany know that? Did she also know I'd moved back home to help my mom after my dad passed away? "Um, yes, it is," I said. "How did you hear about the downsizing?"

Bethany tapped her pen to her lips and stared at the ceiling. "Hmm, I guess you must have told me."

I didn't remember mentioning anything about

my past to her, but I decided to drop the topic and turn the conversation back to her. "Having your daughter work here must keep you two close."

"That was my original idea," she said, "but Violet is starting to forget who's the employer around here and who's the employee. She has all sorts of ideas on how I need to charge my customers more and start offering other products, like home décor items and gardening tools."

"Surely drawing in more customers and increasing profits isn't a bad idea," I said, thinking of all the effort I was putting into promoting Esther's place.

"Business at Don't Dilly-Dahlia is doing fine, and I'm happy with where things stand." She pointed to the wall with the artwork. "She insisted we order those photos, and we've only sold one. Besides, she can worry about taking this shop to the next level when I'm gone and buried and not here to stop her." Bethany gave a little laugh. "And with any luck, that won't happen for another twenty years or more."

I had a sneaking suspicion she'd told Violet that very thing. Maybe more than once. I checked the time on my phone. "If there's nothing else, I need to get back to work."

"Your confirmation was all I needed."

We said our good-byes; then I walked out of the shop and got into my car. I sat behind the wheel for a moment, thinking about Bethany. Her comments about Jason uncovering the town's secrets had rattled me. And how had she known my reasons for returning to Blossom Valley? Was Bethany someone I had to be careful around?

I shook my head to clear away my questions. Bethany had always been perfectly nice to me. Surely I was worrying about nothing.

Chapter 3

Before I returned to work, I swung through the closest fast-food restaurant drive-through and studied the menu options. Over the last few months, my tastes had shifted away from gooey cheeseburgers and salty fries toward fresher fare, partly because I needed to fit into my wedding dress and partly because after filling in for Zennia as the farm's cook a few months back, I was actually starting to enjoy foods without preservatives. Go figure.

After ordering a chicken salad with vinaigrette dressing and adding a chocolate milkshake at the last second for old time's sake, I drove down the highway and took the exit for the farm. I parked in my usual corner spot and hurried into the kitchen to eat my meal before my lunch hour was up.

I was slurping the last drops of my milkshake when Gordon came into the kitchen from the hall. With his slicked-back dark hair, three-piece suits, and pinkie rings, he'd always reminded me more of a mobster from Las Vegas than a business manager. But I knew his integrity was unquestionable, and his concern with keeping Esther's farm and spa thriving never wavered.

When I'd first started working here, Gordon and I had had a somewhat acrimonious relationship, mostly because of his exacting standards and blunt personality. After several months, we'd reached a level in our relationship where I considered us friends, but we still butted heads when it came to marketing budgets and guest discounts. I tended to lean toward the larger discounts and splashier ads, while Gordon watched every dollar and tried to offer the smallest discount possible. We never seemed to agree.

Which is why I'd surprised myself by asking Gordon to walk me down the aisle as a stand-in for my father, now that he was gone. And Gordon had surprised me even more by wholeheartedly accepting my request and seeming downright touched by it.

He watched as I set down my empty shake cup and wiped my mouth with the thin restaurant napkin. "When will your lunch break be over?" he asked.

"Right this minute, actually." I gave up on using the flimsy napkin and went to the sink to wash my hands.

"Excellent. Then it's the perfect time to ask a favor. I need to run into town to meet with the contractor who provides our toiletries and was wondering if you could watch the front desk."

I patted my hands dry on the kitchen towel with the two cows and a pig embroidered on it. "Sure. I could do that. Are we expecting any check-ins?"

"No, but it's good to have someone available in

the lobby in case a current guest has a request that needs to be filled or someone calls for a reservation."

"Consider it done."

He gave a brief thank you and walked out of the kitchen. Once I'd dumped my paper bag from lunch in the recycling container under the sink, I stopped in the office long enough to drop off my purse and put my cell phone in my pocket.

I went up front to take my position behind the counter, noting how silent the lobby was. I drummed my fingers on the countertop and looked out the front window. Several ducks rested on the patch of grass next to the small pond. In the parking lot, a blue jay flew from one tree to another.

When the animals didn't do anything the least bit entertaining, I went over to the sitting area, with its blue-and-white-checked sofa and two blue wing-back chairs, and straightened the half-dozen magazines that littered the coffee table. I noticed a thin layer of dust on the wood and retrieved a rag from under the counter to wipe the surface. That done, I stowed the rag and checked the time.

Good grief. Gordon had been gone for only five minutes.

With no guests in sight, I darted back to the office for a pen and a notebook and then returned to the counter. While I had a few minutes of downtime, I might as well brainstorm ideas on how to best market Esther's farm as a wedding destination. I wrote down anything that popped in my mind, no matter how silly.

I'd just added Wilbur and the other pigs to my list, though I wasn't entirely sure pigs would be a big draw for a wedding, when my cell phone rang. I pulled it from my pocket and checked the caller ID: Private Caller. It was most likely a telemarketer trying to sell me solar panels or housecleaning services, but I answered anyway.

"Hello?"

"Dana, it's Bethany."

Uh-oh.

Why was she calling me when I'd seen her less than an hour before? This didn't bode well.

"Yes?" I asked. I tried to look on the bright side. Maybe she had thought up more additions to the bouquet. Maybe she was going to offer me a discount.

"I've run into a problem with my supplier."

I shouldn't have wasted my time on the bright side. "What kind of problem?" I asked.

"He won't be able to get the color of delphinium you wanted."

Well, that didn't sound so bad, as long as another fall color was available. "What colors can he get?"

"Blue."

Eek. Blue was definitely not a fall color. "Blue won't work," I said, feeling like I was stating the obvious.

"No," Bethany agreed, "but I'm sure you have a backup flower already picked out."

My mind went blank. The moment I'd sat down to study her binder of possible arrangements, I'd latched on to the roses and delphiniums without a second thought. "Unfortunately, I don't."

"That's okay," Bethany said hurriedly. "I have a few possibilities. Maybe freesia or alstroemeria."

I had no idea what either of those flowers looked like. Bethany probably realized that when I didn't respond.

"Here's an idea," she said. "If it wouldn't be too much trouble, maybe you could stop by this evening and take a look at a few selections."

I considered my plans for tonight. I had that dinner date with Jason, but if my trip to the flower shop didn't take long, I would still have time to stop by my apartment for a quick shower and change of clothes before driving to his place. "That'll work," I said.

"Thank you. And again, I'm sorry for the mix-up. I've been doing business with this supplier for at least five years and he's always been reliable."

"Guess there's a first time for everything," I said.

"It had better be the only time if he knows what's good for him," she said, an edge to her voice. I winced as I pictured the tongue-lashing she may have given the guy. When she spoke again, her tone was back to normal. "Don't worry, you'll love the other options. I'll see you this evening."

I ended the call and set my phone on the counter, hoping that by some miracle Bethany would call right back to tell me there'd been a big misunderstanding and everything was back on track.

When my phone didn't ring, I gave up staring at it and returned to my list of perks for a farm wedding. I glanced out the window for inspiration and saw Gordon pull into the parking lot. A moment later, he walked into the lobby, carrying his ever-present clipboard. From the moment Esther had hired Gordon, he'd carried around that clipboard, taking notes on anything that needed to be corrected, fixed, or replaced. I'd even seen him count the plates in the kitchen and record the number. At one time, I'd suggested he upgrade to a personal tablet for convenience, but he'd refused, saying the old method worked fine.

"Any drop-in guests?" he asked.

"None. And no calls either."

He pulled out his pen and wrote something on the clipboard.

I tried to read the page upside down. "Are you making notes on the fact that nothing happened while you were gone?"

"Of course. I've started tracking which days of the week get the fewest walk-in guests and requests for information."

I mulled over how we could use his notes to the farm's advantage. "Are you thinking about running specials on those days to improve the vacancy rate?"

"That's one possibility. Do you have any others?"

I came around the counter so I could see the clipboard and the chart he'd created. "I could increase our online presence those days, tweeting more and posting on Facebook."

"Excellent idea. Let me gather a few more weeks of data; then we'll set some of these plans into motion."

"Sounds good to me." I folded up the wedding list I'd been working on and picked up my pen.

"Now that you're back, I have some work to finish in the office."

I went down the hall to see what was next on my marketing to-do list. I worked in the office for two more hours and then went out to help Esther with odds and ends around the farm, including skimming the leaves out of the pool and hot tub, sweeping the patio, and cleaning up around the picnic tables.

When my workday was finished, I gathered my things and got in my car, my mind full of finding replacement flowers, though I wasn't terribly worried. Bethany had said she had good options to replace the delphiniums, and I believed her. If having to pick a new flower was the worst thing that happened during my wedding planning, I'd consider myself lucky.

Exiting the freeway, I cruised down Main Street and pulled up to Bethany's shop. The Open sign no longer glowed, but I didn't give it a second thought. She was expecting me, after all.

I got out of my car, walked up to the shop door, and grabbed the knob. It didn't budge. I tried again, but the door was locked. Feeling a sense of déjà vu, I cupped my hands on the glass to try to look inside, but I couldn't see anything. The shop was dark.

Where was she? I knew she had my cell phone number. If she'd had to leave unexpectedly, why didn't she call, especially since I was making a special trip at her request?

Maybe she was working in the back, much like

my lunchtime visit. I knocked as hard on the glass as I dared. No one came to the door. I abandoned the front of the store and made my way past the ice cream shop and down the short alley that ran between it and the Prescription for Joy drugstore.

The back parking lot contained a large Dumpster, several empty beer bottles, and a single dirty diaper. Dozens of cigarette butts littered the ground. The back door to Get the Scoop was open, though the screen door was shut. I could hear voices inside as I walked by. The door to Don't Dilly-Dahlia was closed and I knocked, not wanting to startle Bethany by entering unannounced.

No one answered this door either. I tried the knob, expecting it to be locked like the front, but the knob turned easily in my hand. I pushed the door open and stepped inside. The overhead light was off. The only sources of light were from the opened door and the tiny window over the sink.

"Bethany?"

Silence.

Where on earth was she? Why hadn't she called if she needed to reschedule? Since I was already inside, I'd wait a few minutes to see if she came back.

I strode across the room, hit the light switch, and turned around. My breath caught.

Bethany lay faceup on the floor near a worktable. The front of her ivory-colored blouse had turned a violent shade of dark red. What appeared to be blood pooled around her body. Her eyes were wide open, staring at nothing.

My breath started coming in hitches. I felt like my insides had turned to ice.

Now I knew why Bethany had missed our appointment.

She was dead.

Chapter 4

My hand flew to my back pocket, and I fumbled to pull out my cell phone. My heart hammered against my chest as panic swelled inside me. The corners of the phone kept catching on the pocket's seams, and I had to work to yank it free.

I held my thumb over the number nine, but paused before I pushed the button. I forced myself to look at Bethany again. My practical mind told me she was absolutely dead, no question. But what if I was wrong? What if I should be administering first aid?

Cringing slightly, I knelt down and laid my fingers on her neck, where I imagined her pulse should be. Nothing, not even a flutter.

I pulled my hand back and rose, a little unsteady on my feet. I turned away so I wouldn't have to look at Bethany while I dialed the phone and reported what I'd found. Before I hung up, the 911 operator promised me officers were on their way.

With Bethany beyond my help, I moved into the front of the shop and out of sight of her body.

What could have happened to her? What had caused all that blood?

My phone chimed, and I checked it. Jason had texted me: Can't wait to cook you dinner.

Dinner.

The word seemed like a foreign concept right then. How could I think about eating beef stroganoff when there was a dead florist in the next room?

Bile rose up, but I choked it down. I texted him back to tell him our dinner plans were canceled. Not only did the thought of food send waves of nausea roiling through my stomach, but sadly, this wasn't the first time I'd discovered a body. I knew the police might keep me here for hours while they launched their investigation.

My phone chimed again with another text from Jason: What's wrong? Are you sick?

In as few words as possible, I typed that I was at the flower shop and had found Bethany's body.

His response came swiftly: On my way.

While Jason and I had been exchanging texts, I'd noticed the faint sound of sirens getting louder. I watched through the store window as an ambulance pulled up to the curb, followed by a police cruiser. From half a block away, a fire truck was approaching.

I opened the door as two EMTs rushed across the sidewalk and into the shop. One carried a large plastic medical kit.

"Who needs help, miss?" the one with the kit asked.

I gestured to the curtain that led to the back room. "She's through there, but you can't help her now." I hadn't meant to sound quite so dramatic, but the words just sort of tumbled out.

"We'll take a look anyway," he said as he and his partner went through the doorway.

I watched their retreating backs until the curtain swung back into place, then turned toward the door. The police officer was only now climbing out of his cruiser. He shut the car door and headed toward the shop in what I could only describe as a saunter. Didn't he realize this was an emergency?

He finally crossed the store's threshold, but before I could tell him what had happened, I heard one of the EMTs behind me say, "Ruiz, we need you back here."

He brushed past me and disappeared into the back room. I shut the shop door and stood among the flower displays. Seeing all the flowers made me realize I had no one to make my bridal bouquet. I immediately chastised myself for worrying about something as petty as my flowers when Bethany was lying dead back there. I looked out the window, unsure of what to do. Should I go outside to wait for Jason, or stay inside in case the officer had questions?

The front of the store was so quiet that I could hear the ticking of the wall clock and the muffled sound of cars driving by on the street. I was about to text Jason again when the EMTs came out of the back room followed by Officer Ruiz, who was moving with more urgency and talking into the hand mic clipped to his shoulder.

He took me by the upper arm and ushered me toward the door. "Ma'am, I need you to step outside with me," he said in an official tone.

As we stepped out of the shop, a patrol car screeched to the curb and an officer practically leapt out of the driver's seat in his haste to reach the sidewalk.

Officer Ruiz talked to him in a low voice before turning to me. "You need to stay here. Don't leave the area." He and the other officer exchanged a look, and Officer Ruiz tipped his head toward me as if I were about to make a run for it. My gut twisted into a knot. I had to wonder how much involvement the officers believed I'd had with Bethany's death.

Officer Ruiz started back inside, talking into his radio once more, something about a 1-8-7, whatever that was. The radio crackled a reply, but I couldn't make out the words. The door shut with a click, and I was left on the sidewalk with the other officer. He seemed to ignore me while he studied the street, but his occasional glances and the stiff way he carried himself let me know he was well aware I was there. I sighed and got ready for a potentially long wait.

Dusk was settling over the street, and the evening temperature had cooled considerably. I pointed to my car parked nearby. "I'm going to get my jacket."

He gave me a terse nod. I could feel his eyes on me as I walked over and got my jacket from the passenger seat. People were starting to come out of the nearby stores and huddle on the sidewalk, no doubt drawn by the sirens from earlier and the flashing blue and red lights that appeared even brighter in the deepening gloom.

I was zipping up my jacket when I felt a hand on my shoulder. Startled, I whirled around. Jason stood before me. Even under these terrible circumstances, I couldn't help but notice how handsome he looked with his short reddish-brown hair, close-cropped goatee, and warm green eyes. Right now, those eyes were filled with worry. Without a word, he ran his hands over my hair and then pulled me in for a hug. Warmth spread throughout my body as I laid my head against his chest and tried to take deep breaths.

After a moment, he released me and tipped my chin up so we were looking at each other. "Are you all right?"

I nodded and swallowed the lump that had unexpectedly formed in my throat. "I'm in better shape than Bethany."

Jason looked toward the store, though I knew he couldn't see what was going on inside. "Any idea what happened to her?"

Before I could answer, the officer who'd been babysitting me walked over. "I have to ask that you not discuss what's going on here, ma'am."

"But it's only my fiancé," I said, leaving out the fact that he was also a newspaper reporter.

The cop stiffened and put his hands on his utility belt. "Doesn't matter. Until the detective has taken your statement, I can't allow you to speak to anyone."

"I understand, Officer," Jason said. He rubbed my back and leaned down close to my ear. "I'll hang around until you're free to talk, okay?"

I nodded. He took his hand off my back, allowing the cool air to creep through my jacket. A chill shot up my spine.

The officer had hurried over to the storefront, where two people were peering through the flower shop window. I took the opportunity to ask Jason one more question before he could walk away.

"What's a one-eight-seven?"

Jason had been watching the cop at the window, but his attention shot back to me. "What did you say?"

"A one-eight-seven. That's what the other officer said when he was talking on his radio. I assumed it was a police code of some kind. Do you know what it means?"

"Yes, and it's not good." Jason's eyes never left my face. "It means they think Bethany was murdered."

Chapter 5

Murdered? While a tiny part of me had wondered if Bethany had been killed, thanks to the amount of blood and the fact that she'd been fine earlier today, Jason's words still sent a jolt through my system. "You really think she's been murdered?" I thought of Officer Ruiz's change in demeanor when he'd come back out after looking at Bethany's body. No wonder he'd started moving faster after that.

The patrol officer strode back over after shooing away the gawkers trying to see in the window. "Ma'am, I won't tell you again. If you continue to speak to people, I'll need to place you in the back of my patrol car."

Yikes, this guy wasn't fooling around. I held up my hands. "Okay, okay, sorry."

"I'll check in with you in a while," Jason said to me. He walked over to where the ambulance was parked and started talking to the EMTs.

My legs suddenly felt weak, and I eased down so

I could sit on the curb. I rested my elbows on my knees. "Who on earth would want to kill the flower lady?" I asked aloud, though only the cop was close enough to hear me. He didn't answer.

I'd thought Bethany's dying was bad enough, but Bethany being murdered was far worse. I was having trouble grappling with this new information. I stared at the asphalt, mindlessly following a trail of ants as they marched across a jagged crack. The sound of an approaching engine called my attention to the street.

A dark blue Ford Taurus that I knew to be an unmarked car from the Blossom Valley police department pulled up in front of the ambulance. The car door opened and Detective Palmer stepped out.

My stomach, not quite settled after finding Bethany's body, started to churn again. I'd dealt with the detective on a number of occasions, almost always when I'd managed to get involved in a murder investigation. While we generally had an amiable relationship, I was pretty sure he wished he'd see me less often.

As he neared me, I could see his jaw working. He gave me a stern look. "Are you the one who called nine-one-one to report the body?"

I swallowed audibly. "Um, yes."

He muttered something under his breath. "I'll be right back," he said to me.

Giving him my most accommodating smile, I said, "I'll wait for you."

He shook his head and walked past me. I watched over my shoulder as he approached the flower shop. He jerked his head at the officer who'd been watching me, indicating he should come along. The officer gave me a long look, perhaps trying to telepathically warn me to mind my p's and q's, before he and Detective Palmer both disappeared inside.

I pushed myself to my feet, too tense to sit, and started pacing the sidewalk. Surely Detective Palmer wouldn't think I'd had anything to do with Bethany's death, but I knew finding the body put me squarely in the middle of his investigation. That wasn't the place I wanted to be, especially with my wedding coming up.

I turned to make another lap on the sidewalk but stopped short when I noticed my mom in front of me. As usual, she wore slacks and a sweater set. Her salt and pepper hair looked freshly permed.

"Mom! What are you doing here?"

"I heard all the sirens, but I was busy helping a customer." Mom worked part-time at the Going Back for Seconds consignment shop that specialized in women's apparel. Rejoining the workforce had done wonders to help her get over Dad's death, not to mention the extra income helped supplement the small pension she relied on. "As soon as they left, I looked out the window and spotted the ambulance, and then you. I came over to make sure you were okay." She stepped back and looked me up and down. "You're all right?"

"I'm fine." I pulled my jacket tighter around me. "Too bad I can't say the same for Bethany."

Mom's eyes widened. "Has something happened to her?"

There was really no good way to tell her. "Apparently someone killed her," I said.

Mom paled and laid a hand on her chest. "Who would do such a thing?"

"I have no idea. We met at lunch to talk about my flowers and nothing seemed out of the ordinary, but when I stopped by a little while ago, I found her dead in the back room."

Mom's mouth dropped open. "*You* found the body?" She laid her hand on my arm. "Dana, you cannot get involved in a murder investigation. You have a wedding to think about."

I pulled my arm away. "Don't worry. There's no way I'm getting involved. Once Detective Palmer asks me his questions, I'm done. The Blossom Valley Police Department is more than capable of figuring out Bethany's death without me getting in the way."

Mom blew out a breath. "I'm glad to hear you say that. You have enough on your plate."

Detective Palmer stuck his head out the door, scanning the handful of people on the sidewalk until he noticed me.

"Lewis, I'm ready for you," he called.

I squared my shoulders, ready to get the questions over with. "I meant what I said," I told Mom. "I won't get involved."

She gave me a quick hug. "Good. I'll wait for you out here."

I glanced toward the ambulance and saw Jason deep in discussion with the EMTs. I moved at what felt like a glacial pace as I headed for the door, hoping he'd notice me and give me a reassuring sign, maybe a thumbs-up, but he didn't look my way.

Once we were inside the store, Detective Palmer stepped over to the counter, notebook and pen already in his hands. Someone had turned on the overhead lights, alleviating the earlier gloom and emphasizing the beauty of the various bouquets. If I hadn't known poor Bethany had died in this shop, I never would have guessed it.

When I didn't move farther into the store, Detective Palmer indicated the stool I'd sat on only hours ago, chitchatting with Bethany about my flowers. That entire conversation seemed so frivolous now. I slumped onto the stool.

"Tell me how you came to discover the body," the detective said.

I told him everything, from my midday meeting with Bethany to her afternoon phone call to my arrival at the shop. The detective nodded as I spoke, interrupting only to clarify one or two comments, or to ask me for more details.

"And how did Ms. Lancaster seem when you were with her?"

I shrugged. "Fine. I mean, I don't know her very well, but she was as nice and polite as always."

"She didn't seem upset about anything? Or like she was distracted?"

"Not at all."

Detective Palmer reached in his jacket pocket and pulled out a pack of gum. He offered me a stick. When I declined, he unwrapped one and folded it into his mouth. As he did so, he gave me a long, hard look that made my stomach do a flip-flop.

"How about you?" he asked. "Were you upset about anything?"

"Me?" I asked, my voice squeaking.

"Did you find her to be a reputable business dealer, or did you feel she was charging too much for the flowers? Maybe you were dissatisfied with the service in some way."

I stared at Detective Palmer. He couldn't be serious. No way could he be fishing around for a possible motive for why *I* would kill Bethany.

"Of course not," I said. "Why would you even ask that?"

"Just getting a sense of your relationship with the victim."

"It was strictly a business relationship. And one I was very satisfied with." I could hear the defensive tone creeping into my voice, but I didn't care.

"You two never disagreed on anything while you were conducting your business?"

I didn't like where this was heading one bit. I scooted off the stool and faced him. "How long have you and I known each other?"

He held up a hand. "No need to get upset. Please take your seat." He waited for me to sit back down before he continued. "You know I have to ask these questions, especially considering you were the one who found the body."

"But that was just a coincidence! I had no plans to come back tonight until Bethany called and asked me to. If I was going to kill her, which of course I wasn't, wouldn't it make more sense for me to kill her when I saw her at lunch? Why wait and come back tonight?"

Detective Palmer remained expressionless. I would have paid a month's marketing salary to know what he was thinking. "Killers aren't known for their clear thinking. Someone may have thought waiting until the end of the day would reduce the chances of being seen, especially with darkness falling."

"But it wasn't dark when I first got here," I pointed out. "And the killer would have to worry about all the extra witnesses as people got off work. Lunchtime is definitely better for a murder."

Detective Palmer's lips twitched. "I'll be sure and remember that. As it is, we haven't established the time of death yet," he said. "Or found any witnesses who spoke to Bethany this afternoon. Who's to say she didn't die at lunchtime?"

I felt apprehension well up, replacing the indignation. Maybe Detective Palmer didn't know me as well as I thought he did. "I can't have been the only person to talk to her today," I said. Then I thought about how the flower shop door had been locked for the entire morning and Bethany hadn't even noticed. Clearly people weren't beating down her door for flowers.

"We'll see," was all the detective said.

I shifted on the stool. Someone must have talked to Bethany after I saw her. My eyes settled on a vase of ivory-colored roses, triggering a thought.

"Wait!" I blurted out.

Detective Palmer raised his eyebrows.

"Bethany called the supplier and that's when he told her he couldn't get the flowers for my bridal bouquet, remember? That proves I wasn't the last person to talk to her."

"I only have your word that that's what happened, but we'll pull the phone records for the shop and Ms. Lancaster's personal cell."

I settled back on the stool. Once the detective saw the phone records, he'd know I was telling the truth. Of course, if Bethany had called the supplier as soon as I'd left the shop, Detective Palmer might think I'd stayed for the call and then killed her when I'd found out about the flower problem. Then again, even if she'd called much later, that didn't prove I hadn't killed Bethany this evening and then claimed to find the body.

My head was starting to ache. How long until this interview was over?

I glanced out the window and saw that Jason had returned to the sidewalk and was talking to Mom. At least I wasn't alone in this mess.

Detective Palmer asked a few more questions, including whether Bethany had mentioned any additional appointments for the day or if I'd seen anyone in the area when I'd first pulled up to the store. Most of my answers didn't seem to help in the least, and he eventually tucked his notebook out of sight.

"All right. That's it for now. Call me if you think of anything important."

"Of course. I want this solved as much as you do," I said, sliding off the stool. He grunted in response, but I couldn't tell if it was a grunt of agreement or disbelief.

Dashing out of the store before he could think of more questions, I almost ran into Jason as I barreled onto the sidewalk. He grabbed my arms to stop my momentum.

"What's the hurry?" he asked.

I glanced back at the shop, where Detective Palmer was shutting the door. I heard the lock click. At least he was done with me. "Just glad to be out of there," I said.

The number of people loitering around the shop had grown while I'd been inside. The fire truck had left, but the rest of the emergency vehicles were enough to draw the after-work crowd. I started to tell Jason and Mom about my interview with Detective Palmer but stopped when I noticed a woman's voice getting louder.

I could only see the top of her head as she wormed her way through the crowd. "Please, get out of my way, please," she said.

She finally broke free, allowing me to get a good look at her. My heart sank.

It was Bethany's daughter, Violet. She wore a shapeless tank dress over a long-sleeved T-shirt. Unlike her mother's perfectly coiffed hair, Violet's long brown hair was unstyled and possibly unbrushed, providing a sharp contrast to her mother's polished appearance.

She didn't acknowledge Jason, Mom, or me as she hurried up to the shop door and turned the knob. I'd heard Detective Palmer lock the door, so I wasn't surprised when Violet couldn't open it, but she seemed at a total loss when the door didn't budge.

"Why is this door locked?" she practically yelled. Then she turned to the three of us, seeming to notice us for the first time. "A neighbor called to tell me an ambulance was in front of my mom's place. Do you know what's going on?" she pleaded.

Her palpable concern made my heart twist. What were we going to tell her?

Chapter 6

Bethany's daughter rapped on the glass with her knuckles. I flinched at the harsh sound. Now that the sky was darkening, we could clearly see the detective and another officer working inside the lit shop.

"Open up," Violet said to the officers. Even though she wasn't yelling, I was fairly certain the officers could hear her through the glass, but they didn't acknowledge her. She tried the knob again.

Behind me, the crowd started to murmur. Violet whirled around. "Does anyone know if my mom is okay?" She looked at each person in turn until her gaze settled on me and remained there.

It looked like I'd be the one to tell her about Bethany.

I stepped toward her at the same time that I noticed Detective Palmer cross to the front of the store. Relieved, I pointed to him as he reached for the knob. "I think he'll be able to answer your questions." He swung open the door, and the crowd fell silent.

Violet turned to him with a beseeching look. "What's going on? Has something happened to my mom?"

"If you'll come inside, ma'am, I can explain everything."

"Is my mom okay?" she asked again in a much quieter voice. She hesitated a moment before stepping into the shop. Detective Palmer shut the door behind her. As one, the crowd exhaled, and the volume of conversation increased as people started talking amongst themselves again.

I shivered, cold despite my jacket. Jason pulled me close and kissed the top of my head. "Violet will be all right," he said.

"I just feel so bad for her. She's about to find out her mother's dead. I even feel sorry for Detective Palmer, who has to be the one to tell her. I wouldn't know what to say if I were him."

Mom patted my back. "Detective Palmer must have done this before. I'm sure he'll break the news to her as gently as possible."

I leaned against Jason and watched the activity around me. Drivers on Main Street slowed to a crawl as they gawked at the ambulance and police cars, but the crowd on the sidewalk started to break up as people realized there really wasn't much going on. One woman stopped to ask Jason if he could tell her what was happening. He shook his head, and she moved on with a frown.

From nearby, a man called out, "Dorothy! Hey, Dorothy!"

I looked around and saw the owner of the Get the Scoop ice cream parlor next door waving at us from his doorway. Mom waved back, and he stepped around a couple standing on the sidewalk and joined us.

I'd seen the owner many times when I'd stopped by for ice cream, but I'd only ever talked to him about the usual pleasantries, nothing on a personal level. He looked to be in his late fifties or early sixties with short brown hair and a noticeable pot belly that hinted at one too many samples of his own merchandise.

"Dorothy, I thought that was you," he said.

"Mitch, isn't it just terrible?"

He raised his hands, palms up. "I don't know what's going on. I just got here to take over for my afternoon worker and found all these police cars. My employee was too wound up to tell me much of anything."

"You mean you haven't heard?" Mom said. She eyed the nearby couple and lowered her voice. "Bethany has gotten herself killed, the poor dear."

Mitch's eye twitched. "When? How? I saw her this afternoon."

I felt a flicker of hope in my chest. If Mitch had actually seen Bethany in person after my lunchtime visit, that was even better than tracking down the supplier who had spoken to her over the phone.

I shifted out of Jason's embrace. "What time was this?"

Mitch pulled his head back, as if startled by the interruption. "And who are you, young lady?"

Mom put an arm around me and gave my shoulders a squeeze. "This is my daughter, Dana. Dana, this is Mitch."

He smiled. "I should have noticed the resemblance. She's got those beautiful blue eyes of yours, Dorothy. But I'd swear on a stack of Bibles that you're her older sister, not her mother."

Good grief, was Mitch flirting with my mom? Right in front of me? And moments after finding out Bethany was dead?

"Oh, Mitch," Mom said, "you're such a sweet talker." She gestured toward Jason. "And this is my soon-to-be son-in-law, Jason," she said with a note of pride.

The two men shook hands. "Good to meet you," Jason said.

"You too."

Mom rubbed her hands together as if to warm them up, and Mitch said, "Let's get you lovely ladies out of this cold and into my shop."

"Good idea," Mom said. I wasn't sure the inside of an ice cream parlor would be that much warmer than out here on the sidewalk, but at least we could sit down.

Mom walked inside the ice cream parlor, with Mitch right behind her. I couldn't help but notice he had a hand on her back. Mom had dated another man briefly after my father's death, though the relationship hadn't lasted. I'd come to terms with the idea of Mom dating again, but I still felt the need to keep a close eye on any man who showed interest in her. I glanced at Jason to see if he'd observed Mitch's gesture. He had, but gave me a noncommittal shrug.

Once inside, Mom stopped at a small, round table with metal legs and a shiny top. Three chairs sat around it. The entire parlor was done in a 50s-style theme, complete with a checkered floor and old vinyl records stuck to the walls. A jukebox waited silently against one wall.

Mitch pulled out a chair for Mom, and Jason grabbed an extra chair from the neighboring table. We all sat down.

"I love your shop," Mom said as she studied the décor.

"You've got the best dark chocolate ice cream in town," Jason said.

Mitch's chest puffed up. "It's because of the all-natural, top-quality ingredients I use. I can't stand using artificial flavors."

On a normal day, I could talk about ice cream for hours, but this was no normal day, and Mitch hadn't answered my question. "So, Mitch," I said, trying to steer the conversation back around, "you were telling us that you saw Bethany earlier today. When was that exactly?"

He laid his arms on the tabletop. "Around four. I remember because I left right after that to run some errands. Like I told you, I just got back a few minutes ago and found the police all over the place."

The knot that had been holding my stomach hostage since Officer Ruiz had asked me to wait on the sidewalk loosened. Mitch had spoken to Bethany after I had. While it didn't completely clear me, since I could have killed Bethany this evening, instead of at lunchtime, at least it backed up what I'd told Detective Palmer.

"Did Bethany usually stop in?" I asked.

"Most days, so long as she didn't have a lot of customers at her own place. Always ordered a small scoop of pineapple sherbet. Called it her afternoon pick-me-up."

"What did you two talk about?" Jason asked. "Did she give any indication there might be a problem?"

Mitch cleared his throat. "Not that I remember. We talked about the weather and how it's been dragging down my sales. She was telling me how things were slow for her, too, since wedding season's pretty much over. Early November's always hard on both our businesses, though she has Thanksgiving and Christmas to look forward to. She'll be swamped with work soon enough." Mitch looked down at the table. "Or she would have been."

Mom clapped a hand over her mouth and bolted up from the table. I looked at her in alarm.

"What's wrong, Mom?"

She smoothed down her sweater set and brushed off her slacks. "All this talk about work reminds me that I'm still on the clock. I only ran over here to see if you and Jason were okay, but in all the excitement, I forgot that I need to get back." She bent over and gave me a hasty hug, said good-bye to Jason and Mitch, and rushed out.

I watched through the open door as she ran across the street toward the consignment shop. Once she was inside the store, I turned my attention to Jason and Mitch.

"If Bethany stopped by regularly," Jason was saying, "then you must know her well. You've been working next door to each other for years."

Mitch rubbed his chin with the back of his hand. "I wouldn't say that. We mostly stuck to the usual day-to-day stuff. I mean, I knew she was divorced and has that daughter of hers, but not much else. Most times she'd come in, get her sherbet, and leave. She wasn't always the easiest woman to get along with, so I didn't mind that she didn't stick around to talk."

Out of the corner of my eye, I glimpsed Jason sitting up straighter, and I knew he was thinking the same thing I was. Why was Bethany hard to get along with? Did it have anything to do with her murder?

Chapter 7

I saw Jason automatically reach for the notepad he kept in his pocket at all times. He must have changed his mind at the last second, because he reversed course and laid his hand on the table. He probably didn't want to spook Mitch.

"Why wasn't Bethany easy to get along with?" Jason asked. His hand twitched, as if he still felt the urge to take notes.

Mitch opened his mouth to answer, but before he could, Ashlee's high-pitched voice broke in. "There you guys are."

I turned to see her breeze through the door, dressed in her vet scrubs from work. Her hair was pulled back in a ponytail.

"Hey, newsman," she said to Jason. "Covering the murder for the paper?"

Mitch paled. "Newsman? I thought you looked familiar." He pulled back from the table and crossed his arms, not a promising sign.

I tried not to be annoyed with Ashlee. She

couldn't know she'd interrupted an opportunity to find out more about Bethany.

She plopped down uninvited in the chair recently vacated by Mom. "Sure, he's the head honcho for the *Herald.*" She chomped on her gum. "So, what's the scoop?" She looked around the ice cream shop and laughed. "Ha! I made a joke."

"Ashlee!" I snapped. "A woman has died."

Ashlee blushed. "Whoops. You're right. Sorry about that," she said to the table in general.

"How did you find out what happened?" I pointed to her smock. "Weren't you at work?"

"Yeah, but Brittany texted me to say she drove by here a while ago and saw you and Jason in front of the flower place with all the cops and stuff, so she called her friend whose cousin is a police officer and found out the lady who owns the place got shot like fifteen times or something." She blew a bubble, and it exploded with a loud pop.

"Don't be ridiculous," I said. Even if Bethany had been shot, which I didn't know for sure, she couldn't have been shot more than once or twice, based on the amount of blood on her clothes.

"Well, then what happened?" she asked, drumming her fingers on the table.

"We don't know yet," I said.

"Then how do you know I'm wrong?" Ashlee asked in a gleeful tone.

Mitch had been watching our little back and forth as if it were a ping-pong match. He let out a soft groan and started rubbing his temple. A small smile played on Jason's lips. He'd seen Ashlee and me spar before.

I shot Ashlee a look, trying to get her to knock off her antics. "*Anyway*, what were you saying about Bethany?" I asked Mitch, praying that we could somehow get him talking again.

He checked his watch. "Nothing important. Look, I need to get back to work. I have customers to take care of."

I made a show of looking around the empty ice cream parlor. I could have brought the pigs from the farm into the place for a banana split and no one would have been the wiser. "What customers?"

Mitch's face turned red. "We always get a big after-dinner crowd. I need to be ready." He stood.

Jason pulled a business card from the pocket of his leather jacket and handed it to Mitch. "I'll be around the next few days, covering Bethany's death. Here's my card in case you want to talk."

"Sure, sure, sounds great," Mitch said. He dropped the card on the table, where I suspected he'd leave it until we left and he could dump it into the trash.

Ashlee, Jason, and I rose from the table at the same time. I checked my phone and saw it was going on seven o'clock. I felt so tired that I'd half expected it to be closer to nine.

"Say, didn't you see Bethany at lunch today?" Jason asked, breaking into my thoughts.

"She wanted me to verify the flowers for our wedding." *Our wedding.* The idea of getting married and starting a new life seemed at such odds with Bethany's unexpected demise.

"What made you come back after work?" Jason asked.

Ashlee's phone rang. She looked at the caller ID and stepped over to a corner to answer it.

"Bethany called this afternoon to say the supplier couldn't provide the flowers I'd selected for the bouquets," I told Jason. "She wanted me to come back so she could help me decide on an alternate."

He pulled a notebook from his pocket and flipped it open. Now that Mitch knew he was a reporter, there was no reason not to.

"Is that when you found her?"

I tucked a chunk of hair behind my ear and rolled my shoulders to release the tension I felt building there. I knew Jason was simply trying to gather facts about what had happened, but I couldn't help but feel as if he was interrogating me.

"Right. She was lying in the back room. She had blood on her blouse and underneath her."

"No idea what caused it?"

"I'm not a doctor," I said sharply. "She had blood all over her, and she was dead." I felt my face grow hot and felt instantly ashamed at myself for yelling at Jason. "Sorry, I'm just tired."

He pulled me in for a hug. "I'm the one who should be apologizing. You've had a huge shock. I shouldn't be asking you questions right now."

He gave me a gentle kiss, and all the tension eased away.

Ashlee ended her call and rejoined us. Jason and I separated.

"Guess we should reschedule that dinner," I said to him.

He looked at his phone. "No time to make that beef stroganoff, but I could take you to the diner, if you're up for it."

"Not tonight," I said, barely stifling a yawn. "After what happened today, I'm going home to get in my pj's, zone out in front of the TV, and try to forget everything that's happened."

Ashlee let out a squeal and clapped her hands together. "Awesome! We can eat a bunch of ice cream and watch *The Bachelor.* I call dibs on the mint chocolate chip!"

"Wait," I said to Jason, "I think I've changed my mind." But Ashlee was already dragging me outside.

It was just as well. Listening to her nonstop chatter as she critiqued the group of glammed-up women vying for the love of one man, making sure to list the qualities she didn't like about each and every contestant, would keep me from dwelling on finding Bethany's body. At this point, I'd take any distraction I could get.

Two hours later, I was ready to call it a night. Ashlee had polished off her mint chocolate chip ice cream, plus part of my mocha almond fudge. The women on TV had cried enough tears to fill Esther's duck pond.

I pushed myself off the couch. "Okay, I'm spent."

Ashlee stared at me. "But it's barely after nine."

"What can I say? Finding a dead body really took the energy out of me."

"Yeah, sorry that had to happen to you." She frowned. "That totally sucks."

I was oddly touched by my sister's words, such as they were, and almost gave her a hug.

But then she spoke again. "Of course, you've found other people dead, too. Remember that lady from the green living festival? Isn't it getting easier by now?"

"No." Before she could argue, I headed to my bedroom, already imagining my head resting on the pillow.

"Wait!" Ashlee shrieked behind me.

I jerked to a stop, my heart hammering. Slowly, I turned around. "What's wrong?" I asked.

Ashlee rushed over and grabbed my hands. "I just realized the most important thing." Her expression was a mixture of alarm and gloom that made my own anxiety level shoot up.

"What is it?" I asked, wishing she'd hurry up and tell me. Had she thought of a motive for Bethany's death? Was she worried the killer was looking for more victims?

Ashlee gripped my hands tighter. "With Bethany dead, you don't have any flowers for your wedding."

I snatched my hands from her grasp. "For heaven's sake, Ashlee. I don't care about the flowers," I said, as if I hadn't had the exact same thought shortly after finding Bethany's body. Still, it sounded so much more callous when Ashlee said it aloud.

She stared at me with her mouth agape. "You don't care? This is your wedding we're talking about."

"I know that, but they're only flowers. The most important parts are marrying Jason and having our family and friends there to share the experience with us."

She shook her head and made a disgusted sound. "I knew this was going to happen. First you throw this whole thing together in, like, five months or some ridiculous amount of time, when everyone knows you need at least a full year to plan a perfect wedding. Then you pick some shady flower lady who goes and gets herself killed just in time to ruin everything, and you're not even upset about it."

"Bethany wasn't some fly-by-night operator," I said. "She was a well-respected businesswoman who ran that shop for twenty years. And I couldn't possibly have known she'd be murdered when I ordered my flowers from her. It's just a bad turn of events."

"But what are you going to do? You need something to hold when you're walking down the aisle." Ashlee seemed on the verge of panic, almost as though she were the bride without the bouquet.

"I haven't thought about it yet," I said.

"You'd better start. You're getting married in a little over a week!"

Ashlee's panic was contagious. I started pacing in the hallway. "The problem is that Don't Dilly-Dahlia is the only flower shop in town. If I order from a place out of town, I don't know if they'll be able to deliver the flowers fast enough." I tapped my lower lip, considering my options. "If all else fails, I can pick up a couple of bouquets from the Meat and

Potatoes grocery store. They've got a decent flower department." Well, *decent* might be exaggerating a bit, but I didn't have many choices.

Ashlee gasped. "You can't buy your wedding bouquet at the supermarket."

"Why not? I've bought flowers there before, and they always looked nice."

"But it's so tacky," she practically whispered.

"It is not. I'm sure plenty of people have bought their wedding flowers from a grocery store. In fact, one of my friends bought hers at the gas station on the way to the courthouse last year."

Ashlee grimaced, as if the very idea made her nauseated. She snapped her fingers. "Wait, I just thought of something. Violet is Bethany's daughter."

"Right," I said, not sure what she was getting at.

"She brings her dog into the vet's office all the time. I think she even has an appointment coming up. I can call her to confirm and try to find out what's going to happen with the shop at the same time. Maybe she wants to take over the business."

I tilted my head. "I don't know that she'll be ready to make such a big decision. Her mom's been dead less than a day."

Ashlee shrugged. "True, but she may want to keep the shop open in memory of her mom. That means you'd still get your flowers."

"You could be right. And the sooner I find out if I need to start shopping elsewhere for my flowers, the better. It'd be great if you could call Violet tomorrow. Thank you," I said.

"No problem. If you want to show me how grateful you are, you can clean the bathroom this week."

I tried not to roll my eyes. "Let's see what Violet says first."

On that parting note, I headed off to bed. Again. After the day I'd had, I just wanted some sleep.

Chapter 8

The next morning, the alarm sprang to life with a loud blare that yanked me out of a deep slumber. Still groggy, I shut it off and forced myself to get out of bed. Once in the bathroom, I set the shower temperature cooler than usual to help me wake up. When I was done, I wrapped a towel around me, padded out to the kitchen for a cup of coffee with an extra teaspoon of sugar, and returned to the bathroom to get ready. By the time I'd dried my hair and gotten dressed, I was alert enough to face the day, though my neck felt tense. Maybe I'd slept wrong. I grabbed my jacket and headed out.

The farm was quiet when I arrived. An occasional songbird broke the silence as I followed the path past the vegetable garden. Off in the distance, I could see Gretchen at the entrance to the spa, talking on her cell phone. She often had early-morning clients who snuck in a massage or facial before going about the rest of their day. I raised my hand in greeting, and she waved back.

With a few minutes to spare, I headed to the

pigsty to check on Wilbur and his pig pals before I started my workday. Up ahead, I could see a couple of the guests heading toward one of the trails that ran along the back of the property. Most guests didn't venture too far, but the occasional bird or wildflower aficionado would sometimes go exploring.

I found the pigs with their heads in the feeding trough, eating their morning slop. I called Wilbur's name, but he only gave me a cursory glance before returning to his food. I gave him a minute to finish, knowing it wouldn't take long. When the last morsel was gone, he wandered over to where I was leaning against the top railing and snorted at me.

"Good morning to you, too," I said.

He stuck his nose through the gap in the rails and sniffed my pant leg. I scratched behind his ear.

"I don't know if you've heard," I said, "but Bethany, the lady who was providing the flowers for my wedding, was murdered yesterday."

Wilbur stepped back and gave me a wide-eyed stare. I'd have liked to think he actually understood what I was saying, but he probably had indigestion from gulping down his breakfast too fast.

I kept the conversation going. "I was shocked, too, especially since I'm the one who found her. I have no idea why she was killed. Her flower shop doesn't contain enough valuables to make it worth robbing. And while the owner of the ice cream parlor next door hinted at trouble with Bethany, I can't imagine it was anything serious enough for her to be killed over."

Wilbur let out a sigh.

"You're right. I shouldn't worry about it. Detective Palmer is already on the case, and I need to focus on my wedding."

Wilbur snorted his agreement. He wandered over to settle down with the other pigs. I took that as the end of our conversation and went into the house.

Zennia was cooking at the stove. She wore a floor-length paisley-patterned dress that swished around her legs as she moved. Even from the doorway, I could hear her humming, though I didn't recognize the tune.

Hungry diners were due any minute, so I said, "Morning, Zennia. Need any help with breakfast?" I went over to the sink to wash my hands.

She turned from the stove and offered me a smile. "No, thanks. I'm almost finished, and we only have a few guests this morning."

"Okay, then, I'll be in the office." I dried my hands and went down the hall. I spent the morning updating the Web site's blog and brainstorming about the new idea I was working on for holding weddings at the farm. Around ten, Ashlee texted to let me know that she'd called Violet and found out she'd be keeping the flower shop open, even after her mom's murder.

I breathed a sigh of relief. I'd told Ashlee last night that I was okay with buying my flowers at the grocery store, but really, it meant one more task I would have to take care of. Thank goodness that extra worry was now gone.

I worked steadily for the rest of the morning, but by the time noon approached, I'd only finished part of my to-do list. The rest would have to wait until after lunch. I had plans.

Saving my work on the computer, I grabbed my purse and hurried out to my car. As I drove into town, I thought about what I was going to order for lunch.

After Ashlee and I had moved out of Mom's house and into our own apartment several months ago, I'd noticed I was spending a lot less time with Mom. We tried to plan the occasional family dinner at her house, but life had a way of interrupting those plans, and one of us had to cancel more often than not. A couple of months ago, Mom and I had decided to implement a rule that we'd eat lunch together at least once a week, usually at the Breaking Bread Diner. It was our way of making sure we didn't get too out of touch with each other.

I took the off-ramp for downtown Blossom Valley, followed the three other cars that were driving down Main Street, and pulled into the diner's parking lot. The lot was almost full, but I managed to find a space in the corner. I locked my car, trotted to the restaurant entrance, and stepped inside.

The diner's interior was decorated in a tractor theme, an homage to Blossom Valley's agricultural heritage, which included the many pear orchards and grape vineyards that surrounded the town and lined the highway. Photographs of John Deere tractors and farmers plowing fields hung on the walls. Crisscrossed sheaves of dried wheat were artfully nailed over the pie display, although I usually found my attention drawn to the chocolate pudding and lemon meringue pies that filled the case. Shelves too high for children to reach held a collection of toy tractors, while a giant tractor wheel occupied one corner.

Mom sat just inside the door, on a long, wooden bench that held the overflow crowd on the rare occasions when diners had to wait for a table. She'd been perusing the laminated menu, but she looked up when I entered.

I surveyed the dining area and raised my eyebrows. "Are the tables full?"

"No, I thought I'd wait here for you." She rose from the bench and returned the menu to the hostess stand. Shelley, one of the long-time waitresses, saw us and gestured toward an available table off to the side.

We made our way over there. I set my phone on the table and sat down. As soon as Mom took her seat, I rested my arms on the table and leaned forward. "Is everyone talking about Bethany's murder this morning?"

Mom smoothed her napkin in her lap. "Every customer who's come into the store has asked if I know anything. I'm fairly certain half the women aren't even looking to buy clothes today. They just want to hear the scuttlebutt."

"And what *is* the scuttlebutt?" For that matter, what did the word *scuttlebutt* even mean? Didn't you scuttle a ship? What did that have to do with butts? I chided myself for getting distracted by such a silly thought and focused back on Mom.

"I'm afraid I can't help you there," Mom said. "I've been too busy telling the customers I don't know anything to actually find out any new details."

"Maybe there's nothing new to learn," I said. "Bethany was killed less than twenty-four hours ago. And if the police arrested someone, Jason would let me know." At the mention of Jason, I automatically tapped the screen on my phone to activate it, but I had no new messages.

"And Mitch would tell me if he'd learned anything."

"You two seemed pretty chummy last night," I said, tempted to ask about his obvious flirting.

"I don't know about that," Mom said with a little giggle that reminded me of Ashlee when she was excited about a new guy. "But I bet he can help the police with certain information. At the very least, he would know who shopped at Bethany's store regularly or if she was having any issues with the vendors. Word gets around among the businesses on this strip when a company isn't reliable or charges more than they should."

"That's awfully handy," I said, thinking how such a network could really help Esther and Gordon when they needed to contract with a service company. With the farm a few miles outside of town, we didn't exactly have close business neighbors we could rely on.

"They even have monthly meetings to discuss issues that might be affecting all the businesses, like vandalism or loitering," Mom said.

Shelley came over, order pad in hand. "How are you ladies doing on this bright, sunny day?"

I glanced out the window, where I could see the sun struggling to peek out from behind the clouds.

Shelley followed my gaze and then bestowed a

dazzling smile of perfect teeth. "It's always sunny inside the Breaking Bread Diner, no matter what the weather is outside. What can I get you both?"

I ordered a guacamole burger and an iced tea. I'd read somewhere that the avocado in guacamole was good for your heart. Mom requested the chicken breast platter. When Shelley had gone, I leaned forward again. "Between the monthly meetings and Bethany stopping by the ice cream parlor for an afternoon treat, you'd think Mitch and Bethany would have been closer. But yesterday, Mitch said they kept their interactions all business. In fact, he said she could be hard to deal with."

"Mitch said that?" Mom asked.

Shelley brought our drinks to the table. I unwrapped my straw, slid it into the glass, and took a long sip. "So you don't know what he meant by Bethany being difficult?"

Mom stared off into the distance and chewed on her lower lip. "I remember talking to him a few days ago, and he mentioned a meeting with Bethany."

"About what?"

"He didn't say. Only that he hoped she'd see the light and realize what a great opportunity she was passing up."

"What opportunity was he talking about?"

Mom shrugged. "I haven't the foggiest idea, but I got the impression this wasn't the first meeting they'd had. Perhaps they couldn't reach an agreement and that's why he felt she was difficult."

I fiddled with my silverware. "I wish I knew what the meeting was about."

"You should be focusing on your wedding," Mom

said, "not trying to figure out what got Bethany killed."

I didn't answer as Shelley approached the table with our plates. I leaned back to make room. She set the burger before me, gave Mom her chicken, and left a bottle of ketchup in the middle of the table. After we thanked her and she walked off, I took a bite of my burger. The cool and creamy guacamole was a heavenly contrast to the hot burger. Juice from the meat ran down my hand, and I hurriedly wiped it away.

From across the table, Mom watched me and sighed. "I should have ordered the burger."

I nodded toward her boneless, skinless chicken breast sitting on a lettuce leaf. A small pile of white rice and two broccoli stalks sat next to it. "Well, um, I'm sure that chicken is delicious, too."

Mom laughed. "You're a terrible liar, but thanks for pretending."

I uncapped the ketchup bottle and shook it. A red blob plopped onto my plate. "Do you know Bethany's daughter at all? Ashlee said she was planning to keep the store open."

"That makes sense. Violet has worked at the shop for a couple of years, so I'm sure she knows all the ins and outs. Bethany and I were talking not long ago about letting our kids pick their own careers, but Bethany was thrilled that Violet might be interested in inheriting her flower shop one day."

"When I stopped by yesterday at lunch, she mentioned that Violet was interested in changes to the business, but Bethany didn't like any of them. She even joked about how Violet would have to wait another twenty years to get her hands on the shop." I cringed at the memory.

Mom had been about to cut into her chicken but stopped with her knife and fork poised over the plate. "It's like she sealed her own fate."

I took another bite of my burger. "What else did you and Bethany talk about? She mentioned how I'd moved back home after being laid off, and I was wondering how she knew that."

"It might have been from me. Bethany and I would run into each other every now and again since we both worked downtown. I'm sure I talked about you girls quite a bit."

I sipped my iced tea. "What did you think of Bethany?"

Mom cut off a piece of chicken. "She was pleasant enough to talk to, but I wouldn't call us friends. After all, friendship is a two-way street, and as much as Bethany loved to ask questions about my life, she never really seemed willing to share anything personal about hers. In fact, she seemed standoffish most of the time."

I remembered how uncomfortable Bethany's questions had made me. It sounded like she was that way with everyone. "Did she have any close friends?"

Mom dabbed at her lips with her napkin. "Not that I ever knew of, but then, I'd only see her occasionally near her shop, never anywhere else."

We finished eating, and Shelley brought our bill. It was my turn to pay, so I left the tip on the table, and we walked up to the register together. Mom stepped off to the side to touch up her lipstick, while I waited for the cashier to finish ringing up the diners in front of us. Two middle-aged women entered the restaurant and hovered at the nearby hostess stand so they could be seated.

One of the women saw Mom and rushed over to her. "Dorothy, can you believe what happened at the flower shop? Were you working at Going Back for Seconds yesterday? Did you see anything?"

This must have been what Mom's entire morning had been like.

Mom shook her head and plastered on a patient smile. "I was working, but I didn't see anything, Tricia. In fact, I didn't even realize something had happened until I heard the sirens."

"Still, you must be terrified it could happen again."

"I hardly think so," Mom said. "There's no reason to believe anyone else is involved."

Tricia made a tsking sound. "I wish I had your faith. I'm convinced someone else is going to die."

Mom frowned. If it hadn't occurred to her before that the killer might strike again, she certainly couldn't escape the ghoulish thought now. "I'm sure we're all safe. Hardly anyone ever gets murdered around here."

Tricia gave Mom an incredulous look. "Did you forget about that murder at the new day spa a few months ago? And didn't someone else get killed not long before that? This town isn't nearly as safe as you seem to think."

The couple in front of me finished paying and headed for the door. I stepped forward and handed the cashier my tab, along with money I'd pulled from my wallet. As she rang me up, I turned to Tricia.

"I agree with my mom. Bethany's death was an isolated incident."

The other woman, who had remained silent up until now, let out a squeal and pressed her knees together, like a kindergartener who suddenly realized she has to go to the bathroom.

She stretched out her arm and pointed her index finger at me. "Oh my God, oh my God, it's you!"

I took a step back. The change the cashier had been handing me slipped through my fingers. I heard the coins drop onto the glass top, but I kept my eyes on the woman.

Who did she think I was?

Chapter 9

At the other woman's declaration, Tricia's eyes went wide. "What are you talking about, Nola?"

Nola kept her finger pointed at me. "She's the one who found Bethany Lancaster."

I held back a groan. How did she hear it was me?

Tricia brushed past Mom and came over to where I stood. "What did you see? Was it just awful?" From her tone, it was clear she was hoping my answer would be yes.

"I didn't see much," I said. "I stopped by the flower shop for an appointment, discovered Bethany in the back room, and called the police. That was it."

"Did you see any clues, like on TV? They're always finding fingerprints and loose hairs that identify the killer."

I felt like yelling at this woman to stop being so insensitive, that this wasn't some TV show, but for all I knew she was an important customer where Mom worked. I kept my tone even. "I wasn't looking for clues. I was looking to help Bethany."

Tricia's lips formed into a pout, as if she had expected me to say Bethany had written a dying message in her own blood or maybe I'd found a trail of footprints leading straight to the killer's house.

All this talk about the crime scene brought memories from yesterday flooding back. I remembered Bethany on the floor, blood seeping out of her, her eyes open but unfocused. I could feel the guacamole burger I'd eaten start to protest, as if it might rise up in revolt.

"For heaven's sake," Nola said, snapping me back to the present. "Let this poor girl alone. She's been through enough." She looked slightly chagrined. "I should have left you alone, too. I was just so surprised when I realized who you were."

Tricia looked down. "Sorry. I didn't mean to badger you. I'm sure I sound like some excited gossiper, but really I'm terrified. My teenage son works afternoons at Get the Scoop. Thank God he wasn't working yesterday, but I might make him quit after what's happened. He'll be furious, but I can't help worrying that whoever killed Bethany might be hanging around, waiting to kill again."

Nola nodded toward Mom and me. "Maybe they're right, and no one else is in danger."

"I'm not sure I'm willing to take the risk," Tricia said.

I felt a slight pressure on my hand and realized the cashier was still trying to give me the rest of my change. I hastily accepted the handful of bills, picked up the coins that had fallen, and stuffed the money in my pocket.

As I did that, Shelley came up front, grabbed two menus, and led the women to a table, but not before they apologized again. After they walked off, Mom and I made our exit.

"Phew," I said once we were outside. "This must be how celebrities feel. Well, minus the paparazzi shoving cameras in our faces, and all the money and perks that go along with being famous."

"Was it really that bad?" Mom asked. "I thought Tricia and Nola were a bit dramatic, but nothing we couldn't handle."

"You're right, although I do wonder how they knew I was the one who discovered the body." Mom stopped at my car to say good-bye, but I motioned for her to keep going. "I have a few minutes. Why don't I walk you back to work?"

We cut through the parking lot and out onto the sidewalk. Going Back for Seconds was down the next block.

As we settled into a walking rhythm, Mom said, "I'm afraid those women might have found out from me. Remember how I forgot I was in the middle of my shift last night? I had to explain to my boss why I'd been gone so long. I'm sure I mentioned that you were the one who found the body, and she probably told others. You know how fast news spreads in this town."

I exhaled loudly, knowing Mom wasn't exaggerating. Not only did news spread faster than milk spilling out of an overturned carton, the facts had a way of becoming more distorted with each telling. "I bet by the time the gossip makes its way back to you, people will think *I'm* the killer."

Mom shook her head. "No one could ever think my sweet daughter is capable of killing another person."

"You may be a teensy, weensy bit biased, but thanks for the vote of confidence."

Mom came to a sudden stop and stared across the street. "Well, would you look at that?"

I turned to see what had attracted her attention. Violet was out front of the flower shop, sweeping the sidewalk. She wore a dark green canvas apron, maybe even the same one I'd seen her mother wear, over jeans and a T-shirt. The door to the shop was propped open, and the Open sign was lit.

"Wow," I said. "Ashlee told me Violet would keep the business going, but I didn't expect for it to be so soon. She didn't even wait for Bethany to be buried." For one morbid second, I wondered if Violet would be creating the flower arrangements for her own mother's funeral, but I banished the thought from my mind. It was really none of my business. "We should go pay our condolences," I said. I barely knew Violet, but considering I'd found her mother's body, offering condolences seemed like the right thing to do.

I checked for traffic; then Mom and I walked across the street. As we approached, Violet glanced up and stopped sweeping. By the time we reached her, she'd set the broom on its bristled end and was clutching the handle as if it were keeping her upright.

"Can I help you?" she asked in a tone that implied she'd rather do anything but.

Up close, I could smell the cigarette smoke and coffee on her breath. Her brown hair looked just as unkempt as the night before, and her eyes were puffy. Maybe she should have taken the day off.

"Violet, I don't know if you remember me. I met you a few weeks ago when I was here to talk about my wedding order. My name's Dana. I'm the one who . . ." I waved my hand helplessly toward the shop.

Recognition dawned in Violet's eyes. "You found my mom," she said, her voice dull.

"I can't tell you how sorry I am for your loss. Your mom was a lovely person," I said. "So helpful and knowledgeable about her flowers."

This earned a smile. "The customers loved her. This shop meant everything to my mom. Everything," she repeated.

"Please let us know if we can help in any way." Mom pointed across the way. "I'm Dorothy, and I work right over there in the secondhand clothing store."

"Sure, of course. I've seen you around," Violet said, her tone more animated. "And thank you for your offer. I'm handling the situation as best I can, but it's nice to know people care enough to help."

As we talked, I noticed several cars slowing almost to a stop as they eased by the shop. I wondered how many of these drivers were the same ones who had driven by last night when the emergency vehicles were here. Nothing attracted attention in this town like a little murder.

"Someone told me you'll be keeping the shop open," I said. "I'm sure your mother would be pleased."

"You already heard about that? Word gets around quick."

She sounded irritated, and who could blame her? I'd just finished complaining about that very thing. "This place is the only flower shop in town. People must be curious about what's going to happen."

"They don't need to worry," Violet said. She tilted the broom handle against the curve of her shoulder to free up her hands, reached into her apron pocket, and pulled out a pack of cigarettes and a lighter. She shook out a cigarette, flicked the lighter to life, and lit the cigarette's tip. "I plan on running the shop just like my mom, at least for now. People will get their flowers." She exhaled a stream of smoke through her nostrils and squinted at me through the haze. "Including you and your wedding order."

I held up my hands. "I don't want to add to your grief," I said. "If you aren't ready to handle my order, I could buy my flowers at the Meat and Potatoes market so you wouldn't have to worry." I realized I'd essentially said grocery store flowers were equal to ones from a professional flower shop.

"Not that those flowers would be nearly as nice as yours," I added belatedly.

Violet dropped her half-finished cigarette on the sidewalk and ground out the tip with her black tennis shoe. She rubbed her forehead with the back of her hand. "Your order is fairly straightforward, and frankly, I could use the distraction. If I keep myself busy with work, maybe I won't feel so overwhelmed about everything." Her eyes followed the cars that drove slowly by. "And like the whole world's watching to see what I'm going to do."

"The three of us standing on the sidewalk is probably attracting even more attention," Mom said. "We'll get out of your hair."

"Good idea. Maybe I could stop by tomorrow?" I asked Violet. "Your mom wanted to show me a couple of alternate flowers for my bouquet." Too bad I couldn't remember the name of either one of them.

"Tomorrow would be good," Violet agreed. "I'll look over my mom's ledger tonight. She always took meticulous notes."

"Great, I'll see you then. And again, please accept my condolences."

Violet nodded and resumed sweeping. Mom and I paused at the curb for a break in traffic. When the next car slowed down in front of the flower shop, we trotted across the street and said our good-byes in front of Going Back for Seconds.

I hurried back to the diner parking lot, aware that my lunch hour had gone longer than I'd intended, thanks to my talk with Violet. As I stuck my key in the ignition, my cell phone chimed. I checked the screen. Jason's text offered a makeup dinner for the one I'd canceled the previous evening.

I couldn't type my reply fast enough. I mean, sure, one of Jason's home-cooked meals sounded heavenly. But more importantly, I was dying to know what he'd found out about Bethany's murder.

Chapter 10

The afternoon oozed along slower than the organic honey Zennia often bought at the farmers market. After I'd checked the clock for what felt like the hundredth time, my extended workday finally came to an end.

As I saved the document I'd been working on, the office door opened and Esther walked in. "Oh, good, Dana, you're still here."

I swiveled my chair around to face her. "You caught me as I'm wrapping up for the day," I said, hoping she'd take the hint. I was anxious to meet Jason. "What can I do for you?"

"I won't keep you." She held up two spools of wide ivory ribbon in a shimmery fabric that reminded me of the inside of a conch shell. "I wanted to show you the ribbon I found at the craft store. I thought it would look so pretty wrapped around the gazebo posts."

My irritation vanished, replaced by guilt. Here I was trying to rush Esther out of here and all she wanted to do was help me with my wedding. Shame on me.

I stood up and hugged her. "The ribbon is beautiful. It'll look fantastic tied on the posts."

Esther's cheeks turned pink. "I want your big day to be the best it possibly can. You know how fond I am of Jason. And you, too, of course."

"With your help and Zennia's, too, I know my day will be wonderful. I couldn't possibly have planned this wedding without you."

Esther bit her lip and sat down in the metal guest chair near the door. Clearly she had something else on her mind. I settled back into my office chair.

"I heard what happened to Bethany," she said. "Will her passing cause you trouble with your flowers?"

"No, her daughter plans to keep the shop open, and she said she can take care of my order."

Esther's eyebrows came together, causing a deep furrow to appear. "Violet? I never pictured her following in Bethany's footsteps. They're such different people. Then again, she's worked there longer than I ever expected she would, so perhaps she enjoys the business more than I thought."

I almost slapped my forehead as the figurative lightbulb went on. "That's right. I forgot you knew Bethany for years." I studied Esther's face for any signs of grief. "How are you holding up?"

Esther tugged on her blue-and-white-checkered shirt. "Well, of course, I was stunned beyond words when I heard she was murdered. To think someone waltzed right into her shop and killed her is impossible to imagine."

"I'm so sorry. It's hard to lose a friend," I said.

She tipped her head. "She was a good woman, but I'd call her more of an acquaintance than a friend. Once we disbanded the Blossom Valley Rejuvenation Committee, I rarely saw her."

How could I forget the rejuvenation committee, a group of three who were intent on drumming up business in Blossom Valley? I'd helped the committee on several occasions, from setting up a cricket-chirping contest to organizing a green living festival to painting pictures on store windows when I had little experience painting anything, including my own fingernails. I'd done a private dance of joy when the group had broken up, and pushed those memories to the far reaches of my mind.

"Tell me more about Bethany," I said. "From my few interactions with her, she seemed very nice."

Esther started fiddling with the hem of her shirt again, never a good sign. "Yes, she could be nice," she said, pulling on the fabric even harder.

"Could be? Does that mean she normally wasn't?"

Esther let go of her shirt and ran her hands over her legs. "I don't want to speak ill of the dead. Overall, Bethany was as sweet as a bowl of peach cobbler on a warm summer's day."

I kept my gaze fixed on Esther. "What about when it wasn't a summer's day?"

She avoided making eye contact. "Sometimes . . . she seemed a little too interested in other people's lives."

"So she was a gossip," I said. "We've got plenty of those around town." I didn't bother to tell Esther

I'd met two such women at my lunch with Mom today.

She shook her head. "Not so much a gossip. I'd say more of a snoop. She liked to ask really personal questions and was always watching you like she was waiting for the tiniest secret to slip out, like an egg popping out of a chicken."

I cringed at the image, but Esther didn't notice.

"I don't think she passed the information along to anyone," she said. "I got the feeling she just liked knowing everything about a person, especially the stuff they didn't want other people to know."

Esther's description dovetailed with what Mom had told me. If Bethany had pried into the wrong person's life, she might have discovered information that had gotten her killed.

Esther stood up and smoothed out her shirt. "Look at me, babbling on like I am, and here you said you were about finished with work. I'm sure you have plans tonight."

"Dinner with Jason. He's cooking beef stroganoff."

Esther laid a hand on her cheek. "I remember when Arthur and I were engaged. Such a wonderful time." She made a shooing motion at me. "Now skedaddle. You don't want to keep your beau waiting."

I laughed at her antiquated words, but she didn't need to tell me twice. I hurriedly shut down the computer, grabbed my purse and other belongings, and headed to my car. Here I'd been looking forward to what Jason might have learned about

Bethany, but thanks to my little talk with Esther, I might be the one with something to share.

Forty-five minutes later, I had showered, donned a pair of dark jeans and a light blue sweater Ashlee swore was a dead match for my eyes, and dried my hair. After adding a touch of makeup, I grabbed my keys and drove across town to Jason's duplex, which would be my home, too, in another week. I smiled when I saw the porch light already on, a sign he was waiting for me. Mom did the same thing when she was expecting Ashlee or me to visit.

I locked my car and walked up the steps, noting the freshly mowed lawn and carefully swept walkway. My cleaning skills were decent, but Jason's put mine to shame. Maybe I'd place him in charge of the cleaning once we were married. But then, would it be fair to make him cook, too?

Still divvying up the chores in my head, I knocked on his front door. Jason opened it after a moment.

"Hey, gorgeous," he said, pulling me in for a kiss that set my insides on fire.

We broke apart. "Wow, you sure know how to greet a gal," I said.

"Not just any gal. My soon-to-be wife. And there's plenty more where that came from." He winked at me, which only fanned the flames.

He ushered me inside and closed the door. I sniffed the air and picked up a decidedly rich and beefy aroma that made my mouth water.

"Have I ever told you how much I love beef stroganoff?" I asked.

"That's why I made it. Come try a bite." He took my hand and led me to the kitchen, where he dipped a spoon in one of the pans on the stove and held it out for me.

I slurped up the sauce, savoring the rich, salty flavor. "Mmm, so good." I batted my eyelashes at him. "Are you going to cook like this every night after we're married?"

Jason leaned down and gave me a kiss. "Not every night. When I'm under deadline, we may have to rely on sandwiches."

"Or pizza," I said. "Or one of those giant trays of macaroni and cheese I'm always tempted by in the frozen food section. And don't forget there's always ramen noodles."

Jason clutched his stomach. "You and your packaged food. I'm definitely going to be in charge of meals, or I may not survive."

I lightly punched his arm. "My eating habits aren't that bad. I even made a salad for dinner the other night." Sure the lettuce had been buried under a pile of shredded cheese, bacon bits, and ranch dressing, but it was in the bowl somewhere.

"At least you're making progress." He put on an oven mitt, opened the oven door, and pulled out a tray of roasted broccoli. "And here's another chance to eat your vegetables."

I eyed the broccoli. It sizzled on the pan. "I hate to admit it, but that looks pretty tasty. Is that parmesan cheese on top?"

"It adds a subtle saltiness." He pulled two plates down from the cupboard and scooped up a pile of rice that was waiting in the other pot on the stove.

He spooned generous helpings of beef stroganoff over the rice, added a few stalks of broccoli to the side, and carried the plates over to his dining room table, where place settings and glasses of red wine already waited. We sat down to eat.

"Aunt Virginia called this afternoon," Jason said as he lifted his forkful of stroganoff.

"That's your mother's sister, right?"

"Right. She wanted to tell me that Uncle Rick won't be coming to the wedding."

I sipped my wine. "Is he sick?"

"No, he fell off the ladder while cleaning out the gutters and chipped his tailbone. He's not up for traveling."

"Poor guy," I said. "Is Aunt Virginia going to stay home and take care of him?"

Jason shook his head. "Their neighbor will watch him while Aunt Virginia flies out here."

"I'm glad." I caught myself. "Not about Uncle Rick and his tailbone, of course. But I'm looking forward to meeting more of your relatives." Jason's parents visited on rare occasions, but I had yet to meet any other family members.

"I only hope you see Cousin Eddie before we've opened the wine. After a few glasses, he usually starts speaking with a cockney accent and pretending he's in the cast of *Mary Poppins*."

I laughed. "Sounds fun."

"If you say so."

We spent the rest of the meal chatting about other kooky relatives, like my great-uncle Fred, who thought it was hilarious to try to scare me with his false teeth, even though I'd stopped freaking out by the time I'd turned ten.

As soon as I'd finished the last bite and wiped my mouth with a napkin, I said, "Thanks for dinner. Everything was absolutely delicious."

"I aim to please."

I washed my meal down with the remnants of my wine and set the glass firmly on the table. "Since we're done eating, you can tell me all about Bethany's murder, and anything Detective Palmer's shared with you." Though reporters and detectives were often at odds, at least on TV, Jason and Detective Palmer had become friends over the years and sometimes traded bits of information. The detective knew Jason could be discreet when necessary.

Jason wiped his own mouth and set his napkin next to his plate. "I'm impressed you made it through dinner. I figured you'd start asking questions before I'd taken the first bite."

I gestured toward my plate. "You worked hard on the stroganoff. I didn't want to spoil it by talking about murder."

"In that case, how about letting our food settle first? Discussing what happened might give you indigestion," he said with a detectable twinkle in his eye.

"Now you're pushing it." I grinned at him. "Spill it, or I won't tell you what *I* know."

Jason leaned across the table. "And what do you know?"

"You first."

I tried to look fierce, but I was bluffing. If Jason

refused to divulge anything, I'd spill my info in a second.

Thankfully, he didn't call my bluff. "I'll make you a deal," he said. "I told the guy next door that I'd feed his dog while he's out of town. Come help me, and I'll tell you everything I've found out."

"Deal," I said. I held out my hand, and we shook.

We carried our dinner plates into the kitchen. Since Jason had cooked, I handled the dishes while he wiped down the counters and straightened up. That done, we headed to the other half of the duplex.

Cutting past the neighbor's shrub, we walked up to his door. Even before we made it there, I could hear the dog barking from inside, one persistent bark after another, occasionally punctuated with a growl.

"It doesn't sound terribly friendly," I said. "Does it bite?"

Jason pulled a key out of his pocket and inserted it in the lock. "The only real danger is that she'll lick you to death."

"Guess I can take my chances."

He unlocked the door, and I followed him in. Immediately, I felt a series of rapid paw taps on my knees. Jason flicked on the light, and I looked down to see that I was being bombarded for attention by a copper-colored cocker spaniel. It started to whine. I reached down and ran my fingers over its silky fur.

"That's Molly," Jason said. He squatted down, and she abandoned me and ran to him to be petted.

We both showered the dog with affection for a

minute, before Jason rose and led the way to the laundry room, where two dog dishes waited. I filled one with fresh water while Jason scooped dry dog food into the other. After Molly wolfed down her dinner, we took her outside to do her business.

The backyard held a small patio with a kettle barbecue. The rest of the space was devoted to a large lawn and two lemon trees. While Molly romped in the grass, I sat in a plastic patio chair, crossed my arms and legs, and stared hard at Jason.

He gave me a knowing smile. "All right, I guess you've been patient enough." He dragged another patio chair over next to mine and sat down. "What would you like to know?"

"Everything. Start with how Bethany actually died."

"She was shot once in the chest."

I shuddered. "Shot?" I repeated stupidly, though Ashlee had already told me that. Then again, she'd also told me Bethany had been shot fifteen times, so I hadn't put too much credence in her information. I watched Molly sniff around the yard. "That might actually help Detective Palmer. Not everyone owns a gun."

The dog brought a ragged tennis ball over and dropped it at Jason's feet. He bent down, picked it up, and launched it across the grass. Molly bounded after it. "True. Once he has a list of possible suspects, he can check to see if any have a weapon's permit, although someone could have acquired a gun illegally."

"Blossom Valley isn't exactly known as a great

place to buy illegal guns from some guy in a dark alley."

Jason shook his head. "It's more sophisticated than meeting in back alleys these days. You can find someone selling guns on any number of Web sites if you know where to look."

I'd never heard of any such sites, but I took his word for it. "Do they know what time she was killed? Was it right before I got to the shop?"

"Looks that way. Couldn't have been more than an hour before. Probably much less."

I tried not to think about what would have happened had I gotten off work early that day. "Did anyone hear the shot?" I asked. "That late in the afternoon, people would be going home from work, kids are out of school. Plenty of people should have been around."

"The ice cream parlor was packed with a group of kids who'd just won a soccer game. I talked to one of the employees, and she said she might have heard a bang, but with the kids screaming and hollering, she couldn't be sure. A man came out of the store across the street and heard what he thought was a firecracker, but he figured some kids were goofing around in the back parking lot. A few other people reported hearing a pop, and one person even called nine-one-one, but no one looked around for where the sound came from."

Molly brought the ball back. This time I grabbed it before Jason could and heaved it across the yard. "Did anyone at least see anything?"

"The guy who may have heard the shot didn't notice anyone suspicious, but he admitted he wasn't paying attention. The employee at the ice cream shop said she was too busy watching the kids to make sure they didn't drip ice cream on the floor or use up all the napkins. Then two boys started playing tag around the tables, so she had her hands full. The woman who called nine-one-one was fairly close to the flower shop but saw nothing unusual."

I made a mental note not to work in an ice cream parlor if I ever lost my job at the farm. "I don't remember seeing any kids when I tried the front of the flower shop, but maybe they were gone by then." I watched Molly where she was lying in the grass and chewing on her tennis ball. I had a hard time picturing a bunch of kids celebrating a soccer win on one side of the common wall, while poor Bethany lay dying on the other.

I could feel Jason studying me. "You all right?"

"Just got lost in my thoughts for a minute." I straightened in the plastic chair and tried to wave Molly over with her ball. She ignored me.

"So what's your big news?" Jason asked.

I thought about what Esther had told me earlier. Now that I was about to pass it on to Jason, I wasn't sure the information was such a huge deal. "I'd classify it more as little news."

He scooted his chair closer. "Tell me anyway. You never know what's important."

"When I was talking to Esther this afternoon, I recalled that she'd actually known Bethany for a long time. You remember how they were both on that rejuvenation committee?"

Jason put a hand over his mouth, but he couldn't

quite hide the smirk. "Who could forget that albino alligator you painted on the pet store window?"

"It was a cat," I huffed. "Anyway, Esther told me Bethany was a bit of a snoop. Loved to worm everyone's deep dark secrets out of them for her own personal pleasure."

Jason rubbed his goatee. "Are you thinking she was killed when she found out something she shouldn't have?"

"Maybe. It's really the only thing I've heard about her that could possibly provide a motive." Molly finally brought the ball back over, and I tossed it across the lawn again. She ran after it. "Although when I say it out loud, it seems unlikely. If someone is harboring a horrible secret worth killing over, they wouldn't blurt it out to Bethany simply because she asked. When I was talking to her, she tried to ask me how many secrets you knew about the people in town, but I didn't take the bait."

"Still, you might be on to something. I interviewed several owners and employees of nearby businesses and was met with cool responses from more than a few. I got the impression they weren't crazy about Bethany but didn't want to say so. I bet they're more forthcoming with Detective Palmer."

We watched Molly play for a few more minutes. Eventually, she flopped down in the grass, panting. I took that as a signal she was done playing and stood up. Jason followed me inside, with Molly trailing slowly behind. I petted her a few more times; then we went back to Jason's side of the duplex.

"Would you like a drink?" Jason asked once we were inside.

"Thanks, but I need to get going. I have work in the morning."

Jason took my hand and pulled me over to where he stood. I gazed into his warm green eyes and felt a swirl of excitement.

"You sure?" he asked. He leaned down and kissed me.

When we separated, I said, "Maybe not all that sure, but I should go. Work starts early."

He gave a slight bow. "As you wish, milady."

"You should enjoy your solitude. I'll be moving in pretty soon, and then you'll never get rid of me."

"I wouldn't want to."

He walked me to my car, gave me another kiss, and then watched as I drove away. A few minutes later, I parked in my assigned spot next to Ashlee's salsa red Camaro and climbed the outside stairs to our apartment.

When I got inside, I found Ashlee firmly ensconced on the living room couch. She was staring at the television and her favorite reality show, which seemed to mostly consist of twenty-somethings drinking too much and acting stupidly.

I closed the door a little harder than was necessary. The bang jolted her from her hypnotic state.

"Hey, Dana, you totally missed it. Some chick got drunk and climbed on a table to dance, only she fell on this guy who was drinking a beer, and that guy fell backward and knocked over some other guy, who fell in a fish tank."

"Gee, I'll have to catch that episode in rerun," I

said, adding a healthy dose of sarcasm to my tone. I dropped my purse in a chair and then slipped off my shoes before placing them in the hall closet.

"No need. I can rewind it for you."

I held back a sigh. Whoever had invented the DVR, with its ability to rewind live television, really hadn't thought through the possible consequences.

"Is this what you did all night?" I asked. "Watched drunk people fall down?"

"No, I went to dinner with that guy Logan, the one I told you about, but he has to get up early for work, so we didn't stay out late. Now watch."

Ashlee scrolled back to the start of the scene and played it for me. I paid partial attention to the show as I made my way over to the couch and sat down. She froze the playback to the spot where the second guy was about to fall over.

"Look at his face," she said gleefully. "His mouth is totally hanging open. He has no idea what's happening." She pushed play again, and we watched the rest of the scene unfold. I had to admit it was kind of funny, though I felt bad for the fish when the guy landed in their tank.

Ashlee paused the TV again and pointed at the screen. "Yuck, did you see that chick's shoes?"

I tried to find which pair had made her stop the recording, but they all looked perfectly acceptable to me. "There's nothing wrong with the shoes," I said, "but that reminds me I need to check with you about the wedding."

Ashlee turned to me, and her face lit up. "I got this awesome idea today for my bridesmaid's dress. I could cut a slit in the skirt—"

I held up a hand. "Don't even think about it."

She stuck her bottom lip out. "Where's the sex appeal? The dress doesn't even show off my cleavage. Makes me feel like a nun."

A nun in a bridesmaid's dress? "It's a wedding, not a cocktail party. Don't alter the dress."

"Fine. It's your stupid day."

"Keep that in mind." I was starting to see how brides turned into bridezillas. Maybe they all had sisters like Ashlee. "I wanted to make sure you have matching shoes. I didn't even think to ask earlier."

"Are you kidding? I've got at least ten pairs I could use. You know, it's almost too bad Brittany's moving in. I could turn your bedroom into a giant closet."

"I bet Brittany will let you borrow her clothes."

Ashlee smacked her lips together. "You're right. I'm, like, doubling my wardrobe this way, and it won't cost me a thing."

I rose from the couch. "Since the shoe question is settled, I'm off to bed. See you in the morning."

"See ya." Ashlee returned to the TV, where two men were bumping chests, clearly on their way to a fight. Why did my sister watch these shows?

I went into the bathroom to wash my face and brush my teeth. After I put on my pajamas, I crawled under the covers, running through my mental to-do list for tomorrow. Everything on the list was the usual assortment of work items and chores to do at the apartment, nothing out of the ordinary.

Nothing, that is, except my meeting with Violet. I had a feeling that would be anything but ordinary.

Chapter 11

The next morning, I arrived at the farm half an hour earlier than normal. I wasn't sure how long my meeting with Violet would run, and I wanted to get a head start on my workday in case I needed to make up any extra time if our meeting ran over.

On my way past the chicken coop, I noticed the empty basket was hanging on the hook, which meant Esther hadn't been out yet to collect the morning eggs. Might as well start my day mingling with the chickens. I grabbed the basket, unlatched the door, and let myself into the coop.

Berta, the largest and most outspoken of the chickens, watched me as I moved from box to box to collect the eggs. I could hear slightly threatening clucking noises coming from her direction, but at least she didn't try to peck me like she usually did, most likely because I skipped right over her nest. When I finished my rounds and walked out the door, Berta emitted a loud squawk at my retreating back.

I waved over my shoulder. "See you tomorrow."

She probably wouldn't see me tomorrow, since Esther almost always collected the eggs, but I had to let that chicken know who was in charge.

I took the basket of eggs into the farmhouse's kitchen, where Zennia was chopping onions at the counter. I heaved the basket up next to where she was working, grabbing one egg as it threatened to roll off the top of the brimming basket. "I hope you were planning to serve omelets this morning, because the chickens produced way more eggs than usual."

Zennia's eyes widened when she saw the pile. "Must be that new organic feed I started them on. Well, I'm sure I'll find a use for all the eggs. I just need to get creative."

"You could always make egg salad sandwiches or deviled eggs for lunch," I suggested as I went to the sink to wash my hands. "With low-fat mayonnaise, of course."

"Not a bad idea." Zennia set down her knife. "Speaking of deviled eggs, I wanted to go over your wedding menu so I can make sure I'm not leaving out any of your favorite appetizers. We only have a few days left, and I'll need time for grocery shopping."

"Sure. What time works for you?"

"Let's meet around three, right before I leave for the day."

I dried my hands and refolded the towel before setting it on the counter. "See you at three." I grabbed a banana out of the ever-present fruit bowl and went down the hall to fire up the computer.

I was knee-deep in marketing work when Gretchen, our masseuse, came into the office. With her short black hair and nose ring, she added a trendiness to Esther's place that had been missing before, though I was fairly sure the nose ring gave Gordon an ulcer.

"Dana," she said, sitting down in the guest chair. "I just heard about what happened."

With my thoughts on discounts and increasing guest totals, it took me a moment to figure out what she was talking about. "You mean with Bethany?"

She leaned forward. "Is that who owned the flower shop? Did you really find her body?"

Considering Gretchen spent most of her workday in the spa, our paths rarely crossed, and I wasn't surprised she was only now hearing that I was the one who'd discovered Bethany.

"Yes, in the back room."

She blanched. "Wow. That must have been rough."

I nodded. "It was definitely a shock."

"And so terrible, too. I've never been in the flower shop, but I've passed it plenty of times on my way to the ice cream parlor. The lady inside would always wave at me. Was that Bethany?"

"Most likely, unless you saw her daughter, Violet. She's the only other person who works there." I felt a sadness settle over me and changed the subject. "So you like the ice cream at Get the Scoop?"

"I used to love the pralines and cream, but the last couple of times I ordered it, I noticed it tasted funny. Maybe the guy changed his recipe. Or it's the weather. Ice cream never tastes as good on a cold day."

I laughed. "Oh, I don't know. Ice cream always tastes good to me."

"I switched to chocolate chip, which is almost as good." Gretchen stood up. "Anyway, I'd better get back to work. I only stopped in to make sure you're doing okay."

"I'm fine. Thanks for checking."

She left, and I tried to concentrate on my work. I managed to keep myself busy with Web site duties and other marketing odd jobs for the rest of the morning.

As soon as noon hit, I drove to town for my meeting with Violet. I tried to park in front of her shop, but every spot on the block was taken, which was a rare occurrence. I parked on the next block and walked back.

On the way past Get the Scoop, I glanced in the window, wondering if they might be having a giant ice cream sale, but the place was deserted. Why on earth were there so many cars here, then?

I pushed open the door to Don't Dilly-Dahlia and got my answer. At least a dozen people, mostly women, milled around the store. I saw a few customers perusing the ready-made bouquets or studying the coastal photos on the walls, but most didn't seem particularly interested in buying anything.

Violet stood behind the counter, watching the crowd and gnawing on her fingernails. I made my way over to her.

"Is this still a good time for our appointment?" I asked. What little conversation there had been in the shop vanished as soon as I spoke. I felt a dozen sets of eyes fasten on me.

Violet dropped her hand and gave me a curt nod. "Now is the perfect time." She picked up a pen and tapped it on a vase of carnations like she wanted to quiet down a crowd before a big speech, never mind that the group was already silent.

"I'm sorry, everyone," she said. "I'm afraid I have to close the shop for an appointment. If you would like to purchase anything, please make your way to the register. Otherwise, I'll have to ask you to leave."

General shuffling and mumbling broke out as people moved toward the door. I stepped to the side of the counter in case anyone wanted to buy flowers, but no one did. Within thirty seconds, the shop had emptied out, and Violet and I found ourselves alone.

"Has it been like this all morning?" I asked.

She came out from behind the counter, walked to the door, and flipped the Open sign to Closed. "Yes, and I'm absolutely disgusted. You wouldn't believe how many people I had to chase away from the curtain that leads to the back room. They were trying to get a peek at where my mother died, like this is some kind of freak show. It's much worse today than yesterday."

"Maybe you should close the shop for a few days until interest dies down."

"Then people will think I can't handle my mom's death. Or that I'm incapable of running the business." She chewed on another nail. "No, I need to ride this out, whether I want to or not."

"At least you've been working here a couple of years, so that should help. I imagine you already know everything you need to about the flower business."

Violet ran a hand through her long brown hair and sighed. "Not everything. I mostly took care of deliveries and filled the small orders. Mom's the one who handled the major sales and ran the business end. But like I said yesterday, she always took excellent notes, so I'm sure I can figure it out." As if to reassure herself, she pulled out the ledger I'd seen Bethany use and opened it.

I leaned on the counter and tried to read the ledger upside down but couldn't. "Are you the only employee?" I asked. "There's no one else who can help?"

"Nope, it's just me. Mom always had a steady stream of customers, but I wouldn't say business was booming. Between the two of us, we easily managed all the orders. I suggested to her a while back that we could sell other items and expand the business, but Mom was too set in her ways." Violet riffled through the pages of the ledger until she stopped at one. "Let's talk about your flowers."

We spent a few minutes hashing out the options until I'd decided on the alstroemeria to replace the delphiniums in my bouquet. She jotted down notes, promised she'd have no problems supplying the new flowers, and then closed the ledger.

As she slid it forward on the counter, presumably to move it out of the way, a corner caught on the spirals of a small tablet that had been tucked next to the cash register. The tablet shot forward and fell to the floor at my feet.

I bent down to retrieve it and felt the cell phone in my back pocket inch up, as if it might pop out the top of my pocket. I grabbed my phone before it could, set it on the counter, and retrieved the tablet. Violet accepted it with a thanks and frowned at it.

"I found this stuck inside the lining of Mom's purse last night when I was rooting around for her car keys," she said. "It must have slipped through a tear in the lining."

"What's in it?" I asked.

"Hardly anything." Violet flipped open the little tablet and held the page toward me. "All of the pages are blank except this one."

The page was divided into two columns. The heading on the left column read, "CH," and the other heading read, "LM." A series of numbers was listed in the first column, mostly in the hundreds, with the numbers gradually increasing. The column under "LM" was blank.

I looked at Violet. "What do you think the letters mean? Or the numbers?"

"I'm guessing the letters are initials of Mom's customers and the numbers are payments. Mom must have been recording their payments in this notebook for some reason."

I cocked my head. "If your mom was as meticulous about taking notes as you say, I would expect her to keep all customer information in a single ledger. Having two sets of payment records is kind of risky."

"Since it was in her purse, maybe the customers had given her money when she wasn't at the store," Violet said. "These might be friends who paid her when they were visiting her at home or something, and then she transferred the information to her ledger the next time she was in the shop."

"Hmm . . . maybe." Her idea didn't make a whole lot of sense. "Have you compared the initials to the customers listed in her regular ledger?"

Violet tucked her hair behind one ear. "I haven't had the chance yet. I'll do it later. Frankly, I'm not too worried about it."

I dropped the subject. She already had enough to deal with, and here I was pestering her about some little tablet she'd found that might prove completely unimportant. "Okay, well, I'm glad everything is in order, but please let me know if there's anything you need from me."

With a nod to Violet, I headed to the door. Out on the street, an older-model car that had seen better days backfired with a loud bang. I glanced back at Violet and saw her duck behind the counter. Almost immediately, her head rose back into view.

She gave me a sheepish look. "For a minute there, I thought that was a gunshot."

I returned to the counter. "It certainly sounded like one. I don't blame you for ducking down, not after what happened to your mom."

"I told my mom we didn't need that gun."

It took me a second to realize what she was saying. "Wait, your mom was killed with her own gun?"

Violet nodded. "She'd had it for years. Said she

didn't always feel safe working in the evenings, especially in the winter when it gets dark so early. Of course, she never had to use it, not once."

"Where did she keep it?" Had her killer known she had a gun?

"In the back room. On a shelf behind a couple of pots."

"That doesn't sound very secure."

Violet gave me a sharp look. "Hardly anyone ever goes back there, so it's not like every customer who walks in here has access to the gun."

"Huh, okay. It's just that I was in the back room yesterday." Sure, I hadn't noticed the gun behind the pots, but it still seemed unsafe to leave it out in the open.

"I'm surprised," Violet said. "Mom was pretty strict about keeping customers out."

"She wanted to show me a bunch of greenery and thought it would be easier for me to go in the workroom rather than for her to carry it all out. If she let me back there, maybe she allowed whoever shot her back there, too."

Violet paled. "Do you think it was someone she knew? I assumed a burglar came in the back door and she surprised him." Tears formed in her eyes. "I can't help but think how horrible it was that Mom was shot on my day off. If I'd been working with her that evening, she might still be alive."

I went over and laid my hand on hers. "You couldn't have possibly known what would happen."

She sniffed. "I know, but I can't help thinking things might have turned out different."

When she didn't say anything else, I patted her

hand and headed for the door once more. "I should let you get back to work."

"Do me a favor and turn the sign back over on your way out. I think I'm ready for round two." Even as she said it, her fingers flew to her mouth. Her poor nails didn't stand a chance.

"Stay strong," I said. I turned the sign to Open and made my way out of the shop. My stomach growled, and I thought about what I wanted to eat for lunch. I didn't have time for a sit-down meal at the diner, but the idea of a greasy cheeseburger or high-sodium chicken sandwich from one of the fast-food joints didn't hold much appeal.

I glanced around, and my gaze settled on Get the Scoop next door. Looked like my best choice was ice cream. I needed a daily dose of calcium for strong bones, right?

Not sure my logic would hold up under Zennia's scrutiny, I nevertheless went into the shop and up to the counter, where a girl who looked to be fresh out of high school was nodding her head in time to whatever music was playing through her earbuds. When she saw me, she slowly pulled out first one earbud and then the other.

"Can I help you?" she asked.

"I'll take a scoop of vanilla gelato in a cup, please." I'd read somewhere, probably in the same article that touted the benefits of guacamole, that gelato had less fat than ice cream. Not only was I getting a calcium boost, but I was consuming less fat, too. My lunch was practically healthier than a spinach salad.

"That's one of my favorites. The owner uses only natural ingredients, you know."

"Yes, he's mentioned that to me."

The clerk pulled a paper cup off the stack and glanced at me. "Do you know Mitch?"

"Not well. Is he a good boss to work for?"

She nodded. "The best. He comes in at the crack of dawn or some crazy time before any of us get here to make all the ice cream and fill up the display cases. I don't have to worry about any of that. I'm strictly in charge of scooping up orders and ringing up the customers. One time I came into work super early, thinking I could help him make the ice cream and show him what a good employee I am, and he got totally mad at me. Said my place was behind the counter, and he would handle all the work in the back." She filled the cup to the point where I thought the top half of the scoop would tumble out, then stuck a pink plastic spoon in the mountain of gelato. She handed me the cup, and we both moved down to the register, where she rang me up. I noticed her name tag said, NICOLE.

I handed her my money and gestured to the door behind her marked Employees Only. "Mitch isn't back there right now, is he?"

She squinted at the cash register like maybe my gelato order had confused her. "No, he'll be in later." She pushed several buttons and the cash drawer popped out. She gave me my change and slid the drawer shut.

"Too bad. He and I were talking the other night when Bethany was killed, and I was wondering if he'd heard anything more about what happened to her."

Nicole's face brightened, but I chalked it up to an interest in sharing what she knew rather than delight that Bethany was dead. "Can you believe what happened? I mean, I was working right next door when she got shot. In fact, I've been thinking about it, and I'm pretty sure I heard the gunshot, even with all the brats that were in here running around." She put a hand to her heart, and her eyes got big. "I'm just glad *I* didn't get killed, too."

"Lucky break for you," I said. "Any chance you saw anything? A suspicious-looking person entering the flower shop? Or maybe someone lurking near the back door?"

"I wish. My friends would think I was so cool if I saw a real, live killer." She sounded downright wistful for a second, then caught herself. "I mean, don't get me wrong. It's a total bummer that Bethany is dead." Her face brightened again. "I did hear a bunch of yelling, like people were having an argument, but that was at lunchtime, not after work when she got shot."

My skin tingled. An argument at the shop on the same day Bethany had died could easily be connected to her murder. Was this before or after I'd stopped in to see her?

"Was Bethany one of the people yelling?" I asked.

"I think so. I couldn't hear what they were saying, but it sounded like her voice. I was taking the trash out to the Dumpster and her back door was open." She put a hand to her mouth and her eyes got wide, like an actress in a B horror film. "Do you think she was fighting with the killer? Like, maybe I could have been shot, too, if it had happened right then?"

I shrugged. "I doubt it. You said this argument was at lunchtime, right?"

"Or a little after. I guess you're right that it probably wasn't the killer."

I spooned a bite of gelato in my mouth. The rich vanilla flavor spread over my tongue. Absolute heaven. "Did you know Bethany well?"

"Not really," Nicole said. "She used to come in here all the time for what she called her afternoon fix. Then about a month ago, she stopped."

"Do you know why?"

"No, at first I figured she was on a diet. I mean, sure she only ever ordered pineapple sherbet, but every calorie counts, right?" For a second, she sounded exactly like Ashlee, who was almost always on one diet or another. Nicole shook her head, bringing my attention back to the conversation. "Anyway, I said something to Mitch about it, and he told me Bethany was a big chicken and couldn't face him after she refused his deal. He was pretty steamed."

Here was yet another reference to this mysterious business deal. Mitch must have been on the losing end, considering how mad he was.

"No idea what deal he was referring to?"

She tilted her head, as if trying to remember, but then she shrugged. "I don't know. It probably had something to do with Mitch's plans for this place."

My fingers were starting to go numb from holding my cup of gelato, so I switched hands. "What plans?" I asked.

"Mitch is always talking about expanding. Thinks the shop's way too small. He's right about that. When it's summertime, or baseball season, all the kids come in here after their games or for birthday parties. We can barely fit everyone in here."

"Was Mitch trying to buy out Bethany so he could have her space?"

More shrugging. "I think so. She did start showing up again, though. A couple of weeks ago. Looked like she was gloating about something, but she never said why she'd stopped coming in or why she was back."

I heard a customer walk in behind me. Nicole moved down to the display area to wait on them, ending our conversation. I found a seat at a small table near the window and took another bite of gelato. It had softened while we'd been talking, and melted gelato was starting to puddle under the pile in the center, but I barely noticed. I was too busy thinking about Mitch and his expansion plans.

If he kept trying to talk to Bethany, and she kept rebuffing him, that would imply she wasn't interested in selling. I remembered the pride she'd shown when telling me about starting the business from scratch. She certainly hadn't sounded like someone who was ready to sell, especially if she thought Violet was interested in continuing the family legacy. But how would killing Bethany guarantee Mitch could buy her place? Was he banking on Violet not being interested in the business after all and selling to him instead?

And what about this second ledger with the two sets of initials? Did the numbers in the columns really represent payments? If so, the customer in the first column ordered a large quantity of flowers on a regular basis. I could see spending hundreds of dollars on a one-time purchase, like I was for my wedding, but why so often? Esther had mentioned that Bethany liked to extract information from people. Was she blackmailing someone?

The person who had come in for ice cream left, and Nicole went through the door marked for employees. I finished the last of my gelato, stood, and tossed my cup into the trash. Just as I reached the door, Detective Palmer appeared on the other side.

"Good timing," he said.

That piqued my interest. "Oh?"

"I was planning to set up an appointment with you for this afternoon, but then I saw you through the window."

An appointment with a homicide detective? Suddenly the gelato wasn't sitting so well. "Did you have more questions about my finding Bethany? I'm afraid I haven't remembered anything else."

"Not about that exactly." He extended an arm toward the tables. "Maybe we could sit down. This might take a few minutes."

That sounded ominous. Why was he being so vague? The air in the ice cream shop was cool, but I felt much too warm. I picked a table near the front, trying to gain a few extra seconds to gather my thoughts. What on earth did he want to talk about?

I sat down in a chair at the same moment Nicole came out from the back. She gave a little start when she saw me with Detective Palmer, then moved up to the counter and started rearranging the plastic spoons in their holder. I half expected her to cup a hand around her ear in an attempt to hear whatever we were going to say.

Detective Palmer must have noticed her eavesdropping as well, because he pushed his chair back in before he'd even sat down. "We should take a seat outside. For more privacy."

I stood and followed him out of the ice cream shop, and we settled at one of the tables in front. A handful of people were walking along the sidewalk, but no one paid the slightest attention to the two of us.

I placed my elbows on the table. "So, what did you want to talk about?"

Instead of answering me, Detective Palmer pulled a notebook out of his inside jacket pocket, flipped it open, and silently read the page. My skin started to prickle as I waited for him to speak.

At last, he looked up. "Let's talk about the final conversation you had with Bethany Lancaster in person."

"What do you mean? She was confirming my flower order for my wedding bouquet."

"And what was the tone of that conversation?"

I could feel my forehead scrunch up as I mulled over his question. "I would say there was no tone. She asked if I was sure about my choices and if I wanted fern fronds, and I told her that sounded nice."

Detective Palmer consulted his notebook again. "You two didn't argue? Maybe about the cost?"

"No, Bethany's prices were very reasonable." My mouth started to feel dry. "Didn't you already ask me these questions?"

"I spoke with a witness who states you and Bethany were arguing."

Any microscopic beads of saliva that remained in my mouth vanished. Detective Palmer had a witness who said I was arguing with the dead woman? I didn't need to be a detective to figure out what he was implying.

I was now a suspect.

Chapter 12

"Bethany and I weren't arguing," I said, shaking my head. "Besides, we were alone in her shop. In fact, she forgot to unlock the door that morning, and I was her first customer of the day. No one could have overheard us."

Detective Palmer studied me like Berta the chicken had when I was collecting the eggs this morning.

Nicole came out to fill the napkin dispensers on the tables, being careful not to look directly at us as she moved from table to table. She cleared her throat twice, and the sound hit a switch in my brain. I remembered someone clearing their throat like that at Don't Dilly-Dahlia.

"Wait. There was a woman. Is that who's saying these things?"

Detective Palmer waited for Nicole to go back inside the shop and then took out a pen. "Why don't you tell me your side of events?"

I sat up straighter, feeling more confident now

that I had an explanation for the detective. "She came in right at the tail end of my conversation with Bethany. She was picking up an order."

"And that's when she heard you arguing with Bethany?"

I held up my hands, fingers splayed. "We weren't arguing!" I realized I'd practically shouted the words at a man who could snap handcuffs on me at any second. I lowered my voice. "Like I said, Bethany and I never had a single disagreement during any of our meetings." I tried to recall the last conversation I'd had with her. We'd been talking about the flowers and how I was on a budget. Then Bethany mentioned brides who spent huge amounts of money on special orders and how crazy their demands got. It was at that point that the woman had interrupted.

I slapped the tabletop in triumph. "I've got it! I know what happened."

"Do tell," Detective Palmer said.

"Bethany was entertaining me with stories about all these bridezillas who made outlandish requests, like the one who insisted Bethany paint the roses to match the color of her bridesmaids' dresses. I told her that was absolutely ridiculous." I held up one finger. "No, come to think of it, I didn't say ridiculous. I said unacceptable. Then Bethany told me she did whatever it took to make her clients happy. That must have been what the woman overheard."

Detective Palmer jotted notes on his pad. He said, "Hmm . . ." in a way that let me know he wasn't particularly convinced by my story.

"Don't you see? The other customer must have heard the tail end of the conversation and thought I was telling Bethany there was something unacceptable about my own order. She took my comment completely out of context."

"Are you sure you didn't say anything else that would lead her to think there was a problem?"

"Positive." I leaned back in my chair, drained of energy. "What happens now?"

Detective Palmer closed his notepad. "I continue with my investigation."

"But what about this witness? Aren't you going to tell her that she was mistaken?" Even as I said it, I realized how dumb my suggestion was.

Detective Palmer allowed a small smile to slip through. "We don't usually correct witnesses on their recollections."

"Right, of course."

He stood. "Thank you for your information. I'll be in touch if I have any more questions."

I barely acknowledged him as he walked away. I stayed in my seat, marveling at our conversation. I wasn't sure if I should be worried that the detective might suspect me, or ticked off. After all, we weren't strangers. He should know I'd never kill someone.

I heard the shop door open again. Nicole walked over and held out a Styrofoam cup. "I thought you might like some water."

"Thanks," I said as I accepted the cup.

She looked to where the detective was climbing into his unmarked police car. "I should probably tell him about that fight I heard in Bethany's shop, huh?"

I'd forgotten all about that. Did she mean when Bethany and I were discussing demanding brides? The timing worked, but our conversation could hardly be described as one that involved yelling. Then again, the other customer had thought we were arguing, so maybe it was a matter of perspective.

"I think he already knows about it," I said.

"Okay. That's good." She retreated back inside while I took a drink. The cool water felt like ice against my burning mouth, and I gulped it down.

When the last drop was gone, I rose, placed my cup in the trash, and nodded my thanks to Nicole, who was watching through the window. I realized that in my dismay over Detective Palmer's questions, I'd forgotten to mention the little tablet that Violet had found. Then again, those initials and numbers might mean absolutely nothing. Rather than waste the detective's time if I was wrong, I'd wait until I knew more.

A powerful gust of wind blew into me. I shivered, whether from the unexpected cold or the idea that I might be an honest-to-goodness suspect in the eyes of the police, I wasn't sure.

Looking over at the storefront for Going Back for Seconds, I decided to stop in and see if Mom was working. I could use her input on Detective Palmer's latest line of questions.

I barreled across the street, barely managing to avoid the front fender of an SUV on its way past.

The driver leaned on his horn, and I offered a halfhearted wave of apology. Didn't this guy understand that I was involved in a murder investigation? Not to mention, I was getting married in a few days?

After scurrying the rest of the way across, I trotted up the steps. I yanked open the door, and the little bell banged against the glass with a ferocious clanking sound. The handful of customers inside turned to see who was causing the commotion, but I immediately focused on Mom in a nearby corner.

As soon as she saw me, she rushed over and put her hands on my shoulders. "Dana, you look upset. What's the matter?"

I glanced around to make sure we were relatively alone in this part of the clothing store. "I ran into Detective Palmer at the ice cream parlor, and apparently a customer at the flower shop overheard Bethany and me talking the day she died and thought we were arguing. We actually weren't, and I explained what really happened, but I'm worried Detective Palmer believes I got in a big fight with Bethany." I stopped for a breath and then went on. "Is there any chance he might think I killed her?"

Mom pursed her lips. "Of course not. The man knows you. Why, you've even helped him with a few of his murder investigations."

Detective Palmer would probably classify my "help" as interference, but of course, Mom wouldn't say that. "I told him how Bethany and I were talking about her more demanding customers and that my comments were directed at them, but I don't think he believed me."

"I'm sure he did." Mom reached up and smoothed down my hair. "He knows how honest you are."

I found her words reassuring, but I also knew she would have said them no matter what. Still, I felt my heartbeat ease up from its hammering.

"I hope you're right. I mean, even if Bethany and I had been arguing over my order—" I broke off as a woman who'd moved over to our section whipped her head around. She caught my eye and quickly turned back to the rack of clothes she'd been looking through. "Which we weren't," I said loudly, "but even if we were, a tiny argument is no reason to kill a person. Detective Palmer is smart enough to realize that."

"Absolutely." Mom paused. "All the same . . ."

My heartbeat picked up again. "What?"

"Perhaps I should call Harry Wilson. Get his take on the situation."

I took a step back. "Do you really think I need a lawyer?" The last time Mom had contacted the family lawyer was when Ashlee's boyfriend had been killed. Obviously if Mom thought I needed legal counsel, she was more concerned about Detective Palmer's questions than she was letting on.

"No, no, I'm sure you don't," she said. "But I've known him for years and value his opinion."

I wanted to believe her but couldn't quite yet. "Are you sure that's the only reason you're calling him?"

"Of course." She smoothed down my hair again, a calming gesture from my childhood. "Say, why don't you and Ashlee come over for dinner tonight?

We could have a meal with just us girls before you get married."

A home-cooked meal from Mom sounded like exactly what I needed. "I'd love to."

"Perfect. Why don't you text your sister? You know how I don't like to bother her at work with phone calls."

Somehow, Mom was under the mistaken belief that Ashlee only checked her text messages when she was on a scheduled break or at lunch. I knew for a fact that Ashlee grabbed her phone the moment it signaled a text, but I always played along so Mom could keep her faith in Ashlee's work ethic.

"Sure." I reached into my back pocket, but my hand came up empty. I patted the denim, even though I knew the gesture was futile. My phone wasn't there. "Shoot."

"What's the matter?" Mom asked.

"I don't have my phone. Where did I leave it?" I mentally retraced my steps. I hadn't used it at Get the Scoop, nor could I remember taking it out of my pocket like I usually did whenever I sat down. The last place I remembered having the phone was at Don't Dilly-Dahlia, when I'd placed it on the counter. "I think it's at the flower shop. I'll run over there to get it and text Ashlee. I'll call you as soon as she gives me an answer." I gave her a quick hug. "Thanks for all your help."

I went down the steps and to the curb, careful this time to wait for a break in traffic before I crossed the street. On the other side, I pulled open the flower shop door and stepped inside. Violet was talking to a middle-aged man with short brown hair who had his back to me. I checked the counter next to him, where I remembered setting my phone earlier, but the space was empty.

I felt a flicker of panic. Had someone walked off with it after I'd left?

Getting in line behind the guy, I tried not to tap my foot as I waited for my turn. Instead, I studied his suit jacket. I was no expert, but the material looked expensive and fit the man's broad shoulders quite well.

"You're positive your mother never talked about me?" I heard the man ask Violet. His voice sounded strained. His back was ramrod straight.

"I'm sorry, but I already told you no. Mom didn't usually talk about her customers, but rest assured that I follow the same strict code of business that my mother did. The flowers will be top quality and the prices won't change."

"Yes, I'm sure they will be. I thought Bethany might have mentioned me since I'm such a frequent customer."

"And I'm sure she appreciated your business," Violet said, handing him two bouquets of one dozen long-stemmed roses intermingled with baby's breath and wrapped in polka-dotted cellophane. "As do I, Mr., um, Mr. Hawking, is it?"

The man's shoulders relaxed as he accepted the bouquets. "Call me Carter."

I blinked. Carter Hawking. This man had the same initials as the ones in Bethany's extra notebook. Could it be the same man?

Violet thanked him, and he turned to leave. He

would have bumped into me if I hadn't sidestepped out of his path in time.

His eyes grew wide. "I didn't realize anyone else was here."

"I just walked in," I said.

"Well, excuse me," he said, and headed straight for the door.

Violet noticed me and reached under the counter. "I bet you're looking for this," she said as she held up my phone.

I let out a puff of air. "Thank goodness. I don't have the money to buy a replacement."

"As soon as I noticed you'd left it, I put it under the counter for safekeeping."

"Thank you." I jerked my head toward the door. "Who was that?"

Violet looked toward the door, though the man was gone. "A long-time customer, from the sounds of it. He sure was acting strange, though."

"How so?"

"He kept mentioning that the flowers were for his wife, like I might not believe him, and he must have asked me at least three times if Mom had ever talked about him. Maybe she gave him a discount or extra flowers because he was a repeat customer. But if that were the case, why not just ask?"

"Maybe he was hoping you'd be the one to suggest it." Violet didn't seem to know any more about the man, and I wasn't positive he was the same one whose initials were in Bethany's book, so I let the topic drop. I held up my phone. "Thanks again for keeping this for me."

"No problem. Have a good day." She headed to the back room, and I exited the store.

Up the street, I could see the man with the bouquets a couple of blocks ahead of me. On a whim, I went after him. If I could find out more about this guy, maybe I could figure out what those numbers meant in Bethany's notebook. If he really was being blackmailed, I'd pass the information along to Detective Palmer and make him forget all about that lady who thought Bethany and I had been arguing. And if I was wrong, well, no harm done.

I strolled down the street, trying to act natural in case he glanced behind him, but he never looked back. He stopped at a silver Mercedes and reached in his pocket. I slowed down and tried to quell my disappointment. If he drove away, I would have no way to follow him. As I got ready to turn around, he opened the back door of the car and laid one of the bouquets on the seat. Rather than getting in the driver's side as I expected, he returned to the sidewalk and continued walking. I followed.

At the corner, he hung a right, and I quickened my pace. I rounded the corner to find him half a block ahead. He turned up a walkway to what I knew was a small office complex with law and accounting firms. Maybe he worked at one of those businesses, although if that were the case, why park his car so far away?

I waited until he was out of sight and then turned up the same walkway. The complex was comprised of two parallel buildings with a breezeway running in between. Each building had two stories with four businesses on each floor. The doors faced the center aisle, with external staircases on each end. A cement walkway connected the two buildings on the second floor.

I scanned the staircases to see if he'd gone up one of them, but he was nowhere in sight. Anxiety started to work its way through my chest. Which door had he gone in?

The moment I started through the breezeway, I spotted him on the other side of the buildings, at the edge of a small parking lot. I was halfway through the breezeway when he stopped and turned around. I hopped behind a large shrub, hoping I'd disappear in the shadows as I continued to watch him.

He still held the bouquet of roses in one hand. With his other, he pressed a cell phone to his ear.

A moment later, I heard a door open somewhere above me and footsteps clumping down the stairs. An Asian woman a few years younger than me, dressed in a white blouse and a black knee-length skirt, came into view as she pivoted coming off the stairs.

I bent down and pretended to tie my shoe, realizing belatedly that I was wearing slip-ons, but the woman barely glanced my way. She rushed to the back parking lot and into the waiting arms of Mr. Hawking. He pulled her closer to the office building wall, probably to avoid being seen from any upstairs windows. I had to crane my neck to keep them in view as the two engaged in a kiss so passionate that I felt like a pervert for watching them.

Judging by how these two were meeting in a back parking lot, the odd way the man had questioned Violet, and the knowledge that Bethany's little notebook might be for keeping track of her blackmail victims, I had a sneaking suspicion that this woman was not Mr. Hawking's wife. But then, who was she?

Chapter 13

Carter and the woman broke apart from their passionate embrace. The woman clutched the flowers to her chest and glanced down at them every few seconds, the smile on her lips evident even from this distance. After another minute of talking and the occasional kiss, she headed back toward the buildings, sniffing the flowers as she went.

No way would my shoe-tying ruse work a second time. I stood up and headed through the breezeway, as if I was finished with an appointment and on my way out. I stopped at the directory attached to the front of the building and scanned the businesses. As I'd suspected, accountants and lawyers occupied most of the offices.

I heard footsteps moving up a set of stairs inside the complex, most likely the woman returning to her office. Then I heard a man's cough nearby. My blood froze.

Shoot. I should have realized Carter would have to come out this way. What a knucklehead I was. I dropped to my shoe once more, just as he came through the breezeway. I kept my eyes on the ground as he moved past me, shifting a little to angle my back toward him. He probably hadn't paid enough attention to me in the flower shop to recognize me from behind.

I waited in that position until I could no longer hear his footsteps. Then I stood and headed down the sidewalk back toward Main Street and my car. Carter was only a block ahead of me, but he was walking briskly.

He rounded the corner onto Main and stopped at his Mercedes. I considered my options. I could dawdle long enough for him to drive away before I reached his car, or I could bolt past him so fast he would barely have a chance to look at me. In the end, I decided on a steady pace that exuded confidence, like I had a destination in mind. Even if he did recognize me, he'd have no reason to think I'd been following him. Unless, of course, he realized I was the one who'd pretended to tie her shoes back at the office complex.

I sped up a tad at that thought and held my breath as I approached where his car was parked. Through the windshield, I could see him fastening his seat belt. If he noticed me as I went by, he didn't react.

When I reached my own car without incident, I let out my breath, hopped in, and backed out of the parking space. As I straightened out my wheels, I glanced up and saw Carter backing out of his space up the street from me. The impulse was too great. I followed him again, keeping my eyes glued to his back bumper, rather than the dashboard clock that would surely tell me I had doubled my lunch hour. Good thing I'd come in early today.

Carter roared through town a consistent ten miles per hour over the speed limit and rolled through every stop sign rather than actually coming to a complete stop. Apparently the man was a little reckless, which matched my idea of how an adulterer behaved. I kept up my speed so I didn't lose him, though I made sure to stop at every sign and keep two or three cars in between us so he wouldn't notice me.

After several more blocks, he turned another corner, went down half a block, and pulled into a long driveway marked Private. The driveway ran alongside a single-story stucco house with a flower bed full of sprightly daisies out front.

I slowed down and read the wooden sign that swung from the porch roof. It said, HAWKING, STENTON, AND TRUTNER LAW OFFICES.

I turned at the next corner and worked my way back to Main Street and then the highway, thinking about what I'd discovered.

Carter was a lawyer. His girlfriend worked at a law firm. I pictured some sort of lawyer's conference they had both attended, where they happened to sit down on adjoining stools at a fashionable hotel bar and started a conversation that was completely innocent at first. Then one drink followed another, and a relationship had been born.

Was this something I had to worry about with Jason? With his dreamy green eyes and adorable dimples, he'd already caught the eye of more than one girl in town.

I dismissed the idea. I had complete trust in Jason's faithfulness.

Then again, Carter's wife probably did, too. If Bethany had somehow uncovered Carter's infidelity, he might be willing to pay to keep the information quiet, which would explain that secret tablet. And if he'd grown tired of Bethany's demands, he may have killed her rather than risk her exposing his secret.

I realized with a start that I was back at the farm. I'd been so lost in my thoughts that I'd barely paid attention to my driving. I parked in my corner spot and pulled out my phone. Out of curiosity, I opened a search engine in the Web browser and typed in the name of Carter's law firm.

The first search result appeared to be for his Web site. I clicked the link and almost groaned out loud. Carter's firm specialized in divorces. Maybe he could represent himself if his wife found out he was cheating and decided to leave him.

I got out of my car and followed the path past the vegetable garden and pool area, and entered through the French doors that opened to the dining room. With lunch long over, the room was bare and quiet. I darted across the hall to the office, threw my purse in the bottom desk drawer, and texted Ashlee about dinner. Once she accepted, I gave Mom a quick call and then dedicated my attention to the marketing project I'd been working on.

When three o'clock arrived, I stood and stretched, trying to relieve the tension in my muscles from working on the computer for so long. I went into the kitchen to see Zennia.

She and Esther sat at the large oak table, looking at a cookbook. I peered over their shoulders at a picture of a dip with crackers around it.

"That looks tasty," I said. "What is it?"

"Southwestern hummus with baked pita chips, plus I'll add some sliced cucumbers for dipping, too," Zennia said.

Hummus was not something I would ever pick on my own as an appetizer, but if anyone could make it taste good, Zennia could.

"Interesting," I offered. "Have you made this recipe before?"

"All the time," Zennia said. "It's my go-to recipe for parties."

"And we all know someone who has a big party coming up." Esther looked up at me with a wink.

"I mentioned to Esther that we'd be reviewing the menu this afternoon," Zennia said, "and she wanted to sit in. I was showing her a few of my choices."

I bent over and put my arms around both women's shoulders. I gave them each a squeeze.

"Goodness, what was that all about?" Esther asked, patting my arm.

I felt tears spring up. "I can't thank you both enough for all that you're doing. It means the world to me."

A familiar blush crept up Esther's neck. "You've thanked me plenty already."

"I just want you to know how much I appreciate everything. Planning a wedding is way outside my comfort zone, but because of you two, I think I might just pull it off."

"I'm delighted to help," Zennia said. "A friend's daughter is interested in attending culinary school next year and can't wait to assist me with all the prep work. She figures it'll be a good trial run for when she eventually opens her own catering business."

"And I love to help with weddings," Esther said. "Nothing makes me happier than seeing two young people in love and starting a new life together."

"Well, please know how much you both mean to me."

I gave Esther's shoulder one last squeeze and then sat down at the table. Zennia went down the list of appetizers, which included the stuffed mushrooms and a vegetable platter, along with shrimp cocktails with wild-caught shrimp, seasonal fruit, crispy kale with yogurt dip, citrusy crab salad in cucumber cups, and half a dozen other dishes.

"My gosh, Zennia. How are you ever going to prepare all this food?"

"I can do a lot of the prep work ahead of time, and like I said, I have my friend's daughter helping me."

"But it's so much work," I said.

"I can always pitch in," Esther said. "I'll make sure I have the whole morning free to help Zennia."

"And I can help, too, when I get the chance," I said. "At least with the chopping and mixing. Not so much with the actual cooking."

Zennia shook her head. "Nonsense. I don't want you lifting a finger in this kitchen on your big day."

I felt that familiar warmth in my chest. Planning my wedding over the last few months had really reminded me of what wonderful people I had in my life.

Before I could thank Zennia again, Gretchen came through the back door and went straight to the refrigerator. "Afternoon, ladies," she said over her shoulder. She removed a container of yogurt from the fridge, pulled the lid off, and grabbed a spoon from the silverware drawer. She took a seat next to me.

"Dana, I can't believe I never asked you about your wedding flowers when I heard Bethany had been killed. What's going to happen now? Can another florist fill your order in time?"

"Her daughter, Violet, is taking over. She assured me there should be no problems."

Gretchen stirred her yogurt. "I met Violet once. She seemed really nice."

"Yeah, she is," I said. "Where did you guys meet?"

"At a class the library taught over the summer. Well, not a class so much as a place for us writers to meet up." Gretchen blushed. "It's silly really."

Zennia looked up from a cookbook. "I didn't realize you're a writer, Gretchen."

"I'm not," she said hurriedly. "I write short stories sometimes, but not for anyone else to read or anything. I used to love writing when I was a kid, before my mom . . ." Her voice trailed off.

I knew Gretchen's mom had died when she was

a teenager and her dad had worked two, even three, jobs to keep the family afloat. Gretchen had fallen in with a group of questionable kids and gotten into some trouble. She'd eventually straightened out, but she rarely talked about that period in her life.

"I'd love to read some of your work, Gretchen," I said, "if you're comfortable with that, of course."

She focused on her yogurt, but I could see a tiny smile form. "Maybe." She spooned up a mouthful of yogurt. "What were we talking about? That's right, Violet. She was at the meetings, too. I guess she writes plays. They even put on one of her plays at the community college near where she used to live. She said the reviews were really good."

"No kidding," I said. "I wonder if she'll continue that or focus completely on the flower shop." Was writing plays her real passion, and she'd only been working at her mom's shop to pay the bills?

Gretchen shrugged. "I don't know, but she mentioned she was working on another play." She stood up. "I'd better get set up for my next client. Take it easy." We all said good-bye as she walked out.

Esther, Zennia, and I talked over the menu awhile longer before Zennia gathered her things and prepared to leave for the day. Esther decided to go for a walk, and I went down the hall to the office. All this talk about the wedding had given me the urge to call Jason. Besides, he didn't even know what I'd discovered about Carter or my little run-in with Detective Palmer.

Thinking about the detective turned my mood

somber. Maybe it was a good idea that Mom was calling her lawyer.

I shut the office door, sank into the chair, and hit Jason's number on my cell phone.

"Hey, Dana, how's my beautiful bride-to-be?"

"Better now that I hear your voice."

His tone switched from jovial to concerned. "Is something wrong?"

"I'm hoping I'm making a mountain out of a molehill, as they say, but Detective Palmer asked me more questions today."

"Not unexpected. You did find the murder victim."

"Yes, but his questions revolved around a supposed argument another customer overheard between Bethany and me."

Jason was silent a moment. "Supposed argument?"

"We weren't arguing at all, not even close, but a woman heard me say a couple of things and jumped to conclusions."

"You told that to Detective Palmer, right?"

I nodded, not that Jason could see that. "Of course, but I'm not sure he believed me."

"Detective Palmer has to follow every lead, no matter how weak, but I'm sure he believes you. How about I take you out for dinner to take your mind off your troubles?"

"I wish I could, but I'm having a girls' dinner with my mom and Ashlee. It should be a lot of fun. We'll probably spend the whole time talking about the wedding."

"Is Ashlee sad that you're moving out soon?"

I laughed. "Are you kidding? I found her and Brittany measuring the windows in my bedroom for curtains the other day. She can't wait to see me go." I leaned back in the chair and put one foot on the corner of the desk. "Before I forget, I might have some juicy little information for you regarding one of Bethany's customers." I rehashed everything I'd discovered during my lunch break.

When I finished, Jason let out a low whistle. "If Bethany was blackmailing Carter, that would be a solid motive for killing her. But I wish you hadn't followed him. You could've gotten hurt."

I downplayed his worry. "It was the middle of the day with plenty of people around. I'm sure he didn't spot me. Now I need to figure out who the other set of initials belongs to."

"Or you could pass the information to Detective Palmer and let him figure it out. He is a professional."

"I will. In fact, I'd like to think this information will help keep him from focusing on me."

Over the phone, I heard someone talking in the background and then Jason's muffled reply. To me, he said, "I'm waiting for a callback from Detective Palmer to get more details about the crime. I could tell him what you found out and see if he has any other suspects."

"Thanks, but I'd like to call him myself. Show him what an upstanding citizen I am."

"Don't worry. He already knows. Besides, he has plenty of suspects to consider."

I put my foot down and sat up straighter. "Like maybe Mitch? I talked to the girl at the ice cream shop today, the one who was working when Bethany was killed. She said Mitch wanted to buy Bethany out and expand his business."

"I wasn't talking about Mitch, but that's interesting. I heard he wants to buy the vacant building at the end of the street that used to house the auto parts place."

"Really? Then why would he bug Bethany about selling her half of the building?"

"No idea, unless he was weighing his options."

"So who *do* you think the detective is concentrating on?"

"If it were me, Violet. Several people have seen them arguing in recent weeks."

"I argue with Ashlee all the time, but she hasn't pushed me to murder. Yet."

Jason chuckled. "Good thing you're moving out before it comes to that. Anyway, with Violet as Bethany's only living relative in the area and the one who stands to inherit the business, I can guarantee Palmer is taking a close look at her."

"Do you think she knew about her mom's blackmailing habits?"

"Hard to say. Since they lived together and Violet worked for her mom, I'd be surprised if she didn't."

"Hmm . . . maybe," I said. "She didn't seem to realize the importance of that little tablet she found in her mom's purse, though."

"Either way, I wonder if she intends to carry on with the blackmail."

I pictured Violet chewing on her fingernail. "She doesn't seem the type. But I hope you're right about Detective Palmer concentrating on her. I want him to forget all about that lady who said I was arguing with Bethany."

"Like I said, the detective is simply being thorough. But I'd better go. I've got work piling up here."

"Okay, I have a few things to finish up myself."

We said our good-byes. I found Detective Palmer's business card in my purse and called him, only to reach his voice mail. I left a short message asking for a callback; then I got back to my own work.

An hour and a half later, I shut down the computer, gathered my belongings, and headed out the door. As much as I was looking forward to dinner, I couldn't quite shake a feeling of melancholy. Tonight might be the last time Mom cooked for me while I was a single woman. After that, would I still be Mom's little girl?

Chapter 14

On the drive to Mom's house, I thought about what Jason had said about Mitch. Why would he pester Bethany to sell the flower shop and then decide to buy a different shop? Did Bethany refuse his offer enough times that he gave up? And how would her death affect his business dealings? With Bethany dead, Violet was the most likely person to inherit the property. Could he retract his offer from the other place and try to buy the flower shop from her now?

I sighed. I had too many questions and exactly zero answers.

Ashlee's car was parked in Mom's driveway, so I flipped a U-turn at the next cross street and pulled to the curb in front of the light blue single-story home where Mom had lived since she and Dad were first married. I tried the front door and found it unlocked. As soon as I stepped across the threshold, I smelled a chicken roasting and realized how hungry I was.

Mom was in the kitchen, tossing a salad, while Ashlee sat on a bar stool at the counter.

"And then he asked for my number," Ashlee was saying. She caught sight of me. "Finally. I thought I was going to die of starvation."

I half turned toward the door. "In that case, I could always leave again and come back in a while."

Ashlee practically snarled at me. "You're such a brat."

"Girls," Mom said sharply.

"Sorry, Mom," Ashlee and I said in unison. When she wasn't looking, Ashlee stuck her tongue out at me, but I ignored her. Five seconds together in Mom's house, and we were already acting like five-year-olds.

"What can I do to help?" I asked, if only to show my maturity.

Mom picked up a bottle of Italian salad dressing and shook it. "Would you mind setting the table while I finish the salad?"

"Consider it done."

I went to the cupboard and pulled down three plates while Ashlee removed a nail file from her purse and started filing her thumbnail. When she made no offer to assist me, I said, "Hey, how about setting out the placemats?"

She grumbled something under her breath but dropped the file in her purse and slid off the stool. Once the plates and silverware were in place, Mom and I brought over the food, and we all sat down to eat.

Mom laid her napkin in her lap. "I'm so glad you were both available for dinner tonight. It might be a while before we get another chance to eat together."

"No kidding," Ashlee said. "Once Dana gets hitched, we'll never see her again. But don't worry. I'll drag Brittany over here once in a while. She can even sit in Dana's seat. It'll almost be the same as having Dana here."

"I'm not moving to a foreign country," I said. "I'm not even moving out of town."

"Once you and Jason get married, you'll be busy setting up your life together," Mom said. "I remember how it was with your father and me. There's nothing like being a newlywed."

"We'll have dinner together again. I'll always have time for you, Mom." And I would. But I still felt a lump in my throat. Good grief. Why was I so emotional today?

"Knock it off with the sappy stuff," Ashlee said, breaking me out of my thoughts. "Let's eat."

I took a drumstick, while Mom reached for the rolls and Ashlee picked up the salad bowl. She extracted a few pieces of lettuce and a single cherry tomato before digging out all the croutons to pile on her plate.

"Save some for the rest of us," I said.

She handed me the salad bowl. "I love croutons. Even if they are pure carbs."

"Dana, remember that conversation we had earlier?" Mom asked.

My head snapped up. I tried to signal to Mom to stop talking, but she was busy buttering her roll. "I was able to get ahold of Harry Wilson during my afternoon break. He said there's nothing to worry about at this point, but he's available should the situation escalate." So much for not mentioning anything in front of Ashlee.

"Harry Wilson? Isn't that your lawyer?" Ashlee asked. "What'd you call him for? Is Dana in trouble?" She tossed a crouton in her mouth and chomped on it.

Mom mimed a look of apology at me. "Whoops, guess I'm not as subtle as I thought." She set her butter knife down and looked at Ashlee. "Detective Palmer had more questions for Dana today, and I thought it prudent to consult with Harry. You can never be too careful."

Ashlee squinted at me, as if I was a shade of nail polish she'd never seen before. "Why would the detective want to talk to you? You don't know anything."

"Of course I know things," I said, feeling the need to prove to her exactly how much I knew. "I know Mitch wants Bethany's half of the building so he can expand his ice cream business, but it sounds like Bethany wasn't interested in selling. I also know Bethany may have been blackmailing one of her customers." I almost added a neener-neener for good measure, then felt slightly embarrassed that I'd let my sister manipulate me so easily.

Mom picked up the salad bowl. "Blackmail? Really?"

"There might be other victims, too. Any one of them could have killed Bethany."

"That reminds me," Ashlee said. "I was talking to Brittany about the murder, and she said one of her friends buys flowers from that shop all the time. I bet she could tell us something about who wanted to whack Bethany." Ashlee popped another crouton in her mouth and stuffed it in her cheek so she could keep talking. "Her name's Lucia. She works at the drugstore. I see her all the time when I'm over there buying makeup and stuff."

"Would she be willing to talk to you?" I asked.

Ashlee shrugged. "Why not? Everyone likes talking to me. But Lucia always was a weird one, so quiet and nerdy. You probably don't remember her, Dana. She's a couple of years younger than me, so I think you'd already graduated by the time she started high school. She wore glasses and was always carrying around a book."

"What's her last name?"

"Martinez."

"Lucia Martinez." As I said the name, my hands and feet started to tingle. Lucia had bought a lot of flowers from Bethany, and her initials matched those in the second column of Bethany's ledger. Had I uncovered the identity of the other blackmail victim?

We finished our meal, and I cleared the dishes, noting the large pile of croutons that remained on Ashlee's plate. While I shuttled back and forth from the table to the sink, I made a mental note to stop off at the drugstore tomorrow. I needed to buy new makeup for my wedding anyway, and maybe I'd luck out and find Lucia Martinez working, too. Ashlee had offered to talk to her, but I had a feeling I'd better step in and speak to her myself.

* * *

The next morning dawned cool and cloudless. I dressed in brown cargo pants and a long-sleeved work shirt with the name of Esther's farm embroidered on the front.

When I got to the farm, I headed straight to the office to write the day's blog, which covered tips for a better night's sleep. After making several edits, I added pictures of the lavender bushes in the herb garden, since the scent of lavender was supposed to be relaxing. I was getting ready to post the blog to the farm's Web site when Gordon entered the office.

He stopped at the corner of the desk. I continued typing while I waited for him to speak.

When he didn't, I said, "Morning, Gordon. I'm just finishing today's blog if you need to use the computer."

He rested his fingertips on the desktop. "No, thank you. That's not why I'm here."

He didn't say anything else, so I lifted my hands from the keyboard and set them in my lap, giving him my full attention. "Then what are you here for?"

"I wanted to ask you a favor."

He paused, and I took a closer look at him. I'd swear tiny beads of sweat were forming along his hairline, but that could have been little globules of the gel he always used.

"I'd like to bring a lady friend to the wedding."

I stared at him. "Really?" I blurted out before I could stop myself. Sure, Gordon was a fairly attractive, successful guy, but it never occurred to me that he dated. I assumed he spent all of his spare time sitting at home and dreaming up ways to save money at this place. Or else he had a coin collection and spent every evening admiring his haul.

His face turned red. "I understand if it's too late to add to the guest list, with catering requirements and seating and such."

I waved my hand. "No, no, it's perfectly fine. Zennia won't care if we have one more, and there's plenty of room." Now that I knew Gordon had a lady friend, dare I say girlfriend, I couldn't help pressing for information. "What's her name?"

"Margaret," he said after a moment's hesitation. "We met at the Knowledge Sharing Summit convention, a regional event for managers in the hospitality industry. She runs a small boutique hotel over in Mendocino. We found we have many mutual interests."

I couldn't help wondering what those interests were, but knowing Gordon, it was bound to be business related. "Wow, that's great. Looks like love is in the air, as they say."

Gordon grimaced. "Let's not get carried away." He took a handkerchief out of his jacket pocket and blotted his hairline. "Thank you. I'll let you get back to work."

He left the office before I could ask him anything else. Good for Gordon. Maybe having a girlfriend would loosen him up a bit.

I finished posting the blog and spent the rest of the morning researching how effective pay-per-click advertising was, which Web sites I should target, and how much it would cost. When the clock struck noon, I retrieved my purse and keys, and cut through the lobby to the parking lot.

The drive into town was quick, and I soon found myself parking in front of the Prescription for Joy drugstore. Before stepping out of the car, I tried to think of what I needed to buy while I was here. Considering how old and cakey my current collection of makeup had become, I should at least pick up new mascara, eyeliner, foundation, and eye shadow. I thought about texting Ashlee for additional recommendations, but knew she'd have me looking like a Vegas showgirl, complete with glitter.

Running through the list in my head one more time, I got out of the car and went inside. The store was quiet. I glanced around to see if I could spot any employees who might fit Lucia's description.

To my left, a woman with a reddened nose was reading the back of a box of cold medicine while a toddler pulled on her sleeve. To my right, a male clerk with silver hair was ringing up a man in a wheelchair. I could definitely rule out the clerk.

I walked farther into the store, scanning the overhead signs for the makeup section. I got momentarily distracted by a sale on leftover Halloween Oreo cookies but managed to avoid the temptation and find my way to the correct aisle. A cart full of opened boxes sat in the center of the row, and a clerk in a green vest and glasses was shelving a small collection of eye shadows. At first glance, I pegged her as a teenager, but when I took a closer look, I realized she was probably a few years older, putting her closer to Ashlee's age. Could this be Lucia?

She offered me a smile when she saw me and shoved the cart to one side. "Let me get this out of your way." I could see the edge of a nametag stuck to her vest, but it was covered by her long dark hair.

"Thanks."

She turned back to her work and I decided to do some shopping while I tried to think of a decent conversation starter. I scanned the shelves, grabbing my usual combination of neutral and pastel hues.

When I got to the lipstick section, I frowned. I wasn't much of a lipstick wearer, but something as official as a wedding should probably include lipstick. I picked up a tube labeled Peach Fantasy.

"Um, if you don't mind a suggestion?" the clerk said, looking at her hands as if she was afraid I'd refuse.

"Sure. What is it?"

"You might find a shade with more pink," she said. "It would be a better match for your complexion."

I put the tube back. "Which one would you recommend? I don't usually wear lipstick, but I'm getting married soon."

She abandoned the cart she'd been unpacking and came over, obviously excited that I'd asked her opinion. "Congratulations. Then you'll definitely want a shade of red. Nothing too dramatic, of course, but something more bold than an everyday color."

Up close, I could see she was wearing quite a bit of makeup herself, but it was done in such a fashion that it wasn't too obvious. Too bad I couldn't hire her for my wedding day. She brushed her hair over her shoulder, exposing her nametag, and I saw that she was indeed Lucia.

"You seem to know a lot about lipstick," I said.

She selected three tubes in varying shades of red and handed them to me. "My mom's a cosmetologist. She was always practicing on me when I was growing up. I thought about following her into the business, but I already had my heart set on medical school."

"Where do you go to school?" Had Ashlee mentioned anything about medical school last night? Why was she working at the drugstore instead?

"UC Davis, but I'm taking the semester off to earn more money."

The silver-haired clerk popped into view at the end of the aisle. "Hey, Lucia, I'm taking my break."

She gave him a wave of acknowledgment and turned back to me. "Did you need any more help? Otherwise I need to go cover the register."

I looked at the collection of makeup in my hands. "Um . . ." *Think, Dana, think.* "I hear you guys had some excitement around here a few days ago."

Her brow wrinkled. "What do you mean?"

"The lady at the flower shop."

Lucia took a step back and bumped into the shopping cart. An open box of mascara threatened to topple off the top of the stack, and she grabbed it. "Right." She pushed the box back a little until it was balanced again. "I haven't heard much about that."

I raised my eyebrows. "Even with her shop so close? I figured everyone would've been talking about it."

Lucia shook her head and kept her eyes on the cart. "No one here knew her."

Unless there were two young women named Lucia working here who also bought flowers, I knew that was an outright lie. Why would she deny knowing Bethany? What was she hiding?

From the front of the store, I heard someone call out, "Hello?"

Lucia backed up, almost hitting the cart again, the look of relief evident on her face. "I have to get up front." She spun around and trotted toward the registers.

I picked one of the lipstick tubes Lucia had suggested and followed at a slower pace, cradling my selection of makeup. I should have grabbed a basket on my way in.

An older woman was accepting her change at the register when I got to the front. Lucia saw me over the woman's shoulder and pressed her lips together.

Once the customer walked away with her purchase, I stepped up to the counter and set the makeup down. Lucia pushed her glasses up on her nose and began swiping each item across the scanner in rapid succession. By the time I pulled my wallet from my purse, she'd already finished ringing me up and was throwing everything into a bag. I took my time entering my debit card password, but Lucia didn't say anything, intent on her bagging.

"Thanks for your help picking out that lipstick color," I said.

"Sure, no problem." She handed me my receipt

and then looked over my shoulder. "Can I help whoever's next?"

I guessed that was the end of the conversation. I thanked her, but she'd already moved on to the next customer. I grabbed my bag and headed to my car.

As I put my purchases in the trunk, I thought about our talk. Why had Lucia denied knowing Bethany? Was it because she was one of Bethany's blackmail victims, or because she was somehow involved in Bethany's murder? Or maybe both?

I got in the driver's side and pointed my car in the direction of Carter's law firm. As long as I was doing some lunchtime sleuthing, maybe I could learn more about Carter. I wanted something solid to offer Detective Palmer, if he ever bothered to call me back.

I followed the same series of twists and turns as on my earlier visit and parked at the curb. I studied the building. The stucco walls looked freshly painted. The lawn area and flower beds were well-kept, and the lamppost at the end of the walk appeared so new I almost expected a price tag to be dangling from it. The entire setup practically screamed, "Respectable law firm."

After walking up the path, I pulled open the screen door, which didn't dare squeak, and pushed the heavy wooden door inward. The lobby was clean and well-furnished with upholstered chairs and polished light fixtures.

A trim woman not much older than me sat behind a desk. Her light brown hair was pulled back in a chignon, and she wore a beige turtleneck that looked to be of a soft and luxurious material. "May I help you?" she asked.

I glanced down at my faded cargo pants and long-sleeved work shirt, suddenly self-conscious that I looked so sloppy when compared with the receptionist. I'd only thought up my plan on the drive over and had given no consideration to my wardrobe.

Since I was already standing here, I decided to plow ahead. "I'd like to make an appointment."

She nodded briskly and started typing on her keyboard, apparently not as put off by my outfit as I was. "Are you a client of ours?"

"No, I was hoping to speak with Mr. Hawking about a prenuptial agreement."

At this, the receptionist's gaze flew to my clothes, but she quickly recovered and looked back at the computer monitor. "I see." She typed a few more words. "Mr. Hawking charges three hundred dollars an hour, plus expenses."

I gulped. Why hadn't I thought of that before coming? I'd never dealt with a lawyer personally, but of course he would expect to be paid for his services.

Before I could tell the receptionist I'd changed my mind, she went on. "Of course, for new clients, Mr. Hawking offers a free fifteen-minute consultation in which you can explain your situation to see if he can provide the services you're looking for."

I let out a sigh of relief that I was sure the receptionist could hear, though her face remained impassive.

"When would you like to come in?"

"Do you have an opening tomorrow?" I leaned forward slightly to see if I could read what was on her monitor, but the font was too small.

"Mr. Hawking is available at ten-thirty or one o'clock."

Obviously I couldn't interrupt my own workday for my little snooping project. It looked like I'd have to come into town for a late lunch break. "One o'clock would be fantastic."

"Name?"

"Da—" I snapped my mouth shut before I could finish. If Carter had really killed Bethany, I certainly didn't want him knowing my real name.

"I'm afraid I didn't catch that," the receptionist said.

Names flew through my head, and I picked one at random. "Sorry. My name is Daisy Mae Johnson."

She gave me a sidelong glance like she knew I was full of baloney, but ever the professional, she entered the information into the computer. She plucked a card from a holder on her desk, jotted down the appointment time, and handed the card to me.

I nodded my thanks and slid it into my back pocket.

"Have a nice day," she said cheerfully before swiveling in her chair and turning her back to me.

I let myself out of the office, almost whistling as I went. I'd managed to schedule an appointment with a man who Bethany had most likely been blackmailing. Now, I just needed to figure out how to use that appointment to my advantage.

Chapter 15

On my way back to work, I stopped by the closest fast-food restaurant with the intention of ordering a double cheeseburger with fries. All this investigating had me famished.

At the last second, I switched my order to a grilled chicken sandwich. My wedding dress had been fitted weeks ago. I couldn't afford to put on weight and have it be too tight. Wouldn't Ashlee have a field day if I had to use safety pins and superglue when I couldn't zip my dress?

I paid the cashier at the window, accepted my paper sack, and drove back to the farm. Once I'd parked, I went straight into the office and caught up on correspondence while I ate my sandwich. I spent the rest of the afternoon creating an ad for a travel magazine and redoing the photos on the farm's Web site. Feeling like I'd accomplished a good amount of work for the day, I shut down the computer, updated my timecard, and headed out.

Fifteen minutes later, I pulled into my apartment

complex and found Ashlee's Camaro already in her parking space. I pulled in next to her car, noticing a new dent in the right front panel. I knew the one on the left side was from sideswiping a mailbox, and the dent in the back bumper was from a parallel parking attempt. Maybe this one hadn't been her fault for a change.

I locked my car and trotted up the outside steps to the apartment. Ashlee was sitting in her usual spot on the couch, watching a celebrity news program. She straightened up expectantly when I walked in, a smile already forming on her lips. When she saw it was me, she slumped back on the couch.

"Aren't you happy to see me?" I said.

"I thought you were Brittany. She's stopping by in a few minutes."

"Wouldn't she knock?"

Ashlee waved her hand. "No, I already gave her a key to the apartment, since she's getting ready to move in."

I closed the door behind me and set my purse and the bag of makeup from the drugstore on the kitchen table. "How'd you get that dent in your car?"

Ashlee frowned, as if confused. "Which one?"

"The new one on the passenger side."

"Oh, that. I was texting Brittany about this hot guy in the grocery store parking lot and hit one of those little poles they always put up in front of the store. I have no idea why those things are even there."

I didn't bother pointing out the obvious answer,

which was that the poles were there to keep people like Ashlee from driving through the storefront. Instead, I went into the kitchen to see what I could scrounge up for dinner. The freezer contained its usual assortment of entrées, and I opted for the vegetable lasagna. Not only must it contain vegetables, but it was bound to be lower in calories than standard lasagna, right? I popped the frozen meal in the microwave, set the timer, and hit the start button. As I did so, I heard muffled thumping at the front door.

I looked at Ashlee, but whatever was on the TV screen had captured her attention. The thumping noise came again and I went to open the door, curious to know what was making that sound.

A stack of boxes greeted me at eye level. Whoever was holding the boxes was only visible from the waist down. I removed the small box on top to expose Brittany's smiling face.

"Hey, Dana, thanks," she said. She had short red hair with black-dyed tips, reminding me of old-fashioned fountain pens dipped in ink. Her eyeliner, which matched her hair tips, extended past her lash line to form cat eyes. Shimmering aqua eyeshadow covered her lids, and bright red lipstick coated her mouth.

"What's with the boxes?" I asked.

"Ashlee said I could start bringing stuff over. I figured I'd move some of my summer clothes first." She glanced up at the cloudy and rapidly darkening sky. "I won't need my bikini for a few months, not with this weather." She giggled, something she did often.

I cast an accusatory glance back at my sister, but she hadn't looked away from the TV. "I haven't moved out yet," I said to Brittany.

"That's okay. I don't mind." She shuffled past me into the apartment and dropped her stack of boxes by the door.

At the sound of the boxes dropping, Ashlee whipped her head around. "Hey, Brittany, when did you get here?"

Brittany didn't answer as her eyes landed on the bag of makeup. She rushed over to the table. "What'd you get?" she asked Ashlee. She started pulling out items. "Ooh, nice lipstick. Good color. But isn't this foundation too pale for you?" she asked, holding up the bottle.

"That's mine," I said, taking the items from her hand and placing them back in the bag.

Ashlee turned around to study me over the back of the couch. "You bought makeup?" Her incredulous tone was slightly insulting.

"Sure. I wear makeup all the time. I just don't pile it on, like some people I know."

"Touchy, touchy," Ashlee said.

The timer on the microwave *dinged,* and I gave a start at the sound. I'd almost forgotten about my dinner.

I went into the kitchen to remove the lasagna from the microwave, while Brittany flopped down on the couch next to Ashlee.

I grabbed a fork and napkin, set the scalding

entrée tray on a hot pad, and carried my dinner into the living area. I sat down in the wing chair.

"Was Prescription for Joy having a big sale today or something?" Brittany asked. "I could always use some new stuff."

I turned my fork sideways to cut off a piece of lasagna. "No, I decided to splurge and buy all new makeup for my wedding."

"Good to see you making an effort," Ashlee said.

Brittany clapped her hands together. "You know what would be awesome? If I did your makeup for the wedding."

I almost dropped my tray of lasagna. "What's that now?"

"I'm good at it," Brittany said. "I've been doing my own face since I was ten."

I studied her overabundance of eye makeup. "I'm not sure you and I have the same style," I said carefully.

"Don't worry. She won't go crazy," Ashlee said. "She knows you're super plain."

Brittany giggled. "Yeah, I did my aunt's wedding for her third marriage, and she's an old fuddy-duddy, so I couldn't get all crazy or anything. Everyone said she looked fantastic."

"I don't know." I took a bite, mulling over the idea. God knew I was no expert when it came to cosmetics.

"How about I give you a makeover while I'm here? Then you'll have an idea of what you'll look like on your wedding day."

Well, a test run couldn't hurt. Then, when she

made me look like Bozo the Clown, I could say no thank you. Plus, while she was working on my face, I could talk to her about Lucia. "Okay, I'm game."

Brittany squealed in delight, almost making me lose my lasagna tray again. She jumped up from the couch, snatched the bag of makeup off the table, and started setting everything out while I finished eating. When I took the last bite, she grabbed the empty plastic tray from me and tossed it in the trash before coming back and patting the seat of the closest kitchen chair.

"All ready," she said.

With slight trepidation, I moved to the seat Brittany had indicated. Ashlee clicked off the TV and came over to sit at the table with us. Great, just what I needed. An audience.

Brittany started applying a layer of foundation, while Ashlee studied her technique as if there would be a test later. I waited until she started working on my forehead before speaking.

"I bought all this stuff from Lucia this morning. Ashlee says you're friends with her."

Brittany stepped back to scrutinize my face and then moved in for touch-ups. "Sure, Lucia's a total sweetheart. We lived in the same apartment complex when we were kids. Since I was a couple years older than her, I used to babysit her sometimes when her mom was working late. We still hang out. She studies way too much, but I guess she wants to be some kind of doctor or something. She's the first one in her family to go to college."

"She mentioned medical school when I was

talking to her," I said. Brittany started on my eyes and I closed them, crossing my fingers that she'd use a gentler touch than on her own.

"That's a good color for her," I heard Ashlee say. "It'll really bring out the blue in her eyes. Nice pick, Brittany."

Technically, I'd picked out the color, but I didn't bother to mention it.

Ashlee snapped her fingers. "I might have a shade that's even better. Hang on." She headed for her bedroom.

"How often do you and Lucia hang out?" I asked Brittany. Would she know if the other set of initials in Bethany's book belonged to Lucia?

"Not so much when she was away at school, but now that she's home for the semester, I see her once in a while. She doesn't go out a whole lot. Like I said, she's always got her nose in a book." She stepped back for another assessment, frowned, and started wiping my eyelids clean. "I did drag her off to a big kegger Labor Day weekend down in Santa Rosa. You can bet I'm never doing that again."

Brittany was pressing so hard on my eyelids that when I opened them, I saw spots. I blinked to clear my vision. "Why not?"

"She was a total wreck afterward. Super jumpy and nervous."

"Any idea why?" I asked as Brittany started working on my eyelids again.

"Nope, she's kind of a Goody-Two-shoes. Maybe she had a beer or two and felt guilty about driving afterward. 'Course, she sure didn't seem drunk, so

I don't see why she would worry about getting in trouble for that."

All of a sudden, Brittany started laughing, making her hand shake. I resisted the urge to pull my face away before she could do too much damage.

"What's so funny?" I asked.

"I just remembered when she was driving me to the movies a couple of weeks later, and a cop car was driving behind us. She about had a heart attack. She got so nervous she had to pull over and let him pass." She laughed again. "She kept yammering on about how she knew she shouldn't have gone to the party and now they were after her. Like he'd even care she was at that party. After that, I had to switch seats and drive the rest of the way."

Ashlee came back into the room. "Can't find that eye shadow anywhere. I must have gotten rid of it." She shrugged. "The one you have is good enough."

Brittany moved toward me with an uncapped tube of lipstick and such an intent look on her face that I couldn't help but lean away from her. "Hold still," she said.

I tried to relax as I thought about Lucia. Her reaction to being followed by a police officer seemed extreme. What would cause her to freak out like that? Had something happened at the party or maybe later that night? If so, what?

"All done," Brittany said.

I focused back on Brittany. "Already?"

She capped the lipstick. "You didn't want anything too fancy, so I didn't have to do much. Go take a look."

I went in the bathroom, flipped on the light, and looked at my reflection in the mirror. A more sophisticated version of myself looked back. I turned my head one way and then the other, admiring Brittany's subtle use of color. Ashlee and Brittany came in and crowded around me.

"Well, what do you think?" Brittany asked.

"You did a fantastic job. I never could have done this myself."

She giggled. "Does this mean I can do your makeup for the wedding?"

I nodded, unable to take my eyes off my reflection. "I'd love that. Thank you." We all tramped out to the living room once more. I swear I held my head a little higher as I walked.

For the rest of the evening, we sat around and watched a terrible TV show that Brittany picked out, but considering what a great job she'd done on my face, I didn't complain. After she left for the night, Ashlee settled in for a *Project Runway* marathon, and I headed off to get ready for bed. After looking at my reflection once more, picturing how Jason might look at me as I walked down the aisle to join him, I removed the makeup Brittany had applied with only a little extra scrubbing and then donned my pajamas.

As I slipped between the sheets, my mind filled with everything I'd gathered about Lucia tonight. I already suspected Lucia of keeping secrets, and the story from Brittany about how strangely Lucia was acting when she'd seen the police officer driving behind her only added to that suspicion. But what was she hiding? Could it be something Bethany found out about and blackmailed her over?

Somehow, I needed to find out more about Labor Day weekend. And the sooner, the better. I wanted to forget all this murder business and focus strictly on my wedding.

Chapter 16

At work the next day, the morning sped by as my meeting with Carter drew closer. What had I been thinking when I'd set up that appointment? I was already positive Bethany had been blackmailing him, most likely about his affair, so what more did I hope to gain from meeting with him? Did I expect him to admit he killed her?

I was tempted to call and cancel, but then I remembered my little talk with Detective Palmer when he'd asked about my rumored argument with Bethany. Jason and Mom might tell me I had nothing to worry about, but if the police couldn't find strong evidence pointing to a particular person, I'd still be swimming around in the pool of suspects. I needed to see what I could find out before I drowned.

When it was almost time for me to leave, I went into the bathroom and changed from my jeans and farm shirt to a navy blue skirt and a matching blazer with a cream shell top underneath. The outfit wasn't particularly fancy, but it looked decent enough that Carter wouldn't kick me out of his office the moment I walked in. I slid into my flats and headed for the door.

Traffic on the highway was light, and I soon reached the exit for Main Street. Less than five minutes later, I pulled up in front of Carter's office. Inside the lobby, an older woman, wearing a pencil skirt and a silk blouse with a large bow, perched on the edge of a chair in the waiting area. Dyed black hair peeked out from under a wide-brimmed hat. She looked more suited for the Kentucky Derby than a lawyer's office in Blossom Valley. I was glad I'd changed my clothes.

Before I could speak to the receptionist, a man in a black suit and red tie came down the hall. As he approached, the woman rose, and the man took her hands in his. "Mrs. Hencock, so good to see you again. Please follow me. Would you care for a cup of coffee? Maybe tea?" he asked as they made their way in the direction from which he'd come.

When they were gone, I stepped up to the desk and gave the same receptionist from yesterday my name.

"Please take a seat. Mr. Hawking will be with you shortly."

I sat in one of the chairs and winced as my butt hit the stiff cushion. No wonder Mrs. Hencock had sat right on the edge. These chairs were strictly for show.

While I waited for Carter, I texted Jason to see how his day was going. We traded a few texts about a robbery at a gas station the previous night and a dog that had stopped traffic downtown this morning. He then asked me to dinner, to which I agreed, and we texted our good-byes.

For the next few minutes, I used my phone to read the latest world headlines and the entertainment news, though I didn't recognize most of the celebrity names. When Carter still hadn't appeared, I checked the weather forecast for the week. There was a small chance of rain on my wedding day, but how often was the weatherman right?

I moved on to the advice columns, my horoscope, and my favorite comic strips. I was running out of things to read and was about to move on to sports, which I had zero interest in, when I finally saw Carter approach from the hall. Much like the first time I'd seen him, he wore an ultra-conservative, expensive-looking suit. I stood up and tucked my phone in my purse as he reached me and held out his hand.

"Miss Johnson?" he said.

For a second, I could only stare at him, but then I remembered I'd given the receptionist a phony name. "That's me," I said.

I could feel him studying me. Perhaps he'd noticed my hesitation.

"Have we met?" he asked.

Uh-oh. I felt my eyes widen. Did he recognize me from the flower shop, or when I'd followed him? Had Violet said my real name while he was there?

He snapped his fingers. "I saw you in the flower shop the other day."

I forced a smile. "Yes, I remember now. Small world," I said, waiting to see if he'd add more.

If Violet had mentioned my name, he must not have remembered, because he moved on to the business at hand. He gestured down the hall. "Let's talk in the conference room." He turned to the receptionist. "Jennifer, hold all my calls." I'd only ever heard people say that in the movies, but it did have the effect of making me feel important all of a sudden.

We walked down the hall, with Carter matching my pace. When we reached the third door on the right, he opened it and then moved aside so I could enter first.

"Would you like a cup of coffee?" he asked as he pulled out a thick leather chair for me. He waited for me to sit down and then gave it an extra nudge to help push me in, saving me the effort. I had to admit, the guy had polish.

"I'm fine, thank you." I sank into the chair, which was much cushier than the one in the waiting area.

Carter sat down across from me. A legal pad and pen waited on the table before him. "What can I do for you?"

Good question. Normally, I didn't like to lie, but I couldn't exactly blurt out why I was here and expect him to admit Bethany was blackmailing him. For today, I needed to use a little deviousness. "Well, I'm getting married in a few days . . ." I let the sentence dangle, hoping he'd steer the conversation in the right direction.

"Congratulations. It's a momentous occasion."

Well, that didn't help.

"And, of course, I'm sure we'll be married forever," I said. "It's not that I'm thinking of divorce already."

"No, of course not," he said soothingly, "but one should always protect one's assets, in the event of the unexpected."

"Exactly," I said. I sat up straighter in the seat and laid my hands on the table. "I'm ninety-nine percent sure my fiancé would never cheat on me, but I'm sure that's what all women say, even the ones who've been betrayed."

I stared at him, looking for the tiniest hint that I'd struck a nerve, but he didn't so much as flinch.

"I'm sure it won't come to that," he said; then he smiled at me.

What a twerp.

When I didn't say anything, he continued. "It sounds like you're interested in setting up a prenuptial agreement. Is that what I'm hearing?"

"Only to be on the safe side."

He gave a small nod. "Of course. What types of assets would you want to include?"

I started rattling off a bunch of stuff, hoping I was making sense. Lying was much harder than I'd anticipated. "You know, stocks, bonds, things like that. I have a sizable portfolio." Was that even the right word?

"What about property?"

"I have a car." He gave me a quizzical look, and I knew I'd slipped up. "And a beach house," I said hastily. "Yes, the wonderful beach house from dear

Aunt Millie." Was it hot in here? Or was I sweating because I was a liar, liar, with my pants on fire?

Carter scribbled on a legal pad and then tapped his pen. "If you were to estimate, how much do you think your combined assets are worth?"

"Half a million?" I said, though it sounded more like I was asking. He frowned, and I ran through my imaginary list of assets, wondering if I'd lowballed it. "The beach house is small and not really on a glitzy part of the beach."

As I spoke, I realized my plan was going to be a total bust. There had been no small talk, no chance to build a rapport where I could ask seemingly casual questions. On top of that, this guy was a lawyer, a man trained in confidentiality. All this flashed through my mind as I ran through why my imaginary wealth didn't amount to more. "The roof leaks, you know," I finished, my voice getting quieter as I said the last words.

"No, I don't know." He capped his pen, the frown on his face deepening. "In fact, I don't believe you need a prenuptial agreement at all. This beach house sounds like something you invented off the top of your head. If you can't provide evidence of these so-called assets, I can't help you."

"Well, okay, thanks anyway." I stood up, in a rush to get out before he became even more suspicious.

Too late. Carter was on his feet in a flash. He took one step toward the door, so he was blocking my exit. "Why are you really here, Ms. Johnson?" His voice was low and menacing.

My eyes flitted from Carter to the door and back.

Unless I was willing to shove him out of the way, I wasn't leaving until I answered the question.

"I told you," I said. "I was interested in a pre-nup, but after talking with you, I guess I don't need one. If you'll excuse me, I'll be on my way. I wouldn't want to waste any more of your time." I stepped forward, hoping he'd move aside, but he didn't budge. Gone was the solicitous man from earlier.

He crossed his arms. "Not good enough," he said. "Try again."

I swallowed as I thought about what to do. I could lie again, though that didn't seem to be going well. I could demand he get out of my way and hope he obeyed, but then I'd get nowhere with finding out if Bethany was blackmailing him. He seemed like a smart guy. Maybe I could explain the real reason I was here and get his input on Bethany's murder. If he wasn't the one who killed her, he might be willing to offer his own theories.

"Okay, it's like this," I said, trying to keep my tone friendly, even if my stomach felt queasy. "I'm sure you heard Bethany Lancaster was murdered." At the mention of Bethany, his face darkened. "What you don't know is that Bethany and I had been communicating quite a bit these last few weeks, and I was in the flower shop with her that day—" I was about to tell him how I'd found her body and was worried the police might suspect me, but he cut me off.

"So that's your game," he snarled.

"What game?" I asked, at a loss.

He jabbed me in the breastbone with his finger so hard it hurt. "You think you can come in here and squeeze me like Bethany did. Demand those ridiculous payments. Well, you can forget it." He threw up his hand, and I flinched. "Go ahead. Threaten to tell my wife about my little affair."

"No, you don't understand. I'm not trying—"

"I understand perfectly. But I won't be blackmailed twice. I can't believe I allowed it to happen once." He yanked open the door. "Get the hell out of here."

While I wanted to run down the hall to safety, I also wanted to protest my innocence more. Let him know I wasn't some sleazy blackmailer, merely a liar, and a poor one at that. "But if you'll just listen to me for a minute—"

"I'm not interested in anything you have to say."

"But it's not what you think."

Carter pointed toward the hall. "You need to leave."

Clearly, he wouldn't be giving me the chance to explain. I'd already set up the appointment under false pretenses. No way would he believe anything I said now.

Well, fine. If he didn't want to listen to reason, I had better things to do.

I marched out of the conference room with my back straight and my chin up, though I knew my cheeks were flaming. He didn't escort me down the hall this time. I went straight past Jennifer's desk, where I'd swear I saw her smirking, and walked outside. When I got to my car, I threw myself into the driver's seat and let out a huge sigh.

Phew. That definitely could have gone better. At least Carter had confirmed that Bethany had been blackmailing him over his affair. And I'd noticed he hadn't mentioned Violet, so if she knew about the blackmail, she hadn't contacted Carter yet. Even with those two bits of information, I couldn't help but feel disappointed that I hadn't learned more.

I put the key in the ignition and checked the time. Even though Carter had kept me waiting for what felt like forever, my lunch hour was barely half over. What could I do to lift my spirits before returning to work?

I licked my lips as the answer came to me. Ice cream always cheered me up. And Mitch owned the only ice cream parlor in town. My meeting with Carter had completely fallen apart, but maybe I could find out something interesting about Bethany from Mitch. Besides blackmail, what else might have gotten her killed?

Chapter 17

I drove back to Main Street and pulled into a parking space in front of Get the Scoop. As I got out, I noticed Mom's car across the street and remembered how Mitch had flirted with her the day I'd found Bethany's body. If Mitch was working today, Mom might be my best shot at getting him to talk.

I crossed the street, climbed the steps to Going Back for Seconds, and went inside. I spotted Mom the same moment she saw me. She hung up a pair of slacks on a rack and came over.

"Dana, what a nice surprise," she said as she hugged me.

"Hi, Mom." I looked around the store and saw we were the only ones here. "Awfully quiet today."

"We just ended our big fall sale over the weekend. It's always quiet the first few days afterward."

I pressed my palms together as if praying. "Does that mean you have time to go on a little adventure with me?"

Her eyebrows went up. "What sort of adventure?"

I leaned in conspiratorially. "I noticed Mitch seemed quite taken with you the other night."

Mom's cheeks instantly reddened. "You must be mistaken." She paused, cleared her throat, and then added, "Well, you might be right."

"I know I am. Which is why I thought you and I could go get a scoop of ice cream and ask Mitch about his relationship with Bethany."

Mom took a step back and frowned. "You know how I feel about you getting involved in these murder investigations. I wouldn't want to encourage you by helping. You should be focusing on your wedding."

I spread my hands. "The wedding is all set, and you're not encouraging me. I'll be talking to Mitch regardless of whether you come along, but it'd certainly be easier if you were there to grease the wheels. Or should I say grease the ice cream churner?"

Mom chewed on her bottom lip. "I don't know."

Her resolve was clearly weakening. I waited. She tilted her head and tapped her bottom lip. "It would be fun to play detective just this once. I could pump the suspect for information. Isn't that what they say on TV?"

I grinned at her sudden enthusiasm. "We could be like Cagney and Lacey."

"Can I be Lacey?" Mom asked. "I always liked her better."

"You can be anybody you want." I looked around at the empty store again. "But if you come with me, who'll watch this place?"

Mom nodded her head toward the back of the

store. "Annette's working on inventory. Let me tell her I'm taking my break, and then I'm all yours." She dashed to the back room and returned within seconds. "All right, let's go interview our suspect. We need one of those heat lamps to make him sweat. Too bad I don't have a trench coat. That would show him we mean business."

I shook my head as I trailed out of the store after Mom. Exactly what kind of detective shows was she watching?

We crossed the street and entered the ice cream parlor. I felt a thrill of excitement when I saw Mitch behind the counter, rather than the young clerk, Nicole. I slowed my pace so Mom could work her magic.

She walked straight up to the counter and cooed, "Mitch, look at all this wonderful ice cream. I swear, you make the best in town. In the whole state, even." She batted her eyelashes at him.

Maybe I should have cautioned Mom not to lay it on too thick. I wasn't sure if Mitch would be flattered or skeptical.

I needn't have worried. He beamed under Mom's attention. "Thank you kindly, Dorothy. It's the all-natural ingredients that make my ice cream better than most. People can really taste the difference."

Mom nodded. "Absolutely. I've had a hankering for your double chocolate swirl all day. And I'd love it on a sugar cone."

A hankering? Had Mom switched from mysteries to Westerns?

"Coming right up," Mitch said. He grabbed a large metal spoon out of a nearby container, shook off the water droplets, and started to scoop up the rich brown chocolate.

Mom laid a hand on the glass. "You know, I've always admired your business sense. Even with the recession a few years ago, you managed to keep your doors open and do quite well for yourself, from the looks of it."

I bit back a smile. I should have brought Mom to my meeting with Carter, too. I'd forgotten how charming she could be.

"People love ice cream, especially mine," Mitch said. "And even when they're watching their pennies, ice cream is cheap enough to splurge on. I can't take all the credit for my business, though. My grandfather is the one who had the foresight to open the parlor downtown."

"This was your grandfather's place? How wonderful," Mom gushed.

I could practically see Mitch's chest puff up. "I'm carrying on the family business."

He handed the cone to Mom, and she moved toward the register. I stepped up to order. Mitch looked momentarily startled, as if he'd forgotten I was there.

"What can I get you?" he asked. "The same as your mom?"

"Yes, please." I already loved chocolate, so double chocolate could only be twice as good.

He scooped up my portion and handed it over. I held the narrow base of the cone between two fingers while pulling my wallet from my purse.

Mitch held up his hand. "On the house."

"Are you sure?" I asked, keeping my wallet open.

He must need to sell a ton of ice cream to cover the costs of running this place, something that couldn't be easy in November.

"I consider your cones a marketing fee. When people walk by and see you two lovely ladies enjoying your ice cream, they'll come inside to order their own."

I wasn't sure I was enough of a magnet to draw in a crowd, but if Mitch wanted to give me free ice cream, who was I to argue? I closed my wallet, put it back in my purse, and pulled a couple of napkins from the nearby holder. "Thank you," I said. "That's very generous."

Mom and I picked the nearest table and sat down. She looked over at Mitch with a flirtatious smile. "Why don't you join us?" she asked. She gave me an exaggerated wink that I could only hope Mitch couldn't see from where he was standing. Who knew she could be such an actress?

"Thank you, Dorothy. Don't mind if I do." He came around the counter and sat down at our table.

I glanced around the shop. A cluster of local sports team pictures and framed thank-you notes occupied one corner. "You seem to do quite a bit for the community," I said.

Mitch nodded. "It's important for business owners to support their local youth leagues. My grandfather and father always did, and now I do, too. Besides, the coaches and their teams always celebrate their wins in my shop, so I make out all right."

"What a smart marketing strategy," Mom said.

I took a bite of ice cream. Mixes of dark and light chocolate mingled on my tongue. Definitely a good pick. "One of your employees mentioned it can get pretty crowded here in the afternoons."

Mitch nodded. "Some days, it's standing room only. Makes me wish I had this entire building, like my grandfather did."

"Your grandfather used to own the flower shop, too?" I asked.

"Yep, but then the business took a turn for the worse, and he had to sell half the property to keep afloat. I'd love to get my hands on the other half again." His eyes gleamed. "I could add tables, open a cookie station, an iced coffee bar . . ." His voice trailed off as he became lost in his thoughts.

"If you want to buy the other half of this building, why did you make an offer on that property down the street?" I asked.

He reared back his head as if I'd hit him in the face with a scoop of ice cream. Clearly he didn't think anyone knew about the offer, but so what if they did?

"What are you talking about?" he asked.

I tried to keep my answer vague, since I'd gotten the information from Jason. "I heard a rumor that you placed a bid on that old auto parts place. Is that so you can add the cookie station and the other things you were just talking about?"

His face turned red, and he started to tap his fingers rapidly on the table. I glanced at Mom, and she raised her eyebrows at me.

"I'm only wondering," I said, "because someone else told me you wanted to buy the flower shop."

Mitch tugged at the collar of his polo shirt. "I like to keep my options open. Don't want to put all my eggs in one basket and all that." He stood up so fast, his chair wobbled and I thought it might tip. "If you ladies will excuse me, I have work to do." With a hurried smile at Mom, he strode behind the counter and through the employee door.

Mom turned to me, her eyes wide. "What was that all about?"

"I don't know, but he sure was acting odd," I said.

She took a nibble of her cone. "Do you think I should ask him out to dinner? See what else I can find out?"

"Absolutely not, Mom. For all we know, this man could have killed Bethany." Wow. Wasn't she the one who always lectured me about safety?

Mom patted my hand. "I suppose you're right. Besides, we learned a little bit about Mitch today. It's a start."

But not much of one. All we'd confirmed was that Mitch wanted to expand his business. He'd talked about how important it was to buy the other half of his grandfather's original building, but it couldn't be too critical to him if he was interested in a different location. The big question was why he'd acted so squirrely when I'd mentioned it.

Mom held out her arm so I could see the watch on her wrist. "You know I don't like to nag you, but shouldn't you be getting back to work?"

I looked at the time with a jolt. Here I'd gone from being finished with Carter's appointment too early to return to work to now being late.

"You're right." I jumped up from the table and

tossed my napkins in the trash. Mom followed me outside, and we said good-bye before she headed back to work. I got in my car and sped back to the farm. Fortunately, Gordon wasn't waiting in the lobby, tapping his foot and preparing a lecture on tardiness.

I was breathing a sigh of relief when I opened the office door and came face-to-face with him. Shoot.

"Hi, Gordon," I said too brightly. "How's your day going?"

"I can't complain." He held up a stack of index cards. "I was using my lunch break to work on my wedding toast."

"How nice of you," I said, sidling past him to place my purse in the desk drawer.

"In it, I was going to mention your dedication to your job, except I see you've taken another long lunch."

I sat down in the desk chair, clasped my hands on my stomach, and looked up. "Well, since we don't have set lunch hours, I'll be making up the extra time at the end of the day."

"I suppose I can leave that part in then," he said as he erased something on an index card.

"Are good employee skills usually listed in wedding toasts?" What would he mention next? That my pigsty mucking skills were unrivaled? That my e-mail punctuation was impeccable?

Gordon twisted one of his pinkie rings. "I must confess, I've never written a toast before."

No kidding. Seeing the worry on his face, I felt a pang of remorse at teasing him, even if it was mostly in my own head. "You know what? Neither have I. Write whatever you'd like. I bet it will be perfect."

He touched the knot in his tie, as if for comfort, and nodded. "Maybe I'll look up some examples on the Internet later." He walked out of the office, muttering to himself about sentiment and mushiness.

I got to work and soon found myself immersed in discounts, ads, and reservation rates. Even with the added minutes from my late lunch, quitting time arrived before I knew it. I powered down the computer, gathered my belongings, and stopped by the kitchen to see if I could find an apple for Wilbur from the fruit bowl Zennia always kept on the counter.

Picking a shiny red one, I went out the back door and past the herb garden, noting how the scent of rosemary filled the air. I stepped onto the patio, where a couple was playing backgammon at one of the picnic tables, cut past the redwood tree, and went up the path that led to the pigsty.

Wilbur already stood at the fence, as if he knew I was coming for a visit. I patted his bristly head and handed him the apple. Then I leaned on the fence while he ate his fruit.

"How's it going, Wilbur?" I asked.

He snorted in reply.

"Good to hear," I said.

He snorted again.

"Me?" I asked. "Life's okay, except the police might suspect me of killing that flower lady I was telling you about." Wilbur didn't reply this time, so I kept talking. "I'm sure I'm blowing everything out of proportion, but I did find her body. And some lady swears I was arguing with her, even though I wasn't. But Detective Palmer knows me and knows I'm not the killing type. At least he has other people to investigate."

Wilbur pawed at what little remained of his apple and glanced up at me.

"Who, you ask? For one, the creep who's cheating on his wife. Bethany was blackmailing him, and there may be other victims to consider, like Lucia from the drugstore. And there's always Mitch, who could have killed her over the sale of her shop, even though he's supposedly made an offer on another property, so I'm not sure. And there's Bethany's daughter, I guess, although I don't know why she would kill her mom, unless she was in a hurry to take over the flower shop." I sighed.

Wilbur stepped forward, stuck his snout through the fence rails, and bumped my leg. He wagged his curlicue tail.

I patted his back. "Thanks for your support. I'm sure everything will get sorted out."

And if it didn't, I could only hope the extra stress didn't ruin my wedding day.

Chapter 18

Half an hour later, I'd showered, blow-dried my hair, and donned black leggings and a cable knit sweater. I'd even gone the extra mile by adding earrings and a touch of makeup for my dinner with Jason.

The doorbell rang. I went to the door and opened it, already smiling in anticipation of the evening. Jason was dressed in crisp blue jeans and a white button-down shirt. The little flecks of gold in his green eyes sparkled in the porch light, making my heart do a flip-flop.

When he saw me, he let out a low whistle. "Well, hello there." He stepped inside and pulled me in for a kiss that made my toes curl.

"Yowsers," I said after we'd pulled apart. "I hope you continue to greet me like this once we're married."

"Count on it. Every day."

I grabbed my purse off the table and checked to

make sure I had my keys. "Carter should take lessons from you on how to be a good husband."

Jason's brows came together. "Is this the same Carter who Bethany might have been blackmailing?"

"The very same. I had a little chat with him today. I'll tell you about it on the way to dinner."

Jason gave me a troubled look but didn't say anything as we stepped out of the apartment. I locked the door before we headed down the stairs to Jason's car in the visitors' parking space.

Once there, Jason held the door open for me and I slid in, leaning back into the cushioned seat. He went around to his side and got behind the wheel. As he backed out of the space and drove to the Breaking Bread Diner, I filled him on everything I'd learned during the day, from Carter's admission to the affair and blackmail to Mitch's original plan to buy the rest of the building his grandfather once owned.

I skipped over the part about Carter blocking the door during my visit and poking me with his finger. I hadn't been hurt, and besides, Jason couldn't do anything about it now. There was no reason to upset him and spoil the evening.

The restaurant was fairly empty, and we had no trouble being seated. Once we'd placed our orders, our food arrived in record time. As if by mutual agreement, we dropped the topic of Bethany's murder while we ate. It wasn't that appetizing a topic.

"When does your brother get into town?" I asked.

Jason cut into his steak. "He and his wife are

coming two days before the wedding. They'll stay at my place in the spare bedroom."

"I assumed your parents would be staying with you."

"They'll be at one of the hotels in town. They didn't want to impose. I told them it was no trouble, but they insisted, so I offered the room to my brother."

We spent a few minutes talking about where our other relatives would be staying and for how long. When I'd finished the last bite of my grilled fish, Jason leaned across the table and said, "Feel like a little bowling?"

The last time I'd gone bowling, I'd accompanied Ashlee and Brittany on a man-hunting mission. Neither one had picked up a spare, but they'd both managed to pick up a guy.

"Sounds fun," I said. "I've been working on my technique." A bit of an exaggeration, but I knew Jason's competitive side would immediately kick in.

He waggled his eyebrows. "Your technique, huh? Are we still talking about bowling?"

I felt my face grow warm and shot him what I hoped was a mysterious smile. "Maybe."

We left the restaurant and drove across town to the bowling alley. Living in such a small town, going bowling and seeing a movie were the two main options when it came to nightlife. Luckily, Jason and I enjoyed both.

At least a dozen cars were parked in the bowling alley lot, but we were still able to score a lane. After stopping at the shoe rental counter, I changed into my bowling shoes, picked a ball that was light enough I wouldn't embarrass myself, and plugged our names into the machine.

While Jason put on his shoes, I sat down in the plastic chair next to him. "Has Detective Palmer shared anything with you about Bethany's murder?" I asked.

"Not much. He's more closemouthed than usual. Did you tell him about the blackmail?"

"I left him a voice mail, but he hasn't called me back." I felt my chest tighten. He hadn't returned my call and wasn't sharing information with Jason. Was it because he considered me a viable suspect? Would I be getting married in a Blossom Valley jail cell?

Jason must have noticed my concern, because he said, "He's probably swamped and doesn't have time for either of us. I'm sure he'll call when he has the chance."

His answer made sense, but if the detective was really so busy with Bethany's case, wouldn't he want to return my call as soon as possible to see if I knew anything that might help? "He hasn't given you a single update?" I asked.

"He mentioned no one has a solid alibi. Mitch checked in on the ice cream shop once or twice that day, which puts him right next door to the scene of the murder. He said he was running errands the rest of the time, but doesn't remember talking to anyone who could back up his claim. Violet was home alone, but she has no way to prove that."

"What about Lucia? If Bethany really was blackmailing her, she has a motive, too."

Jason finished tying his shoes and stood up. "I don't know if she's even on the detective's radar. Not to mention, we know little about her. She may not belong to those initials in Bethany's notebook. LM could stand for someone else."

"Maybe, although it is curious that a girl who has to skip a semester of school because she can't afford the cost would buy flowers all the time." I grabbed my bowling ball. "But let's worry about that later. Right now I need to concentrate on beating the pants off of you."

"If your plan is to get my pants off, I may let you win," Jason said.

I tossed a smile over my shoulder and stepped up to the lane. Five seconds later, I had my first gutter ball.

Jason had the good grace not to comment as I moved aside so he could take his turn. He got a strike. Of course.

"I'm letting you take the lead so you won't be too embarrassed when I beat you," I said.

He gave me a quick kiss on the lips. "Whatever you have to tell yourself."

Four frames later, I was bowling slightly better, but Jason was winning by a significant margin. I decided to distract him.

"Hey," I said as he picked up his ball from the ball return. "Do you remember anything big happening Labor Day weekend?"

He frowned. "Do you mean here in town? There's always the parade."

I shook my head. "More like a news story about someone getting busted at a big party or a drunk driving arrest, anything like that. Brittany told me that she took Lucia to a party on Labor Day weekend, and Lucia started acting weird after that, especially the one time a cop was driving behind her."

"Let me think about it," Jason said. He released the ball and knocked down only six pins, the worst he'd done so far. Maybe my plan to distract him was a good one.

Once the ball came back, he took his second turn and picked up the spare. So much for messing up his game. Maybe I should have fluttered my eyelashes, like my mom had with Mitch.

I tried to copy what he'd done but only managed to knock down seven pins total. I flopped down in my seat. "Think of anything?" I asked in a last-ditch effort.

Jason smirked at me like he knew what I was doing. "Afraid not, but when we're done here, why don't you come over to my place and we can research it?"

If this was a first date, I might suspect his offer was akin to the old "Come up to my room to look at my stamp collection" gambit, but I knew Jason literally wanted to do research. Of course, we could always make time for a little stamp-collecting action when we were done.

"What are you smiling about?" he asked, snapping me out of my reverie.

"Maybe you'll find out later," I said with a wink.

He gave me a curious look and then bowled a strike. I managed to follow that up with a spare, my first of the evening. A few frames later, the game was over.

I returned my ball to the rack and then swapped out my shoes and took them to the counter, while Jason did the same. We made our way to the exit. For a second, I thought we'd make it out of the bowling alley without Jason gloating, but right as he pulled open the door, he said, "You know, you might want to change your bowling technique. It doesn't seem to be working out so well."

"It was an off night. I'll beat your pants off of you next time."

Jason gave me a salacious grin. "Strip bowling. I like it."

When we got to his car, he stepped up next to me and whispered in my ear, "I could give you lessons, you know." His breath was warm on my neck. He pulled my arm back and mimed rolling a bowling ball. His touch made the little hairs on my arm stand on end. "I have a special technique of my own."

I swallowed hard. "Lessons are always good, especially private ones."

He kissed my neck and released my hand. "I thought you might agree."

Jason held open the car door for me before going around to his side and starting up the engine. Within minutes, he was pulling into his driveway. Once we were inside his place, I sat down on the leather sofa.

"So," he said, "are you sure you want to do this research?"

Not wanting to get sidetracked, I nodded. "Better now than later. Go ahead and grab your laptop."

He retrieved it from where it perched on an end

table, set it squarely on the coffee table, and fired it up. Settling in next to me, he started typing. "Let's check the *Herald* first. I don't remember covering any major events that weekend, but someone else could have handled a smaller story, like a drunk driving arrest."

He brought up the newspaper's Web site and clicked the search function. He narrowed the range to the week before and after Labor Day weekend and entered "alcohol" and "party" as keywords. I watched over his shoulder, but none of the results looked promising.

"Do you have other information we can work with?" Jason asked.

I felt a ball of frustration form in the pit of my stomach. "No, but there must be some reason Lucia started acting odd after that Labor Day party."

"There could be a lot of reasons, none of which would make the paper."

I rubbed my forehead. "I know it's a long shot. Let's try the *Press Democrat.* Brittany said the party was down in Santa Rosa, so if something happened there, it might not have made the *Herald* anyway."

He entered the *Press Democrat*'s URL and squinted at the page as it loaded. He repeated his search criteria, but again, we found nothing of interest. Jason leaned back and stroked his goatee. "Are you sure alcohol was involved?"

I considered the question. "Brittany mentioned it was unusual for Lucia to go out drinking. I must have made the connection in my head that alcohol was at the root of the problem."

Jason scrolled back up to the top of the screen. "Okay, let's take alcohol out of the equation and do a blank search for only that weekend." He hit a few keys, and I leaned in to get a better look at the results.

"Nothing, nothing, nothing," Jason muttered as we sorted through the list. He scrolled through another page of results. "This looks interesting."

I straightened up to read the headline: BICYCLIST INJURED IN HIT-AND-RUN ACCIDENT. I scanned the article and felt my pulse quicken. The Saturday before Labor Day, a woman had been struck by a car while riding her bike on a narrow two-lane road outside of Santa Rosa. Witnesses who passed the accident said a young lady was rendering aid, but when the ambulance arrived, the EMTs reported the bicyclist was alone. The police were able to obtain a general description of the woman and her car, but so far the driver had not been identified.

I laid my hand on Jason's knee and turned to look at him. "What if Lucia was the driver?"

Jason tapped the screen. "There's no way to be sure. The article doesn't provide enough details."

"You're a reporter. Don't you have access to the police reports?"

"Sure, but that can take time. I imagine the reporter who wrote this article already viewed the report and would have included any details that seemed important."

"Maybe. I still think Lucia might have been the driver. It happened on Labor Day weekend, and running away from an accident would explain why Lucia was so jumpy when that policeman was following her weeks later."

Jason didn't look convinced, but I felt like I was making headway. The timing and location matched with when Lucia had started behaving strangely.

That meant I might have uncovered her secret.

Chapter 19

Jason and I didn't find any other search results that looked promising. After another fifteen minutes of clicking links and scrolling through lists of headlines, we gave up.

That was fine by me. While I couldn't be positive Lucia was responsible for the hit-and-run accident, it was my best lead. I needed to think of a way to contact her again to find out more. I'd lucked out when I'd found her at the drugstore, but she might get suspicious if I appeared in the cosmetic aisle again so soon, especially if I started asking questions.

If Lucia really was the driver in the accident, how did that connect to her flower purchases? With the way Bethany liked to probe people's secrets, she could have tricked Lucia into letting her guard down on one of her many visits to the shop. If Lucia told her about the accident, Bethany may have jumped at the chance to blackmail her.

"Earth to Dana," Jason said.

I realized that Jason had been talking to me the entire time I'd been thinking. I'd missed every word he'd said.

"Would you mind repeating that?" I placed my hands in my lap like a contrite schoolgirl and smiled up at him so he'd know I was paying attention.

"I forgot to mention at dinner that I verified the tux rentals today. Is there anything else you need help with?"

Dozens of thoughts jumped around my head, but none remained in place for long. After a moment, I shrugged. "I can't think of anything specific."

"Let me know if that changes. I want to help." He kissed my forehead.

How had I gotten so lucky? "I'm sure I'll be a mess on our wedding day, but right now, everything seems to be on track. Of course, that doesn't stop me from waking up in the middle of the night and panicking that I've forgotten something important." I leaned into him, and he rubbed my thigh.

"The day will be great," Jason said, "even if one or two things go wrong. Marrying you is the most important thing."

I gave him a kiss. "At least we've only invited family and close friends. Can you imagine the extra work if we were having one of those huge weddings with three hundred people? I don't know how anyone can pull off a wedding like that. No wonder couples hire wedding coordinators."

I'd swear I felt Jason shudder. "I'm glad we stuck to the basics," was all he said.

"Me too." We fell silent. Between the warmth of

Jason's touch and the late hour, I felt my eyelids droop.

I glanced at my phone and reluctantly rose. "I'd better leave before I fall asleep right where I'm sitting."

"If your goal is to stay awake, I know a way to make that happen," Jason said, standing up as well. His inviting tone let me know exactly how he planned to keep me awake.

"Easy does it," I said with a laugh. "You need to save that energy for after our wedding."

He pulled me close. "Don't worry. I have plenty of energy."

I tilted my head up, and he gave me a kiss that reached from the top of my head to the tips of my toes. "Maybe I don't need to rush off right this minute," I said when I caught my breath. I leaned in for another kiss, and Jason pressed his lips against mine. As he ran his hands along my back, I marveled at how I was soon to be Mrs. Dana Forrester.

I arrived at work early the next morning, eager to write up my blog about how to clean out a teakettle. The idea had come to me the other night, when I'd made myself a cup of tea before bed, only to find strange bits of a mysterious gray substance floating in my cup. Once I'd posted my suggestions, I responded to the handful of new comments from yesterday's blog and checked the farm's e-mail account.

With the correspondence out of the way, I dug

out my list of reasons to hold weddings at Esther's farm and reviewed my ideas. I'd originally placed Wilbur and his pig pals as a highlight, but now I had to question my judgment. Did a bride really want to see pigs at her wedding? I shuddered at a vision of muddy hoofprints splattered across a white bridal gown train as a herd of pigs thundered past Esther's makeshift altar. I deleted Wilbur from the list.

I spent the better part of the morning adding more ideas, none of which involved farm animals. When my eyes began to burn and my back started to protest, I took that as a sign I needed a break. I stood up and stretched before wandering into the kitchen, where I found Zennia slicing mushrooms at the kitchen table. Wafts of steam rose from the contents of a pot simmering on the stove.

"What's on the menu for today?" I asked her as I went to the refrigerator for the pitcher of lemonade that always waited there.

She tossed the mushroom slices into a bowl and started cutting up another one. "I decided to go simple today and make mushroom, spinach, and mozzarella panini with roasted red pepper soup on the side."

What Zennia considered simple would easily take me all day to prepare. Good thing Jason wasn't marrying me for my cooking skills. I poured the lemonade into a glass and sat down.

I let out a sigh. "It feels good to take a break." I watched Zennia slice another mushroom. The rhythm was almost hypnotic.

"How are the wedding plans coming along?"

"So far so good. I'm planning to run into town during lunch to check on my flower order with Violet, but it's more for peace of mind than anything else."

Zennia nodded. "Don't underestimate the importance of a peaceful mind. Surprises can be disruptive to your overall well-being." She glanced at the clock. "Speaking of surprises, I didn't realize the time. The guests will be arriving in the dining room any minute." She carried the bowl of sliced mushrooms to the counter. "Dana, if it's not an imposition, would you mind ladling out the soup while I get started cooking the panini?"

I finished my lemonade, took my glass to the sink, and washed my hands. "Of course not. I can help serve, too."

"I don't want to interrupt your lunch plans. You said you were going into town."

"It can wait." I took down a stack of soup bowls while Zennia heated the griddle and assembled the sandwiches. We worked in companionable silence as I lined up the filled bowls on the table and helped put the sandwiches on plates.

When everything was ready, I filled a pitcher with water and carried it to the dining room. Most of the tables were occupied with diners waiting for their lunches. I left the water on the sideboard and went back to the kitchen for the first bowls of soup. More guests filtered in as Zennia and I delivered the food, but the two of us easily met the demand. When everyone was happily slurping and munching, I returned to the kitchen to help clean up.

I picked up a sponge to wipe down the table, but

Zennia practically swatted it out of my hand. "Don't even think about it. You've done enough already." She pointed to a single remaining sandwich sitting on a plate. "I made an extra one for you."

A few months ago, I would have cringed at the thought of eating a sandwich comprised mostly of vegetables, but my taste buds were slowly evolving. Now, the sight of the sandwich, especially the melted cheese oozing down the side, made my mouth water. "Thanks."

I took the plate into the office, sat down at the computer, and brought up a Web site for a competing spa. While I read about their offerings to see how they compared to Esther's and whether we should add to our own list of services, I ate my sandwich and tried not to spill bits of mushroom on the keyboard.

Once I was finished eating, I scanned a few more Web sites, taking notes as I read, and then pushed back from the desk. With my keys and purse in hand, I headed down the hall and out the door.

The afternoon air was chilly. Ominous-looking clouds scuttled across the sky. I tried not to think about rain on my wedding day as I got into my car and backed out of my space, but each passing day seemed to be cloudier.

On the drive into town, I considered why I was even going. I didn't really need to visit the flower shop. If I wanted a status update, I could easily call Violet and save myself the cost of gas. But with my wedding so close, I wanted to be sure Violet knew what she was doing. I needed to see her in person and hear her confirmation. I hadn't suffered from any pre-wedding jitters yet, but I suspected they lurked just under the surface.

Exiting the highway, I drove down Main Street and parked in front of Don't Dilly-Dahlia. I was momentarily tempted to pop into the drugstore and see if Lucia was working, but I'd already decided against that strategy. I shouldn't second-guess myself.

I went inside the flower shop and spotted Violet in the far corner, arranging a collection of small bouquets in a large container. Her back was to me.

"Hi, Violet," I said.

The sound of crinkling cellophane must have blocked my arrival, because she gave a startled cry and dropped the rose she'd been holding. She whirled around, a hand to her chest. She let out her breath when she saw me. "Oh, it's you."

I crossed the shop to join her. "Sorry. I didn't mean to scare you. I was in the neighborhood and thought I'd stop in."

Looking slightly embarrassed, Violet lowered her hand, almost knocking into the handles of the pruning shears sticking out of her apron pocket. "That's all right. I guess I'm still a little jumpy." She bent down and retrieved the rose from the floor. The shears threatened to slide out, but she kept them in place with one hand. "Mom and I kept meaning to install one of those chimes that goes off whenever someone opens the door, but we never got around to it. I'd better put it on my list of things to do."

"List?" I glanced around the shop. "Are you planning a lot of changes?"

"Not really. I've had a running list since I started working here, not that my mom ever agreed to any of them."

"I have an ongoing to-do list myself, but I never seem to cross anything off it," I said. "Maybe your mom was the same way."

Violet shook her head. "No, she just didn't like any of my ideas."

I pointed to the pictures and paintings of the beach and redwoods. "Bethany told me selling the artwork was your idea."

"That was the only thing she allowed me to add to the merchandise." She scowled. "She complained about them all the time. Said they weren't selling fast enough." She chewed on her bottom lip. "Was there something I could help you with?"

"I wanted to see how everything was going with my wedding bouquets."

"Fine. I spoke to the distributor this morning and your order is on schedule." Her scowl was back. "I would have called you if there was a problem."

I offered her a smile. "Of course. I'm not implying I don't trust you, but I'd understand if you were more focused on what happened to your mom, rather than what's happening at the shop. Flowers must seem so unimportant."

She closed her eyes in a long blink, as if trying to compose herself. "I can handle your flowers. You don't need to worry about a thing."

I'd obviously hurt her feelings, and I scanned the room for a new topic. "These are pretty," I said, pointing to a cluster of small red flowers. "What are they?"

Violet squinted at the flowers and shrugged. "Maybe it says on the tag."

I raised my eyebrows and read the name on the sticker. "Matsumoto Aster."

Shouldn't she already know that? I'd swear Bethany had said Violet started working here a couple of years ago, giving her plenty of time to learn what types of flowers the shop sold.

"That's right," Violet said. "I knew it was some kind of aster."

"Must be hard to remember all the names."

"Flowers were always Mom's thing." She plucked a dead petal off a nearby mum and dropped it on the floor.

I watched it settle next to another one already there. "Your mom seemed to think you were interested in taking over the business one day."

"She did think that, didn't she?"

I studied Violet, but her expression remained impassive. Her answer implied that Bethany may have overestimated Violet's interest in the flower shop.

"What about all the changes you have planned?" I said. "You *are* going to keep the shop, aren't you?"

Violet started gnawing on her thumbnail. "Well, it's mine now."

Not exactly a direct answer.

After a second, she sighed. "I came up with those changes because I knew my mom would keep me working here for years, if she had her way, and I wanted to have a small say in how Mom ran the business. I mean, I like this place well enough, and God knows Mom absolutely loved it, but there are better ways to make a living."

"Like through your writing?" I asked, remembering how Gretchen had mentioned meeting Violet in a writing group at the library.

She gave me a sharp look and gnawed on her nail faster.

"You wrote a play for one of the community colleges, didn't you?"

Violet's face broke into a grin. "Did you see it?"

"I'm afraid not, but someone told me about it and said you got rave reviews."

She nodded eagerly. "I did, I really did. I told my mom about it. I was even considering a writing career, but Mom really likes my help here. I mean, liked."

"So you've given up writing altogether?"

"No, I've kept writing, but Mom thought it was silly, so I'd work late at night after she went to bed. I didn't want to cause any arguments." A shadow crossed her face, and her eyes narrowed. "Heaven forbid I do something my mother didn't approve of."

In one smooth motion, Violet pulled the pruning shears out of her apron pocket and snipped a rosebud off its stem. It plunged to the floor.

"You can't always do what your mom wanted," I said. "You are an adult."

She looked at me, and I saw a coldness in her expression that sent a chill down my spine. "I tried telling that to my mom, not that she ever listened. She expected me to do her bidding all the time with no complaints." Her eyes took on a glazed look, and she snipped the head off another rose. "Violet, deliver these flowers." Snip. "Violet, sweep the floor." Snip. "Violet, forget about your stupid writing. You'll never succeed anyway." Snip.

I stared at the pile of rose buds on the floor. "You can make your own decisions," I said soothingly, as if trying to calm a cornered animal. "Your mom isn't here to tell you what to do anymore."

"But think of the years I've wasted," she said. "A newspaper reviewer said I was the next Eugene O'Neill. I should have focused on my second play, rather than shoving all the drafts to the back of a drawer. Now I've missed my chance to keep the momentum rolling and make a name for myself."

I took a step back, alarmed by the gleam in her eye. "It's never too late. Surely there will be other chances."

"I don't know that for sure." She turned her attention to a fall floral arrangement of carnations, roses, and day lilies, attacking the bouquet in a series of savage snips. Bits of stems and blooms showered down like rain. I could only watch in stunned silence, wondering what had happened to the docile Violet I was so familiar with.

A sudden rush of street noise behind me announced that someone had opened the door. Violet looked up and the wild look in her eye winked out like a cell phone screen when the battery dies. I turned to see an elderly woman with a hunched back shuffle into the store.

I swiveled back toward Violet. She slid the shears

in her pocket and stood there as if nothing out of the ordinary had happened.

"Can I help you?" she asked the woman, offering a polite smile that didn't hint at the damage she'd done to the flowers only moments before.

"Don't let me interrupt." She raised a gnarled hand toward me. "This young lady was here first."

"I was just leaving," I said. I looked at Violet again, wondering if I should leave this woman alone with her, but the woman was already listing her order while Violet nodded along complacently. Whatever demons had set Violet off were gone.

With their attention on the order, I pulled open the door and left the flower shop, wondering at Violet's mental state. Though she'd only been butchering flowers, I'd seen a dark side to her that I'd never imagined. Had Bethany somehow set off Violet before she'd died, and it had resulted in her death? Or was she simply expressing her grief now that Bethany was gone?

I shook off the thought and reached in my pocket for my car keys at the same time I heard Mom calling my name. I looked around until I saw her waving at me from across the street. Checking for traffic, I trotted over, the incident with Violet already fading as Mom gave me a quick hug in greeting.

"Hi, Mom. Working today?"

"Only for another hour, but I'm glad I saw you. I was going to give you a call later."

"What about?" I asked.

She tilted her head toward the Get the Scoop

storefront. "I went in for ice cream yesterday evening and had a chance to talk to Mitch."

I held up my hand. "Wait. You're not playing detective without me, are you?"

Mom opened her eyes wide, obviously trying to look innocent. "Would I do a thing like that?" she asked. "I merely felt like a scoop of vanilla. If Mitch happened to be there, and felt like talking to me, maybe about Bethany's murder, it would only be polite to listen to the man, wouldn't it?"

I tried to suppress a smile but failed. "I wouldn't want you to be rude. Did Mitch have anything to say, maybe about Bethany's murder?" I added with a wink.

Her eyes lit up. "My goodness, yes. I didn't get all the details, but he said he was working on getting a bank loan and talking to contractors. Whatever he's planning must be a big project. They'll have to tear down a wall and redecorate everything and put in all sorts of counters and fixtures and such. The list went on and on."

"These changes must be for the auto parts store he wants to buy. Sounds like he'll have to practically gut the place."

"He didn't mention where he was making these changes, but I can ask him at the symphony next week." She glanced up at the sky, as if thinking. "Of course, that seems so far away. Maybe I should ask him to dinner."

She seemed to be talking more to herself than to me, but I still reached out and grabbed her shoulder. "Hang on a second. What are you talking about?"

"There's a performance down in Santa Rosa next week. I happened to mention how much I like the symphony, and Mitch asked if I'd like to go. But if we want to find Bethany's killer, we need information now, not next week. That's why I should ask him out before then."

I stared at my mother. Had she gone mad?

"What?" she asked, all innocence.

"After all the times you've lectured me to be careful, you're actually considering asking a potential killer out on a date?" My voice reached a pitch I didn't know it could. "I told you the other day that it's too dangerous for you to see Mitch alone."

Mom blushed in full force. "I guess I got carried away. I never realized how much fun being a detective could be, and to be perfectly honest, I don't believe for a second that Mitch is the killer. Frankly, I enjoy the man's company, whether it's at the symphony or having dinner together."

My mom was starting to sound like Ashlee, putting her love life before her safety. I tried to reason with her. "Let's not forget someone has died here. While you might be confident he didn't kill Bethany, I'm not so sure. If you start asking too many questions, he'll wonder what you're up to." How many times had Mom given me the exact same lecture about pretending to be a detective? "Promise me you won't ask him out. I'm not thrilled you're going to Santa Rosa with him either."

"Fine, I won't ask him to dinner. If the police don't figure out who killed Bethany in the next few days, I'll skip the symphony, too, even if Mitch is a handsome and charming man."

"Thanks," I said. "I appreciate the sacrifice. With any luck, the cops will catch the killer, it won't be Mitch, and you and he can have a lovely time together."

A woman came out of the clothing store, and Mom watched her walk past. "I'd better get back to work. I didn't expect to talk to you for so long."

"Thanks for letting me know what you found out from Mitch."

Before she turned away, she asked, "Do you have any last-minute wedding tasks you need help with? I'm not working tomorrow, so I'm available."

"I only need to put together the wedding favors, which won't take any time at all. Thanks anyway."

"Call if you think of anything else or need help with the favors."

I nodded my thanks and then ran back across the street before an approaching car could flatten me. I gave Mom a little wave and got in my car.

Once inside my Honda, I sagged against the seat, surprisingly tired. I'd told Mom that I didn't need any help for the wedding, but clearly planning for the big day and worrying about being involved in Bethany's murder were starting to take their toll. The workday was only half over, and I already felt ready to call it quits.

I started up the car and headed toward the Daily Grind. What I needed was a pick-me-up, one with lots of caffeine and sugar. After all, I'd eaten Zennia's healthy, vegetable-filled sandwich. One little frappé wouldn't hurt.

On the short drive, I shook my head at my mom's antics and then mulled over my conversation with Violet. I felt sorry for her. Flowers clearly held no interest for her. The only time I'd seen her animated was when she'd been talking about writing.

Had Bethany insisted Violet keep working at the shop, causing her to bottle up a slow-simmering rage? Had Violet finally blown her top and killed the one person she believed was standing in the way of her writing career?

Chapter 20

The inside of the Daily Grind was a mix of new technology and old country. Behind the counter, shiny stainless-steel espresso machines hissed and steamed, while in the pick-up area, jars of locally made jams and honeys crowded for shelf space on a display case near the newspaper stand.

I got in line behind a man in khaki pants and a polo shirt who was talking into his Bluetooth earpiece. He mentioned toeing the line, leveraging best practices, getting the manager's buy-in, and other business jargon that meant little. I tuned him out and thought about Violet again.

She had to be in her early thirties, if not older. Would a woman that age allow her mother to dictate her career choice? It seemed like Violet had, but at what expense? She clearly held plenty of resentment toward her mom. Why not cut the cord and pursue her dream?

Maybe Violet felt indebted to her mother since Bethany had created a position at the flower shop after Violet had been laid off from her job. Or maybe Violet wasn't capable of making such a monumental decision on her own and allowed her mom to pressure her into staying, even if she wasn't entirely happy with the decision.

Then again, everyone had their breaking point. Maybe Violet had reached hers. Bethany may have tried to control Violet one too many times, and Violet had snatched the gun from the back room and shot her.

But would Violet be able to hide her guilt from the police? I knew firsthand how intimidating Detective Palmer could be during questioning. I imagined Violet would crack under the pressure.

The businessman in front of me placed his order and moved to the side. I stowed my thoughts for later and stepped up to the counter to order a mint chocolate chip frappé. In an effort to make it a little healthier, I told the barista to hold the whipped cream.

After I'd paid for my drink, I moved to the pick-up area and perused the assortment of local food items, noting that they'd added a selection of caramel sauces since my last visit. The barista called my name, and I retrieved my frappé. I stuck a straw in my cup and was heading for the exit when a figure in the far corner of the coffeehouse caught my eye.

A woman in a black pantsuit sat at a small table, with a briefcase at her feet. Even with her head bowed and her long black hair partially blocking her face, she looked familiar. It also looked like she was crying, if her shaking shoulders were any indication. As I watched, she brushed the hair away from her face, exposing her profile, and my sense that I knew her from somewhere grew. I racked my brain as to where I might have met her, but the information stayed just out of reach.

The woman ran her fingers under her eyes, then rose with a furtive glance, hurried over to the cart that held a collection of creamers, sugars, and stirrers, and pulled out a handful of napkins. She glanced at me for a second before dropping her gaze, but that second was all it took for me to remember where I'd met her, or at least seen her.

It was in the back parking lot of the office complex where she presumably worked. The woman was Carter's mistress.

She hurried back to the table, holding the napkins to shade her eyes, as if trying to cover her crying. She needn't have worried. Everyone was too busy staring at their smartphones or talking to their companions to notice.

She sat back down at her table, and I made my way over. As I got near, she looked up at me, new tears fresh on her cheeks. Based on what little I'd seen of her, I'd assumed she was quite young, but up close, I could see the start of crow's feet at the corners of her eyes and detectable lines around her mouth.

"Sorry to bother you," I said. "But I noticed you seem upset. Are you all right?"

She threw down the sodden napkin she'd been

clutching. "I'm fine," she said. The single sob that slipped out begged to differ.

I sat down across from her, torn between finding out information about Carter and helping her with whatever was causing her distress. "You don't seem fine. Is there someone you'd like me to call for you?"

She shook her head. "No, I have no one."

A melodramatic exaggeration if I'd ever heard one. "I've heard talking to strangers is easier than talking to your closest friends," I offered. Someone, somewhere, had told me that once, although I had no idea if it was actually true.

"There's nothing to talk about." She plucked a fresh napkin from the small pile before her. "I've been dumped."

I stared at her. Carter had dumped her? When? Why? I eased back on the seat and tried to think of a neutral comment. I didn't want her to realize I already knew about her and Carter. "It's always tough when a relationship ends, especially if you weren't expecting it."

She dabbed at her eyes. "I told myself not to get too attached. I'm certainly old enough to know better. Plus, more than one of my friends has been in this exact same situation, so I know how it usually ends."

"What situation's that?"

"Women letting their boyfriends string them along for years while promising to leave their wives, when, of course, they never do. Yet, here I am, acting like a total schmuck and doing the opposite of what I tell my friends to do. This is the last time I date a married man."

I couldn't believe this woman was openly admitting to her affair with Carter, without a hint of remorse. Maybe that theory about talking to strangers was true after all.

"If you already knew the outcome, why didn't you drop him?" I asked.

She set her mouth in a hard line. "Because our relationship was different."

I blinked. Surely every woman who had dated a married man felt their relationship was different.

Carter's girlfriend must have noticed my doubts. "Well, it was," she said in a defensive tone.

"Of course," I said, not wanting to argue. "Different how, exactly?"

"He clearly loves me." She leaned across the table. "Do you realize he's sent me a dozen red roses every week for months? What other guy does that? And he's always surprising me at work. And leaving little notes on my car. He even took me to Fort Bragg for a romantic dinner a few weeks ago."

Well, sure. He probably didn't know anyone in Fort Bragg. "Sounds like quite the guy," I said.

She tilted her head. "You know, I think you're right."

"That he's quite the guy?"

She laughed, making her appear much younger for those few seconds. "No, that talking to a stranger is easier than telling a friend. I do feel better."

I held out my hand. "Well, at the risk of not being a stranger anymore, my name's Dana."

She shook my hand. "Phoebe, Phoebe Chan.

You're also right about him being quite the guy." She played with the strand of pearls around her neck. "I should have realized something was up. He stood me up on Friday night. That's the first time he's ever canceled without calling. Maybe his wife had some kind of medical emergency. If she wasn't so sick, I know everything would be different."

I leaned forward. "What's wrong with his wife?" I asked.

"He doesn't like to talk about it. Probably because her situation is so sad."

Or maybe because she wasn't really sick.

"He did tell me that she has to stay in bed all day and almost never leaves the house," Phoebe said. "It's some sort of terminal illness. He said she's taken a turn for the worse and that's why we can't see each other anymore." She broke into fresh sobs.

I glanced around the coffee shop to see if anyone had noticed. An older gentleman in a suit gave me a sympathetic smile.

I turned back to Phoebe. "Why would her declining health force you to break up?"

She wiped her eyes with a napkin. "He said the guilt was too much. Every time he looks at his wife withering away, he worries that she somehow knows about me, and that's why she's getting sicker."

More likely Carter had grown tired of his girlfriend and wanted an easy way to dump her. Who could argue with a story about a dying wife?

"One of his best qualities is how dedicated he is to her," Phoebe said, "even if she treats him badly. He wouldn't dream of abandoning her when she's so ill. He takes his wedding vows seriously."

I used all my willpower not to gag on my frappé. Apparently the irony of her comments completely escaped her. "His wife doesn't treat him well?" I asked.

"She's just so demanding. The poor man works all day and then has to come home and practically be her servant. But he does it anyway, without a word of complaint, I'm sure." Phoebe gave a wistful smile. "There I go again, blathering on about what a great guy he is. I sound like some silly schoolgirl." She swept her long dark hair over her shoulder. "I don't think I've accepted that he doesn't want to see me anymore." Her face grew dark. "Especially after everything I've done for him."

"Like what?" I sipped my drink, feeling as if I was caught up in a soap opera.

"I kept our little secret, for one thing," she said. "I never objected when he brought takeout to my apartment instead of wining and dining me at a nice restaurant. That's why the dinner in Fort Bragg was so special." She sighed, no doubt remembering the evening.

"What a trooper," I said dryly, but she didn't seem to notice my tone.

"That's only the beginning. I made sure I was available whenever he called at the last minute." Her eyes narrowed to slits. "Do you have any idea how many nights I sat home hoping he'd call? And he just dumps me like this?" Her voice got louder. "I'm a professional woman. I deserve better!"

Uh-oh. Maybe Carter's plan to escape the relationship for the good of his sick wife wasn't such a smart one after all. "Are you going to tell his wife?" I asked.

Phoebe wrapped the napkin around her fingers so tightly, the flimsy material ripped. "I should, you know. If only his wife weren't so sick. I don't want to be the one who pushes her over the edge. What if the news kills her?"

I heard a chime coming from the direction of Phoebe's briefcase. She slid her hand into one of the side pockets and pulled out a cell phone, checking the screen.

She gasped. "Is it that late already? My boss is going to kill me." She dropped the phone back into the briefcase pocket and hastily gathered all the crumpled napkins into a ball. "How do I look? Is my mascara smeared?"

"Nope, you look great."

Phoebe stood, deposited the wadded-up napkins and her cup in the trash can, and slung her briefcase strap over her shoulder. "Hey, thanks for listening. It was a big help." She rushed out of the coffee shop, taking any additional information she might have shared about Carter with her.

That was okay. She'd given me plenty to think about. I just needed to decide if her relationship with Carter, and their breakup, was somehow connected to Bethany's murder.

Chapter 21

After I'd finished the last drop of my frappé, I drove back to work. A light rain dampened my hair and clothes as I crossed the farm's parking lot toward the lobby, my mind wandering back to my chance meeting with Phoebe at the Daily Grind.

Poor, gullible Phoebe. Why had Carter chosen now to dump her? Had he needed to kill Bethany before he could break up with her?

I considered the possibility and then shook my head. Even with Bethany dead, Carter had to worry Phoebe would tell his wife about their affair. Bethany's murder didn't change that.

Perhaps the breakup wasn't related to Bethany's death at all. Maybe their relationship had reached its inevitable end and the timing was a coincidence. Carter might have simply decided he wouldn't allow Bethany to blackmail him anymore and gotten rid of her.

Feeling like I was no closer to finding Bethany's killer, I spent much of the afternoon working on a new brochure in the office before taking the digital camera outside to snap pictures of the vegetable garden, particularly the broccoli plants. Tomorrow's blog would include a recipe for healthier guacamole, with chopped-up broccoli florets replacing part of the high-fat avocado. I'd never tried the recipe myself, but it was one of Zennia's favorites.

After I'd finished taking photos, I went back inside, put away the camera, and gathered my belongings, surprised at how fast the afternoon had sailed by. Jason was getting together with a few of his buddies tonight for his bachelor party. While he was enjoying one of his final nights as a single guy—hopefully without any strippers—I was looking forward to a quiet evening at home, double-checking the RSVPs, tallying up our expenses to make sure we were within budget, and watching TV while I assembled the wedding favors.

I said good night to Gordon and left through the lobby. Once in my car, I drove down the highway and took the exit for downtown Blossom Valley. The Open sign for the flower shop glowed brightly in the encroaching dusk. I wondered how Violet felt about working evenings in the shop where her mother was murdered. I certainly wouldn't want to be there alone, especially after dark.

A few minutes later, I pulled into my parking space at my apartment complex and shut off the engine. Ashlee's Camaro sat in the space next to mine. Her being home might mess up my plans for a relaxing evening, but I could always hang out in my room if she turned the volume up too high on whatever reality show she was sure to be watching.

For a second I considered adding noise-canceling headphones to my wedding registry, but I'd be moving out soon enough.

I climbed the stairs and unlocked the door to the apartment. As I pushed it open, I could hear voices coming from down the hall. Ashlee must have company. I shrugged out of my jacket and headed to my room to hang it up.

As I got closer, I realized the voices were coming from my bedroom, not Ashlee's.

What the heck?

I stuck my head inside and froze. Ashlee and Brittany stood in one corner, blowing up balloons. Mom and Esther each struggled with the shrink wrap on packages of streamers, while Zennia sat on my bed with a stack of index cards and several pens. Lucia and Gretchen crouched in the corner, trying to untangle a garland of tiny wedding dresses.

When no one noticed me, I cleared my throat and said, "What's going on?"

Everyone whipped their heads in my direction, while Ashlee let go of her partially filled balloon. It flew around the room with a loud farting sound before dropping to the floor.

There was a pregnant pause; then Brittany threw her arms wide. "Surprise!"

A huge grin spread across my face as I realized what was happening. Mom rushed over and gave me a hug.

"I know you said you didn't want a shower, but it didn't feel right. I told your sister this morning, and she took over from there."

Ashlee snatched the balloon up off the floor and

started stretching it out. "Yeah, only I had to help with an emergency dog surgery during lunch, so I couldn't get started until I got off work. I texted Brittany, and we ran over to the drugstore for party supplies. That's where we ran into Lucia."

Lucia gave me a small wave and a shy smile. "I hope you don't mind that I came along. It sounded like fun."

"Of course not," I said. "The more the merrier."

As I looked around the room, I couldn't seem to stop smiling. My family and friends were really throwing me a bridal shower. Even though I'd said I didn't want one, deep down, I really kind of did.

Zennia took up the narrative. "When we all got here and found the girls hadn't had a chance to decorate, we all jumped in."

"But wouldn't it be easier to do this out in the living room?" I asked.

"Yeah, but if you walked in on us, we wouldn't be able to surprise you," Ashlee said. "My room's a mess, so that only left your room to work in. I thought we'd hear you come home, and we'd hit the lights and all jump out at once."

Gretchen laughed. "Guess we messed up the surprise part."

I shook my head. "No, I'm definitely surprised. And thrilled. This means a lot to me."

Everyone started talking at once as they gathered their supplies and carried them out to the living room. I glanced in the kitchen and saw bags of chips, a carton of dip, a sandwich platter, and a cake box on the counter that I'd somehow missed on my way in.

"Let's get this party decorated," Mom said.

We all set to work. Ashlee and Brittany resumed blowing up the balloons while the rest of us put up streamers, the garland that Gretchen had finally managed to untangle, and a sign that read CONGRATULATIONS, with each letter made out of miniature brides and grooms. I found myself smiling as I helped decorate for my own surprise party.

"All this work is making me hungry," Ashlee said as she taped a balloon to the end of the coffee table.

Brittany giggled. "Me too. Let's get the food out."

I went with them into the kitchen, where Ashlee pried the clear plastic cover off the sandwich tray and Brittany pulled open a bag of chips.

"Dana, can you get out the drinks?" Ashlee said, nodding toward the fridge. "We're making mimosas."

"Whoo-hoo!" Brittany hollered, making me wonder if she hadn't already sampled one.

Gretchen came into the kitchen. "Ashlee, where did you want me to set up for the facials?"

"The kitchen table is fine. We can put the food on the coffee table. But let's wait to do the facials until after we play that game Zennia made up."

"Okay. I'll wait and set up later," Gretchen said.

She went back to the living room while I opened the fridge and found bottles of champagne and cartons of orange juice. I grabbed a few and carried them to the counter, then opened the cupboard to see how many clean glasses I could scrounge up.

Lucia came into the kitchen. "Can I help with anything?"

"Know how to open champagne?" I asked.

She took the closest bottle and started to remove the foil around the cork.

Brittany watched her and sighed. "I love a good party. Lucia, remember that awesome Labor Day party we went to?"

Lucia let out a little gasp and dropped the foil on the floor. She scrambled to pick it up, obviously agitated.

"It sounded like the best party ever," Ashlee said with a pout. "Next time you'd better invite me."

"I did invite you," Brittany said, "but you'd started dating that drummer and he had some gig that weekend."

A dreamy look came over Ashlee's face. "I almost forgot about Tommy. That guy was a master with his hands, and I'm not talking about what a good drummer he is."

"And you're not still dating him?" I asked, casting another glance at Lucia. She'd turned her back to us and was lining up the glasses I'd taken out of the cupboard.

Ashlee shook her head. "Too many groupies. You should have seen the way the girls threw themselves at him."

My sister didn't normally let a little competition get in her way. These groupies must have been prettier than average, or more aggressive.

"Besides," Ashlee said, "he was too flaky. Not like Logan."

"Logan? Isn't that the guy you've gone out with a couple of times already?" I asked. Ashlee dumped most guys by the third date, ready to move on to someone new. I had to wonder when Logan's expiration date would hit.

Ashlee shrugged. "I like hanging out with him."

Brittany grabbed two chip bags and picked up the dip. "Ashlee, help me carry the rest of the food to the living room."

Ashlee took hold of the sandwich tray. "Right behind you." They headed out of the kitchen area, leaving me relatively alone with Lucia. With all the excitement over the surprise party, I'd all but forgotten how I'd wanted to ask her about the night of the hit-and-run accident. This might be the perfect time to talk.

I moved next to her. "Boy, sure sounds like I missed quite the Labor Day party," I said as I pretended to busy myself with the glasses, too.

"I guess," Lucia mumbled.

"What was it like?"

"Everyone hung out, listened to music, the usual."

"And drank beer, if it was anything like the parties I used to go to." In actuality, I'd never been much of a partier, but didn't all parties have beer?

Another shrug. "I didn't stay long." She looked longingly at Ashlee and Brittany, who were over by the coffee table, laughing about something.

"Wasn't it down in Santa Rosa?" I asked. "That's a long drive for a party."

She abandoned the champagne bottle and pulled

an orange juice carton toward her. She twisted the top. "Brittany really wanted me to go. She thought I'd have fun."

I could barely hear her over the buzz of people talking in the living room, but based on her tone, it sounded as if it had been anything but fun.

"That's cool." I paused, wondering how to work the conversation around to the accident. "I always worry about driving home in the dark down in that area, with those windy roads. Makes it hard to see any bicyclists in the dark."

Lucia whirled toward me and bumped the orange juice container, hard. It teetered on the edge of the counter for one long second and then fell to the floor. Orange juice gushed out the open top. I knelt down, grabbed the carton, and tipped it upright to stop the flow.

Lucia covered her mouth with her hands. I noticed they were shaking. "I'm sorry," she said. "I'm so sorry."

Everyone rushed over to the kitchen entrance, and I held up my hand to stop them from coming in. "Nothing to worry about. We just spilled some juice."

Mom went to fetch the mop from the utility closet. I glanced at Lucia and saw that her eyes were filling with tears.

"I'd better go," she said. "I have to get home." She hurried from the kitchen and out the door without a backward glance.

"Maybe I should find out if she's okay," Brittany said.

"No, let me," I said. I stepped around the spilled

juice and headed for the door. This was turning out to be quite the bridal shower.

Once outside, I scanned the parking lot and saw Lucia already opening her car door. “Lucia, wait,” I called down the stairs.

She glanced up at me and slowly closed her car door. I trotted down the steps and over to where she stood.

“What is it?” she asked.

“I wanted to make sure you were okay.” In the glow cast by the parking lot lights, her eyes looked puffy. “Are you?”

She nodded. “I have a lot on my mind. That’s all.”

“Does it have anything to do with the Labor Day party?” I held my breath.

Her head snapped up. “How did you know?”

“Every time someone mentions it, you get upset. Why don’t you tell me about it?”

My apartment door opened, and Ashlee stepped out. “Hey, you coming back up?” she called.

From behind her, the pop of a champagne cork sounded. At least the party was still going on. Too bad I was out here in the parking lot.

“Give me another minute,” I called.

Ashlee shrugged and disappeared into the apartment, shutting the door behind her.

I turned back to Lucia. She was wringing her hands and staring at her feet.

As gently as I could, I asked, “Were you the driver who hit the bicyclist?”

Lucia burst into tears. I gave her a few seconds to compose herself and then said, “Why don’t you tell me what happened?”

She sniffed. "I was driving home from that party. It was dark, like you said, and I don't always do so great on the freeway at night. I decided to take the old highway, the one that runs parallel to the freeway, since hardly anyone uses it."

"Sure, I know that road," I said.

"Everything was fine at first," she went on, "but then I came around a curve too fast, and all of a sudden, I saw some lady riding her bike in front of me." Her voice rose in pitch. "I couldn't help but hit her. I mean, she wasn't even on the side of the road or anything. I slammed on my brakes, but . . ." She let the sentence hang.

"I read in the article that you took off before help arrived," I said. "Why didn't you stick around?"

Lucia twisted her fingers together. "I'd only had one beer, but it might have been enough to show up on a Breathalyzer test. I wasn't supposed to be driving at all. I would have been in big trouble."

"Why's that?" I asked, keeping my eyes on her face.

"I was always running late for class and didn't pick the best places to park. I got so many parking tickets that they suspended my license."

Driving on a suspended license? Ouch. Hitting someone on a bicycle after drinking? Double ouch.

"I'm on a partial scholarship. They might have revoked it if I'd gotten arrested," Lucia said. "They already did me a huge favor by letting me take the semester off. I couldn't risk getting caught."

"So you hit someone with your car and just left?" I couldn't help asking.

"It wasn't like that," Lucia said. "I don't know

how everything went wrong so fast, but I stopped, I swear I did."

I believed her. The article had mentioned a young woman providing help before the paramedics arrived. That must have been Lucia.

"I thought she was dead when I first got out of the car." Lucia winced at the memory. "She was lying in the road, not moving. But when I got closer, she started to moan." She put a hand to her heart. "I nearly jumped out of my skin. Then I noticed her phone on the ground next to her and used it to call nine-one-one. I stayed with her until I heard the sirens from the ambulance. Then I jumped in my car and barely made it out of there. I actually passed by the ambulance, but I don't think they got a good look at me."

I tried to imagine what it had been like for Lucia that night: The guilt of running someone down, the fear of being arrested, the uncertainty of what to do. No wonder she was still such a wreck.

Lucia let out a long breath. "I feel so much better after telling you. I've had everything bottled up inside me. Whenever I see a policeman, I think he's coming to arrest me."

"Have you considered going to the police? Telling them what happened?"

"Every day, but I'm just so scared." She lifted her head and squared her shoulders. "But maybe I should tell them. Otherwise, I'll never be free of what happened."

"It's the right thing to do," I said.

She nodded. "I'll go to the police tomorrow."

I gave her a hug. After a pause, she hugged me back.

Ashlee came back out. "Hey, you guys, everyone's asking where you are. Come on up."

"Be there in a sec," I said.

"Fine, but if you're not here pretty quick, I'm drinking your mimosa." She stomped back into the apartment.

"You should really get in there," Lucia said. "I've already taken you away from your party for too long."

"I have one more question," I said. "Did Bethany from the flower shop find out you were the hit-and-run driver?"

Lucia's eyes widened. "How did you know?"

"I found your name in a notebook. Well, your initials anyway. I assume she was blackmailing you?"

Lucia shook her head. "No, she wasn't."

I scrunched up my nose. "Really?" Then whom did those initials belong to?

My cell phone rang before I could ask her more. I pulled it out of my pocket, my finger at the ready to reject the call, but I froze when I saw the screen. Detective Palmer's name stood out in stark relief.

My insides turned to jelly. What did the detective want now?

Chapter 22

I stared at my cell phone as it continued to ring. Why was Detective Palmer calling me? Had he realized I'd been telling the truth about that supposed argument with Bethany and wanted to apologize? Or had he unearthed something else he could use against me?

Lucia nodded toward the phone. "Are you going to answer that?"

I looked at her as if she were speaking pig Latin. "What?"

"Are you going to answer your phone?" she repeated, giving me a quizzical look.

"Right, the phone. Of course I'm going to answer it." But before I could, the ringing stopped. "Oops, guess I missed it." Thank God. "Say, did you want to come back upstairs with me?"

Lucia shook her head. "I think I'll go home. But thanks for the talk. You've helped a lot."

"I'm glad. Well, good night."

She got in her car, and I turned toward my

apartment. I still held my phone, and the bell signaling I had a voice mail *dinged.*

I forced myself to take a deep breath. Maybe Detective Palmer was calling for a reason unrelated to Bethany's murder. I'd read in the paper about a bowling fund-raiser the police department was organizing. Maybe the detective didn't know what a bad bowler I was and wanted me to join his team.

Yeah, right.

I gave a little wave to Lucia as she pulled away and then accessed my voice mail.

"Miss Lewis, this is Detective Palmer." At the sound of his voice, I felt an involuntary shiver. "Please call me at your earliest convenience." He recited his number and then clicked off.

The message didn't tell me anything, but the fact that he'd addressed me by my last name instead of my first let me know he was serious. This was no bowling invitation.

I sighed. No sense putting off the inevitable. If I didn't do this now, I'd spend the rest of the night worrying about why he'd called. But I'd make the call in my room, not the parking lot, where anyone might overhear me. I climbed the steps and opened the apartment door, hoping to sneak into my room unnoticed. No such luck.

"There's the bride-to-be," Mom said when she spotted me.

I held up my phone. "I need to make one quick call and then I'm all yours."

"But what about the party?" Ashlee asked.

"Yeah, you're the guest of honor," Brittany said.

"This will only take a minute. I promise."

I went into my bedroom and shut the door. For a long moment, I sat on the edge of my bed and stared at the wall. When I felt calm enough, I called the detective.

He answered before the first ring finished. "Palmer here."

"This is Dana Lewis. I got your message, Detective Palmer," I said, using the same formal tone that he had.

"Thank you for returning my call so promptly, Miss Lewis," he said with the tiniest hint of sarcasm. I wasn't sure if that was a good sign or not. Did that qualify as banter?

He cleared his throat and continued. "I wanted to go over your statement and clear up a few things. Let's start with your first meeting with the victim the day she was killed."

"Again?" I said before I could stop myself.

"Is that a problem?"

I felt myself blush. "Of course not. I'm just surprised, that's all." Geez, wasn't I Little Miss Unhelpful? "I want to assist however I can," I added to let him know we were on the same side.

"Good, then start with your first meeting."

I rehashed my conversation with Bethany, though I noticed I wasn't quite as sure about the exact words in our conversation anymore. Maybe the music I could hear from the other room was distracting me, reminding me that I was missing my party.

"And the only person you saw was the woman who came in at the end of your conversation?" Detective Palmer asked, breaking into my thoughts.

"Right," I said. "The woman who mistakenly thought Bethany and I were arguing."

I was hoping Detective Palmer would agree that the woman had been wrong, but he switched topics. "What about Violet?"

"I didn't see her at all. Both Violet and her mom said it was her day off."

"Huh," Detective Palmer said.

His response gave me pause. Was that a "huh" of surprise? Or was he simply moving the conversation along? Too bad we weren't talking in person so I could see his expression. Then again, even when I could see his face, I never had any idea what he was thinking.

I finished running through the events of the day with him, amazed at how quickly the finer details were already starting to fade from my memory. After a few more questions, he ended the call, leaving me to wonder what it was all about.

I got up and opened the window, letting in the brisk night air. I checked the clock and was surprised to find our conversation had taken less than ten minutes.

But why had the detective called at all? I'd told him nothing new. I hadn't remembered anything else that might help. Was he simply letting me know he hadn't forgotten about me? Was this some sort of mind trick detectives used to keep people on their toes?

Someone banged on my bedroom door, and I jumped.

"Come on, Dana! It's party time!" Ashlee yelled through the door.

"I'll be out in a minute," I called back.

She opened the door. "You mean that?" she asked, a mimosa clutched in her hand. Brittany hovered behind her.

"Yes, I'll be right there."

She pointed at me. "Okay, 'cause Mom really wants you out there, plus it's time to start the games."

"And we can't dress you up in toilet paper if you're not there," Brittany said with a giggle.

Not waiting for an answer, Ashlee pulled the door closed, leaving me alone once more. I shook my head at the two of them and then sank down on the bed to call Jason.

"Hey, gorgeous. What's up?"

His voice instantly put me at ease, and I leaned back against the pillows. I could hear talking in the background, making me wonder if he'd gone into the office for some reason. "Detective Palmer just called."

"What did he want?" His voice held a touch of curiosity, nothing more.

"I don't know, but isn't that bad? I don't think he considers me a serious suspect, but I could be someone he's got his sights on, right?"

"No, the police talk to everyone involved in a case multiple times, especially a murder investigation. You have nothing to worry about."

I nestled farther into the pillows. "I found his call unnerving. He got me so rattled, I forgot to tell him all the information I've found out." I heard a shout in the background, followed by cheering. "Are you at work?"

There was a pause. "I'm at my bachelor party."

I slapped a hand to my forehead. "I can't believe I forgot. I'll let you get back. Besides, I have my own party here."

"What party?"

"Ashlee and Mom threw me a surprise bridal shower."

"Nice. Then you should forget about Detective Palmer and go have fun. But before you do, I found out today that Mitch made another offer on the flower shop. He wants to buy it from Violet."

I pushed off from the pillows and sat up straight. "When did this happen? What about the auto parts place?" None of this made any sense. I'd assumed that Mitch's bank loan and talk with contractors was related to the auto parts store. Were these his plans for the flower shop instead? Why hadn't Violet mentioned it when I'd spoken to her earlier? Or had she been too busy reliving her resentment toward her mother?

"My source said he hadn't made a formal offer on the other property. He must have wanted to try for the flower shop one more time with Bethany out of the way."

I shivered at the wording. Bethany was out of the way all right. I told him about Mom's conversation with Mitch. "Maybe when Mitch told my mom about breaking down a wall, he meant the one between the two shops. Last time Mom and I were in there for ice cream, he mentioned how his dream was to one day buy the other half of his grandfather's property and make it whole again. He must figure Violet isn't as attached to the shop as her mom was."

"I'd bet on it," Jason said. "But let's worry about it tomorrow. Go enjoy your party."

I briefly considered telling him about Lucia's confession, but now wasn't the time. Tomorrow would be better. "You too. I love you."

"I love you, too."

My insides always felt warm and fuzzy whenever Jason said that. We hung up, and I took a moment to savor the feeling.

Ashlee's loud laugh sounded from the living room, reminding me that I still had a party to enjoy. I rose from the bed, flipped off the light, and headed out of my room.

Tonight, I'd celebrate. Tomorrow, I'd find out just what Mitch had planned for the flower shop. And whether he'd killed Bethany to achieve that goal.

Chapter 23

The bridal shower went on for another two hours. After everyone teamed up to create wedding dresses out of toilet paper, we played the game Zennia invented, where everyone tried to name vegetables that started with the letters in the word *wedding*. I came in last.

After that, we ate the cake Ashlee had bought, and Gretchen gave everyone facials while we chatted about everything from our childhoods to Mom and Esther's favorite parts of being married. The evening was so much fun that I almost didn't want it to end, but everyone eventually left, except Brittany, who crashed on the couch after having one too many mimosas.

I went to bed, where I tossed and turned most of the night, finally drifting off in the wee hours. When I awoke just after seven, I panicked that I was late for work, until I remembered that I was scheduled to take the morning off. With the wedding only two days away, I needed to try on my dress with the veil, make sure I had all the little extras, including something old, new, borrowed, and blue, and practice walking in my heels so I wouldn't fall on my face on my way down the aisle. I also wanted to do all of this at a time when Ashlee wouldn't be home to watch me and offer unsolicited advice.

I could hear Ashlee and Brittany moving around in the kitchen, so I stayed in bed and relaxed until I heard the front door open and close. Then I threw back the covers, got up, and headed for the shower. Twenty minutes later, I was in the kitchen, toasting a bagel. Once it popped up, I slathered on a healthy layer of vegetable-flavored cream cheese, wondering if it counted as a serving of vegetables.

With my breakfast ready, I sat down on the couch in my bathrobe and ate while watching a news show. The apartment was so peacefully quiet, even with the low volume of the TV, that I found myself eating slower than usual.

When I'd polished off the last bite, I washed my plate and went into my bedroom. Tucked in the far reaches of my closet, protected by a plastic bag, was my wedding dress. I slid the hanger along the rod, unzipped the bag, and took out the garment to lay on the bed.

Maybe it was because I spent my days in polo shirts and jeans for work, or maybe it was because the dress represented such a momentous occasion, but just looking at it took my breath away. The tiny beads on the bodice sparkled. The lace flowers on the skirt looked almost too delicate to touch.

I shed my robe and gingerly stepped into the dress. I sucked in my breath as I slid the zipper up, worried I'd put on weight since my fitting, but everything fit as it should. I might even have enough room in the waistline to enjoy a piece of cake at the reception.

I slid my feet into my white satin shoes and walked around the apartment a few times. I only stumbled twice, both times over the same throw rug near the kitchen. I'd have to watch out for similar obstacles at the farm as I walked across the back patio. Then again, Esther didn't have any throw rugs on her patio, so I most likely didn't need to worry.

When I felt confident in my shoes, I removed them and slid the dress off, careful not to step on the lace. I hung it back up and smoothed out a handful of tiny wrinkles. Once I'd wrangled the plastic bag over the dress, I zipped it up and secured it in the closet. I gathered my blue garter belt, my mom's pearl necklace, an old lace handkerchief that had belonged to my grandmother, and a new bracelet I'd found a few weeks ago on sale, and placed everything in a velvet-lined case that I then stowed in my dresser.

While I brushed off my shoes and put them in the corner of the closet, I thought about my conversation with Jason the night before. Would Violet sell the shop to Mitch now that her mother wasn't there to stop her, and use the money to launch her writing career? Or had she known her mother hadn't wanted to sell to Mitch and would refuse his offer out of a sense of loyalty?

I looked at the clock and found I wasn't due at work for quite a while, giving me plenty of time to assemble the wedding favors, since I hadn't done so last night. After that, a trip downtown might be in order. With the detective still calling me up to ask questions, I wanted to talk to Mitch and find out why he'd set his sights on the flower shop once more. Considering he was trying for a bank loan and talking to contractors, he must expect Violet to agree to his offer. I had to wonder if he'd killed Bethany to clear the path for his plan. No way could I let Mom anywhere near this guy until I knew what was going on. She'd promised not to ask him out on a date, but that didn't mean she wouldn't accept a request from him for dinner or a movie.

I grabbed the box of favor supplies, carried it to the living room, and set it on the coffee table. I left the miniature mason jars in the box and unpacked the pre-printed labels, jelly beans, ribbon, and tulle to wrap around each jar. Flipping on the TV for company, I arranged the items in assembly-line fashion before pulling out the first jar and filling it with jelly beans.

As I worked, I remembered how Ashlee had called me Martha Stewart one time. Her observation couldn't have been further from the truth. Most of the labels were slightly off-center, every jar had a different number of jelly beans, and I could barely form a bow with the slippery satin ribbon, let alone tie a symmetrical one. But the guests were coming to the wedding to see Jason and me get married, not to receive a perfectly decorated mason jar.

I finished the last one, carefully placed each tulle-covered jar back in the box, and stowed the box in my bedroom. Not sure I'd have time to return to the apartment before going to work, I dressed in my usual work shirt with the name of the farm stitched over the pocket, a pair of jeans, and my sneakers. I ran a brush through my hair, applied a touch of lip gloss, and went out the door.

As I went down the steps, I noticed that the sky was overcast. The pavement in the parking lot was wet, implying that the threat of rain had become a reality sometime during the night.

I told myself not to worry. The wedding was still a few days away. Just because it had rained last night didn't mean it would rain again. With that thought, I climbed into my car.

Five minutes later, I was pulling into a parking space in front of the Get the Scoop ice cream parlor. Until recently, Mitch had opened his shop early each morning, but I'd noticed he'd pushed the opening time to eleven a while back. I never did understand why he opened so early, except during the summer. Surely not too many customers wanted cold desserts first thing in the morning, especially in November.

Even with the later opening, I saw him most mornings on my way to work and knew he often arrived early to sweep the sidewalk in front of his shop or set up the outside tables and chairs.

Today, the tables and chairs were already in place, but Mitch was nowhere in sight. I glanced next door at the flower shop, wondering if Violet was available to talk, and then shook my head. I really needed to speak with Mitch first.

I walked to the entrance of the ice cream parlor

and pulled on the handle. Locked. No surprise since the shop was technically closed.

Through the window, I could tell the lights were on, but I couldn't see anyone moving around. I cupped my hands against the glass, leaned forward, and strained to see behind the counter.

As I breathed on the glass, it created a fine layer of haze, and a jolt of déjà vu shot through me. Wasn't this how things had started when I'd found Bethany's body? First I'd tried to see into the shop and then I'd gone around back, only to find her dead.

I shuddered at the memory and took a step back before immediately admonishing myself. Bethany's murder had been a one-time occurrence. I couldn't freak out every time I looked through a window.

I knocked on the door louder than necessary and waited. After a moment, I knocked again. I glanced at the tables and chairs in front of the shop. Had Mitch set everything up and then run an errand? Was he the type to leave the lights on when he wasn't there?

I gnawed on my lower lip, debating whether I wanted to risk checking the back door. Then I squared my shoulders. No way was Mitch dead in the ice cream parlor. When had I become such a wimp? With a final glance at the glass door, I marched around the corner and through the small alley that led to the back parking lot.

A white delivery truck with a picture on the side of a little kid holding an ice cream cone sat in the lot. The truck's back doors were wide open, revealing plastic-wrapped tubs of ice cream stacked on pallets. Thick white mist wafted out the open door, as if from a fog machine.

To the side of the truck, Mitch stood with the driver. They appeared to be talking while Mitch was signing the man's clipboard. I was so relieved he wasn't dead in the back of his store that I yelled out "Mitch!" with way too much enthusiasm. The truck driver gaped at me. Mitch jerked his head around.

He thrust the clipboard at the deliveryman, who fumbled with it. Then he stepped in front of the guy and held up one hand. "We're not open yet. You'll have to come back." Apparently he wasn't as glad to see me as I was him.

"I know. I wanted to talk to you."

He glanced at the deliveryman. "I'm busy right now. I don't have time to talk."

"It'll only take a minute."

"I don't have a minute. Really, it's not a good time." Mitch licked his lips, appearing more nervous than angry. What was wrong with him? Maybe I should have brought my mom along to woo him with her feminine wiles. Never mind, then he'd want to ask her on a date.

"It's about the flower shop," I said, not sure if I was helping my cause or hurting it. Then again, this conversation couldn't go much worse than it already was.

Mitch sighed and motioned toward the alley with the back of his hand. "Fine. Go back to the front. I'll be with you as soon as I'm done here."

"I'll be waiting." At least he was agreeing to speak with me. Unless, of course, he was planning to run out the other side of the parking lot to the street and take off for parts unknown. I wandered back to the front of the shop, mulling over why the sight of me would trigger such a strange reaction. Was he anxious about whether Violet would accept his offer and worried I'd somehow mess it up? That couldn't be it. He'd been acting funny before I even mentioned the flower shop.

From the direction of the back lot, I heard the rumble of a truck. The ice cream deliveryman must be getting ready to leave. I'd seen that logo on the side of his truck somewhere else.

With a jolt, I suddenly realized where. If I was correct, Mitch had some explaining to do.

I ran back through the alley just as the truck pulled out of the lot. I screeched to a halt in front of Mitch, pointed at the truck as it drove away, and put my hands on my hips. "Do you want to tell me what's going on here?"

Chapter 24

Mitch took a step back, avoiding my gaze. "What's got you all riled up?"

I pointed once more at the truck, which was far down the block. "That truck."

Still not looking at me, Mitch rubbed the back of his head. "What about it? I'm just getting my ice cream supplies."

I shook my head. "Not supplies. Ice cream. You're buying cartons of ice cream from that guy."

"What? No way," Mitch protested, but it was all for show. His words were as hollow as an unfilled cone.

"I got a look inside the back of that truck. It was full of already prepared ice cream. What happened to making everything on-site? With all-natural ingredients?"

Mitch leaned toward me. "Keep your voice down. I'm trying to run a business here."

"By lying to your customers?" I hadn't planned on speaking so bluntly, but my mom was interested in dating this guy. I couldn't let her go out with someone so dishonest. "I recognize that logo. I used to buy that brand at a discount grocery store when I was living in the Bay Area. And I'm fairly certain most of the ingredients came out of a chemical factory."

Mitch rubbed the back of his head again. "Look, business this time of year is brutal. Even with the after-school crowds, it's all I can do to keep the doors open, let alone pay for these all-natural ingredients. You got any idea how much those cost?"

"But people think they're spending their money on a good-quality product when they're not. That's false advertising, which is a crime, the last time I checked." If this guy would lie about a major part of his business, what else would he lie about? Did I really want my mom dating someone who couldn't be trusted? And should I really be talking to the guy in a secluded back parking lot mere feet from where a woman had been shot?

He spread his hands. "Look, I've only been buying from that company the last couple of months, when the weather turned and sales dropped. I'm cutting corners anywhere I can, including pushing my opening time back. I thought being open early in the morning would let customers buy ice cream whenever the mood struck, but instead I ended up paying my employees to stand around and twiddle their thumbs. Once business picks up, I can go back to buying the good ingredients and making my own ice cream again."

"Do your employees know?" I had a hard time picturing fresh-faced Nicole lying about what she was selling.

"No, I've been real careful. The shipments come early morning when I'm here by myself. The only reason the delivery guy was late today was because of an accident on the highway. I transfer the ice cream from their cartons to my own tubs in the display case, stuff all the empty cartons into trash bags, and drive a couple blocks to throw the bags in the Dumpsters behind the furniture store. Then I come back here before any of my workers arrive. I even leave mixing bowls in the sink sometimes to make it look like I used them."

He seemed almost proud of his duplicity, but to me, that was a lot of effort for an ice cream scam. Then again, it might be necessary if Mitch wanted to stay in business. If news of his deception leaked out, customers might never buy ice cream from him again. It would be the same if Zennia decided to start using non-organic vegetables without telling our customers. We'd be out of business for sure.

"What happens if sales don't pick up?" I asked.

He glowered at me. "They will. I'm the go-to place in the spring to celebrate baseball games, plus I've been drawing in the soccer crowd, and once school's out for the summer, I'll have kids in here all day. Besides, if I can expand this place like I want to, I can guarantee profits will double. Every day, I see people driving around town with those giant iced coffees from the Daily Grind clutched in their hands. I plan to get a share of that business."

"Is that why you made an offer to Violet?"

Mitch jerked his head back. "Word sure gets around fast. How'd you hear about that?"

"A friend mentioned it," I said vaguely, not

wanting to put Jason in a tight spot. "How did she respond?"

"She hasn't yet. Said she needed to think about it, but she's just playing hardball. She has about as much interest in the flower business as I do. Probably hoping I'll up my offer if she drags her heels, but I know she'll cave eventually."

If he was right about Violet, then Bethany's murder couldn't have come at a better time for him. "What about the old auto parts store? Didn't you already make an offer there?"

"I told the owner I was giving his place some thought and might be interested in buying the space. But it never went beyond that, which is why I was trying to keep that on the hush-hush. Wouldn't want Violet to find out I had my eye on another place. She might get her feelings hurt and turn down my offer out of spite." He gestured to the building behind him. "You know my grandfather used to own everything here. I want to rebuild what he once had. Besides, ice cream parlors make it or break it on foot traffic, and that other place is too far down the strip. No one's going to drive out of their way for ice cream when they can just as easily stop by the grocery store."

True enough. It would have to be some pretty special ice cream for me to go out of my way to get it. Of course, now that I knew Mitch's ice cream wasn't special at all, I might not bother to stop by here anymore either.

"Do you think you'll have better luck getting Violet to sell than you did with Bethany?" I asked.

"Can't hurt to try. Right?" He glanced at the back

door to the flower shop, but it was firmly shut. "I only hope her mom didn't open her big mouth."

I raised my eyebrows. "About what?"

Mitch cast his eyes my way and then down. "Nothing. Forget I said anything."

I stared at him a moment. "Did Bethany find out about your little ice cream switcheroo?"

He blew out a mouthful of air. "She was always sticking her nose where it didn't belong. She saw the delivery truck here a couple of times and wormed the information out of me."

Much like I had done. "Well, it's a pretty big truck and a pretty small lot. She was bound to notice."

"I guess," he conceded. "But when she figured out what was going on, she should have offered to help me out, being a fellow business owner herself. Instead, she used it as leverage. Told me to stop bugging her to sell her shop or else she'd tell everyone I was buying my ice cream on the cheap."

So that's why Mitch had suddenly dropped the idea of buying Bethany's half of the building before her death, and why Bethany started coming back for her daily sherbet fix, looking smug. She'd had him over a barrel, or at least an ice cream tub.

"Once I saw she'd keep her mouth shut so long as I didn't ask to buy her store again, I started looking around for another spot. The only one I could find was the auto parts store, but it wasn't the best spot, like I said, so I didn't make an official offer. Then Bethany got killed, and I figured I'd see what happened with her place." He glanced at his watch and flinched. "Listen, I gotta get that ice cream swapped out before any employees get here."

He headed toward the back door of the parlor but swung around before he reached it. "Hey," he said, "do me a favor and don't tell anyone, all right? Like I said, it's only temporary until business picks up."

I didn't answer, not sure what I planned to do. But you could bet I wouldn't be recommending his ice cream to any of my friends.

"Tell your mom hi for me, too, would you?"

No way could I guarantee that either. Not after what I'd learned.

He raised his hand in departure and disappeared into the shop, while I stood there, thinking.

Once more, Bethany had managed to pry a secret out of someone and use it to her advantage. Mitch had said Bethany kept quiet once he stopped badgering her about selling her shop. Did he believe she'd stay mum forever? Or had he killed her to make sure his secret would be buried right along with her? And how could I keep my mom away from this man until I knew the answer?

Chapter 25

I walked through the alleyway and around to the front of the ice cream parlor as Violet came out of the flower shop next door. Her long brown hair was pulled back in a low ponytail. Over her jeans and a T-shirt, she wore the same dark green apron with the large pockets as yesterday, but with no sign of the shears poking out of a pocket. At least she hadn't been decapitating any more flowers.

Instead, she fished around in one of the pockets and pulled out a cigarette and lighter. She lit the tip, put the lighter away, and then noticed me as I neared my car. "Hey, Dana. Were you coming to see me?" She exhaled a stream of smoke.

I went over and joined her by the door, making sure to pick the side where the wind wasn't blowing. "No, I had to talk to Mitch for a sec. While I was over there, though, he did tell me about his offer on your place."

Violet had been lifting the cigarette to her lips but stopped. "Oh, that."

"Are you going to accept?"

She dropped her barely smoked cigarette on the sidewalk and stubbed it out with her shoe. "I don't know. I feel like I'd be dishonoring my mom if I sold her shop to him, especially so soon after her passing."

Gone was the anger and resentment I'd seen on my last visit. An air of sadness hung over her. Before I could think up an appropriate platitude, she perked up. "But forget about me. You have a wedding coming up. How's that going?"

"Great. At least I think so. I keep feeling like I'm missing something."

"It's at that organic farm, right? It must be fun to decorate out there."

"Yes, in fact the decorating has been easy with all the flowers and plants already out there. Plus the flowers you're providing, of course." I smiled at her, but then a thought crossed my mind. We were setting up the archway, and tying the ribbon around the patio posts, but still . . .

"Is something wrong?" Violet asked.

"Talking about the decorations reminded me that I'd meant to decorate the chairs somehow, maybe with bows or slip covers, but I forgot." Darn it. I knew I'd forget something at the last minute. "I'd better hurry and check the craft store when I'm done with work today. But what if I find the perfect bows and they don't have enough in stock?"

Violet snapped her fingers. "I might have a solution for you. Mom kept a fairly large supply of bows and ribbons, things like that, for our floral arrangements. I'd be happy to lend them to you."

It was all I could do not to jump up and down. "Would you really? That would be a huge help."

"No problem. I'll have to find the exact bows I'm thinking of, so it might take me a while to gather everything together, but tell you what. I'll drive out to the farm later and drop off the box."

I shook my head. "Don't go to any trouble. You're the one doing me the favor, and I can drive back here to get the box whenever you're ready."

"It's no trouble," Violet said. "I was thinking about visiting the farm later today anyway so I could get an idea of what sort of vegetation is already out there. It'll help me decide how much greenery to add to the bouquets."

"What a clever idea." Maybe she was more interested in flowers than I'd given her credit for.

"My mom always said you have to envision the location to produce a fabulous wedding bouquet to match."

She put her hands in her pockets, feeling around inside. "I could have sworn I had some paper in here," she muttered. "I kind of know where the farm is, but as long as you're here, maybe you could give me exact directions."

"Sure. It's just off the highway, near Pear Tree Lane. Do you know where that is?"

She turned to go in her shop. "Come on in so I can find a pen and paper and write it down."

I followed her inside. She walked straight to the counter, where she found a pencil and piece of paper. I slowly recited the directions, watching over her shoulder to make sure she wrote them down correctly. When she was done, she folded up the paper and slipped it in an apron pocket. "I'm not sure when I'll get out there, probably later this afternoon."

"That's fine. I took the morning off, but I'll be there for the rest of the day."

I turned around to leave just as the front door opened. Carter entered, his gaze on his cell phone. He was wearing his usual suit and tie. He glanced up as he moved into the shop, and our eyes locked. He briefly broke his stride and then moved past me without a word.

"Mr. Hawking," Violet said, "I received your voice mail. You only want a single bouquet of roses from now on?"

I looked at him at the same moment he looked at me. I must have been smirking, because he scowled and turned back to Violet. "Yes, it's for my wife," he said, enunciating each word.

"She's a lucky lady," Violet said.

If only Violet knew the truth, I thought as I took my smirk outside. Apparently Phoebe and Carter were through for good, since he was no longer buying her flowers. While I'd love to think Carter was done cheating on his wife, Ashlee swore that once a cheater, always a cheater.

My phone vibrated in my pocket and I pulled it out. Speak of the devil. I had a text from Ashlee, asking me to pick up toilet paper sometime today. Considering I was mere steps from the drugstore and was thinking about going home for a quick lunch anyway, I texted her back a confirmation.

As I was putting my phone in my pocket, Carter came out of the flower shop with a bouquet of red roses in his hand. He walked in my direction, head down, and I shifted to the side so he wouldn't bump into me as he moved past.

"Beautiful flowers," I said to him.

He spun around. "What?"

I took an involuntary step back at his fierce expression, but I quickly regained my composure. "I said the flowers are beautiful. Only one bouquet today?"

His jaw clenched, and he surveyed the block, probably checking for anyone who might have heard me, but no one else was nearby. "What business is it of yours, Miss Johnson?"

I was momentarily distracted by his use of my fictitious name, but then I said, "Well, none, of course. Only I ran into Phoebe yesterday, and she told me you two had broken up." I pointed to the flowers. "Guess she was telling the truth, if you're only buying the one bouquet today."

He tightened his grip, and the cellophane wrapper let out a crinkle of protest. "You claim you ran into her, but I suspect you arranged the meeting. I already told you I won't be blackmailed again."

Sheesh, maybe I should have kept my big mouth shut. I held up my hands. "Blackmailing isn't my style. I'm just wondering why you'd break up with Phoebe now."

"Again, none of your business."

"But with Bethany dead, you're free to carry on your affair forever, or at least until your wife finds out some other way."

Carter gave a humorless laugh. "You want to

know the irony of the situation? I was all set to break up with Phoebe before Bethany found out about us, only I didn't have the chance. Then Bethany started in with her demands."

"So why not drop Phoebe and call Bethany's bluff?"

"The damage would have been the same if Bethany told my wife. I figured as long as I was paying her, I should at least receive some benefits from my transgression."

Ick. It was bad enough he was an adulterer, but to only sleep with poor Phoebe because he was paying Bethany? Not cool.

"Since I'm no longer buying Bethany's silence, I've lost interest in Phoebe again." He adjusted the knot in his tie with his free hand. "Satisfied?"

"Yes, I didn't mean to upset you."

Carter rolled his eyes and walked off.

Remembering my errand for Ashlee, I walked the short distance to the drugstore. As usual, the place was practically deserted this late in the morning on a weekday. I followed the signs to the bath tissue aisle and searched for the sale items, knowing that if Ashlee were doing the shopping, she'd splurge on the more expensive three-ply. Nothing was too good for her bum.

I grabbed a value pack of the discounted brand and started toward the checkout aisle. I paused, wondering at the chances Lucia was working today, or if she was locked up in a jail cell after confessing to the police about the accident. She'd told me Bethany hadn't been blackmailing her, but I hadn't found anyone else whose initials matched the ones in Bethany's notebook. Had Lucia been lying to me, or was I missing something?

As if on cue, she walked past the end of the aisle and I started after her.

There was only one way to find out.

Chapter 26

I dashed down the row after Lucia, hugging my large pack of toilet paper to my chest. When I reached the main aisle, I looked in the direction she'd been heading and then the opposite way, but she was nowhere in sight. I speed-walked across the store, checking each row as I passed, but I couldn't find her. In the last row, I noticed a pair of hinged doors at the other end that led to an employee area. They were swinging slightly.

Holding my purchase, I hurried over and pushed through one of the doors. The back section of the store was much darker than the front, and I paused in the gloom to allow my eyes to adjust.

As I waited, I heard footsteps coming toward me from around the corner. A second later, Lucia came into view, a price-marking labeler in her hand.

"Excuse me, customers aren't allowed back here. If you're looking for the restroom—" She broke off when she recognized me. "I didn't realize it was you, Dana." She glanced at my toilet paper. "Did you need a price check?"

I lowered the package, feeling like an idiot for running through the store with it. "No, I saw you head back here and wanted to find out how you were doing."

"Okay, but nervous. I'm going to the police station as soon as my shift is over."

"I'm glad you haven't changed your mind." I gripped the package in my hands. "While I've got you here, I wanted to ask you something about the accident."

Her eyes narrowed. "What now? I already told you everything that happened."

I heard movement behind me and turned to look. A man in a short-sleeved white dress shirt and a clip-on tie came in through one of the swinging doors. His name tag declared he was the manager.

He frowned at me. "Did you need something, ma'am?"

Lucia tensed but remained silent, her eyes on her boss.

I tried to think of a valid reason for being back here. "Um, I was looking for the bathroom," I said, since that's what Lucia had originally assumed I needed.

The manager raised his eyebrows at the package I clutched in my hands, and I felt my face grow warm. I could only imagine what he thought I needed twelve rolls of toilet paper for.

"It's in the other back corner of the store," he finally said.

"Gee, I'm not good with directions. Maybe she could help me find it?" I asked, gesturing at Lucia.

My face only got hotter at my ridiculous request. I made a mental note to never shop here again.

The manager seemed momentarily stymied, but then recovered. "I suppose that would be all right." He turned to Lucia. "Help this customer, please, Lucia, and then return to stocking the Christmas tree lights."

Christmas tree lights? It was the beginning of November! Whatever happened to Thanksgiving?

"Yes, sir," Lucia said. She led the way out of the back room and I followed. Together, we headed to the opposite corner of the store. I glanced back to find the manager watching us.

Lucia stopped when she reached a small hallway. It held two restrooms and a drinking fountain. She turned to me with folded arms. "Whatever you want, you'd better make it quick. I know my manager's keeping an eye on me, and I need this job. You already know that."

I set the package of toilet paper at my feet. "Look, I'm not trying to cause you any trouble, but last night you told me Bethany wasn't blackmailing you over the accident. I'm positive she was."

Lucia surprised me by laughing. "Is that what this is about? The blackmail? You can't blackmail someone who's broke."

"But she tried?"

"She did. I stopped by the shop to place an order—I'd been ordering these little bouquets for weeks by this time—and Bethany started asking me who they were for. She wouldn't stop pestering me with her questions." Lucia looked at her hands. "I'm still not sure why I told her what happened. I mean, I'd been keeping my secret this whole time from everybody, even friends and family. I think I was just tired, tired from trying to hold it all in. I hadn't been sleeping that great, or eating much. And she seemed so nice and sympathetic, like she really wanted to help me with my problems. It was almost like talking to my mom." She passed a hand over her eyes. "Before I knew it, I blurted out the whole story and how I send the woman flowers after her physical therapy sessions to cheer her up. I realized later that Bethany was only pretending to be nice to me so I'd tell her my secret, but by then it was too late."

A lump formed in my throat. I already knew Lucia was carrying around a lot of guilt. Sending flowers to the victim was her own form of penance.

"The next time I went in the shop, Bethany started hinting around about how tough it was for a single businesswoman to make a living and how a little extra money could make all the difference. She practically called me a liar when I told her I couldn't help her out, but then I reminded her that if I had any money, I'd be at school right now, not working here. After I explained it that way, she seemed to get it."

I nodded along as she spoke, realizing why there had been no dollar amounts under Lucia's initials in Bethany's notebook. Lucia simply didn't have any cash to give her. At least not enough to bother with.

"You must have some money," I pointed out. "I've had to order several bouquets and boutonnieres for my wedding, so I know buying flowers once a week can't be cheap."

"I wasn't planning to do it for as long as I have," she said. "Originally I was only going to buy flowers once or twice, but I think about the accident every day. I needed to do something to keep from obsessing over it. Besides, they're only carnations and daisies. Those are about the cheapest flowers you can buy."

"How do you even know where to send the flowers?"

"I heard the woman ended up at the hospital here in Blossom Valley. I have a friend who works there. She told me about the physical therapy appointments. I figure the flowers aren't much, but maybe they brighten her day." Lucia studied her hands again. "I never sign the cards, but she must know that they're from whoever hit her. I hope she knows how sorry I am. I'm just glad she never tried to track me down through the flower shop."

I didn't point out to Lucia that she still might. But since Lucia was planning to tell the cops everything, it didn't really matter.

"Once Bethany realized you didn't have any money, she just dropped the whole thing?" I asked.

Lucia nodded. "She never seemed all that interested in the money anyway, even though she gave me a hard time about it. I think she really liked knowing my secret. She'd hint around about it every time I went in there, but I was too scared to get my flowers somewhere else."

The manager's voice boomed behind me, interrupting our conversation. "Everything all right, ladies?"

I gave a little start and turned around, offering

him a big smile. "Yup, turns out the lock on the door doesn't work, so I needed someone to stand guard."

His eyes narrowed. Even if I ever did want to shop here again, he'd probably have me banned for acting so strangely. I could already imagine my picture tacked up next to the cash registers, like those people who wrote bad checks.

I bent down and retrieved my toilet paper. "Guess I'm ready to leave." Before I walked away, I turned to Lucia, who was once more watching her boss. "Thanks for your help, miss. I'd never have found the bathroom without you." I only hoped I hadn't somehow gotten her in trouble.

I headed to the front of the store, the manager close behind. There were three people in line at the only open checkout lane. The manager took my package of toilet paper from my hands, moved over to another register, and said, "I can ring you up right here." He was clearly done with my nonsense.

After I paid for the toilet paper, I left, wondering as I did so if I was any closer to figuring out who had wanted Bethany dead. Violet had ended up with a store she didn't seem to really want, and Carter had dumped the girlfriend Bethany had been blackmailing him about. Even when Bethany was alive, Carter seemed to have no trouble paying her off. As for Lucia, Bethany's other blackmail victim, she really had no reason to kill Bethany, especially since Bethany had kept her secret even when she received no money in return.

That left Mitch. I really wanted him to be innocent, for Mom's sake, but he seemed to benefit the most from Bethany's death. If Violet accepted his offer to buy the flower shop, he'd realize his dream of restoring his grandfather's property to its original state, plus he might be able to get his business back on track. Maybe Detective Palmer would reach the same conclusion and arrest him. Then I could focus squarely on my wedding and forget everything else.

I opened the trunk of my car and loaded in the toilet paper. Once behind the wheel, I checked the clock and found I had just enough time to run home for a quick lunch. Then I'd head to work. With no looming deadlines, I felt confident it would be a quiet afternoon.

Chapter 27

With my head full of thoughts about the wedding, I drove home. I frowned when I saw Ashlee's Camaro in its regular parking space at the apartment complex. If Ashlee was home, why had she texted me to ask if I could run an errand for her?

I grabbed the toilet paper out of the trunk and climbed the stairs to the apartment. Inside, Ashlee was sitting on the couch in her veterinarian smock, with her blond hair swept up in a bun. I tossed the giant pack of toilet paper onto the coffee table in front of her. Startled, she glanced up from the court show she'd been watching.

"Thanks, sis. I knew I could count on you," she said.

I put my hands on my hips. "If you were planning to come home for your lunch break, why didn't you pick up the toilet paper yourself?"

Ashlee snuck a peek at her show. "You said you were taking the morning off, so I figured I'd give you something to do. Plus, I'm kind of short on cash right now."

I gritted my teeth and stalked into the kitchen area. There was no sense in pointing out to Ashlee that I had plenty to do on my morning off, especially with my wedding so close. I'd only be wasting my breath. Besides, in a few short days, she wouldn't be my constant problem any longer.

That thought cheered me up, and I found myself humming as I dug through the refrigerator and pantry for something to fix for lunch. I managed to dredge up two slightly stale slices of bread, some packaged turkey, a couple of wilted lettuce leaves, and a tomato that was a little softer than I liked but edible. Not the best sandwich in the world, but considering I usually grabbed fast food or zapped a frozen meal in the microwave, it was definitely an improvement.

While I put everything together, Ashlee came over and leaned her elbows on the counter. "What's with the humming?" she asked.

I couldn't exactly tell her I was rejoicing over how soon I was moving out. Instead, I said, "Just thinking about the wedding."

Ashlee snorted. "About how you're going to be tied down to the same guy for the rest of your life? That's, like, forever, you know."

I sliced the tomato. "That's what makes me so happy."

She rolled her eyes. "You're hopeless." She toyed with the phone charger that was sitting on the counter. "Do you think we'll still hang out after you get married?" Her voice was softer than usual, and I paused in my slicing. "I mean, Brittany's going to be an awesome roommate," she said. "It's just, you know, you and I always watch the Oscars together, and the Emmys, stuff like that."

I set the knife down. "Of course we'll get together. Not everything's going to change. I'll still mock you for dating the wrong guys, and so many of them. You'll make fun of me for getting married. It'll be like I'm living here with you, only I won't be buying your toilet paper anymore."

"I'm sure I can get Brittany to do that," Ashlee said. "But you'll be spending every minute with Jason. You might not have time for me."

I felt a knot form in my chest. Could my sister actually be feeling lonely? "Jason and I aren't joined at the hip," I said. "Besides, he likes you, too. I'm sure we'll have you over for dinner. You just better hope Jason's the one who does the cooking."

Ashlee pretended to gag. "Dinner with a married couple? Are you guys going to wear matching aprons? And make us sit at an actual table?" She put her hands up. "I don't think I'm ready for all that grown-up stuff."

I picked up the knife and resumed slicing the tomato. "You'll get used to it. And then, one day, you'll turn into a grown-up, too."

"Hardy har har. I'll never let that happen." Ashlee went back to the couch and turned up the volume on the TV. Clearly she was all done talking about being adults.

I finished making my lunch, added a pile of chips to the plate, and carried everything into the living room, where I ate my sandwich and Ashlee stole most of my chips. When the pile had dwindled to a handful, I turned the plate around to save a few for myself and swallowed the last bite of turkey.

"You all set for your honeymoon?" Ashlee asked when her show went to commercial.

"I need to buy a few more things, like new sandals." I probably should have used my morning off to go shopping, but too late now. "We'll only be gone for five days, so it's not like I have to pack a lot."

Ashlee threw herself back on the couch. "Yeah, but five days in Hawaii. I'm sooooo jealous." She straightened up. "Hey, do you want me to keep an eye on Jason's place while you're gone? I mean, it'll be your place by then, too."

I still thought of Jason's place as his own, but she had a point. I needed to start thinking of it as our place. "I'll ask Jason," I said, touched by the offer.

"I hope he says yes." Ashlee picked up her phone from the coffee table and started texting. "After that party I threw when you were out of town last month, I think the management's keeping an eye on me. I can't risk having any more parties here."

Of course that's why she was offering to help. I should have known. "I'm not letting you watch Jason's place so you can invite a bunch of your friends. Give me a break."

"Seriously? I'm doing you guys a favor here. The least you could do is let me have a few friends over."

"Forget it. But I'll bring you a souvenir from the honeymoon." I stood up and carried my plate to the sink, shaking my head at Ashlee. I could only imagine how many parties she and Brittany would try to have once I moved out. "Hey," I called to her, "when management evicts you, don't even think about asking to move in with Jason and me."

Ashlee scrunched up her nose. "As if. That would be almost as bad as moving back in with Mom." She touched her bottom lip with her index finger. "Although, didn't you tell me he has a spare room?"

Sheesh. I shouldn't have brought it up.

I wiped down the counters, made sure I'd put away all the sandwich makings, and said good-bye to Ashlee. She gave me a thumbs-up in return. I headed out the door for work.

Rain drummed steadily on my car's roof as I drove down the highway, and I started thinking up alternate plans for the ceremony. If we moved all the tables to one side, we might be able to squeeze all the guests into the dining room. Otherwise the lobby was another option, although that space was even smaller. I blew out a breath. Man, I hoped this rain was only temporary.

Once at the farm, I parked in front of the main house and hurried through the lobby door. Gordon stood at the reservation desk, crossing off something on his clipboard. Based on his satisfied smile, he'd had a productive morning.

"How's it going?" I asked.

He paused. "No guest complaints today, which is always a good sign."

"How could there be, with you running the show?"

He looked up, probably wondering if I was mocking him. When he saw I was being sincere, he went back to his clipboard. "That reminds me . . ." He lifted up the paper he'd been working on and scanned the one underneath. "This is coming along pretty well. Know any words that rhyme with reliable?"

Man, he'd better not be working on my wedding toast. "How about certifiable?" I said.

He looked up at the ceiling, considering. "That won't work, but I'll think of something else."

I glanced toward the parking lot, but no cars had pulled in. I turned to Gordon. "I'm expecting someone to stop by here in a while. Could you let me know when she arrives please? Her name is Violet."

"I can do that. I'm assuming she won't interfere with your work duties."

Same old Gordon. At least he was reliable. Maybe even certifiable. "She won't." I went down the hall and into the office, where I typed up the day's blog and posted it to the farm's Web site.

As I turned my attention to the handful of e-mails waiting for me, Esther walked past the office, reminding me that I wanted to ask her a question. I hurried to the doorway and called after her, "Esther, do you have a minute?"

She stopped and came back to where I stood. "What is it?"

"I was thinking about the decorating I need to do on the patio for my wedding. I realize it's not until Saturday afternoon, but would you mind if I started decorating the patio tomorrow? I know we'll have a few guests checking in, but I'd be sure to keep out of their way."

"Of course I don't mind. I'm sure you have a million other things to take care of on your wedding day."

I nodded. "Exactly what I was thinking. The more I can check off my to-do list ahead of time, the better I'll feel."

Esther patted my shoulder. "The whole day will be right as rain, just so long as it doesn't really rain." I must have looked as panicked as I felt because Esther hurriedly added, "Not that there's a possibility. It's California, after all. The forecast always calls for blue skies and sunshine. I'm sure this storm won't last." She sighed. "What a weekend. A wedding one day and a memorial service the next."

For a second, I wondered who died, but then I realized she must be talking about Bethany. While I had no reason to go to her service, other than to snoop around, I imagined Esther would. She and Bethany had known each other for years.

Esther pursed her lips. "I didn't mean to cast a cloud over your special day. I shouldn't have mentioned Bethany's service."

"That's all right. Is Violet arranging everything?"

"As far as I know, although it's an awfully big job for one person. That's why every member of my Bunco group is bringing a casserole or dessert to the gathering after the service."

Sometimes Esther reminded me of a mother hen, the way she was always watching after others. "I'm sure Violet appreciates the gesture. You're very thoughtful."

She pooh-poohed my compliment with a wave of

her hand. "It's the least I can do. I feel so sorry for that woman."

"Losing a parent is always tough," I said, remembering my own grief when my father had died. I automatically reached up to my neck and touched the St. Christopher medal he'd given me years ago and that I always wore.

Esther nodded. "Yes, and people are often left with guilt when someone close to them dies, even when there's nothing to feel guilty about. I know I felt that way when my sweet Arthur passed on to that great big farmhouse in the sky."

"I wonder if Violet feels the same. After all, she had the day off. If she'd come to work instead, maybe whoever shot Bethany wouldn't have done it."

Esther tilted her head. "But I saw Violet at the flower shop that day." She shrugged. "I bet she just dropped by for a minute. She seemed to be in an awful hurry."

Goose bumps popped up on my arms. I was certain that when I'd talked to Bethany the day she'd been killed, she'd said Violet had the day off. Violet herself had told me she hadn't gone to the shop. Could Esther be mistaken? "Are you positive it was Violet?"

"Sure. I walked right past her on my way to the drugstore. I said hello, but I guess she didn't hear me. She seemed upset."

"And it was the same day Bethany was murdered?"

Esther thought for a moment and then nodded. "Yep, one of my prescriptions had run out, and I was down to my last pill. I'm positive it was the same day."

"What time was this? Did you tell the police?"

Esther blanched. "Should I have? It was right after lunch, hours before poor Bethany died. Besides, I'm sure Violet told the police she was there."

Not if she'd been planning her mother's death at that time. The fact that she'd been there after lunch rather than closer to when Bethany was killed didn't change her lying to me. But why? What was she hiding?

"Are you all right, dear?" Esther asked. Worry lines appeared around her eyes. "Do you think I should tell the police after all?"

"Yes, absolutely. I can give you Detective Palmer's number. I have one of his cards." I went over to the desk, pulled open the bottom drawer, and grabbed my purse. As I searched through the contents, I remembered how the detective had asked me if I'd seen Violet that day when I'd stopped in to talk to Bethany. At the time I'd thought it was an odd question, but maybe Esther wasn't the only one who'd noticed Violet downtown.

I found the card and handed it to Esther. "Here you go."

"Thanks." She checked her watch. "I have just enough time to call before heading off to my Bunco game."

Once Esther left, I sat down in the office chair and thought about why Violet might have lied. Even if she'd killed Bethany, that was much later. She didn't need to lie about visiting earlier, even on her day off. I stopped by the farm on occasion if I'd left something here that I needed or I wanted to help out for a special event. Was she worried the police would see her as a suspect and thought it was better to lie?

I stood up and stuck my purse back in the drawer. I could sit here all day and come up with theories, but only Violet could tell me the answer. And as luck would have it, she was due at the farm this very afternoon.

In fact, she might be on her way right now. Maybe she was already here. I practically sprinted to the lobby to find out.

Gordon glanced up when I burst in from the hall. He frowned.

"Violet isn't here yet?" I asked, though of course I could see he was alone.

"I said I would let you know when she arrived."

"Well, you never know when we might have a sudden surge of guests that would keep you from notifying me."

Gordon swept his arm in front of him, indicating the empty lobby. "As you can see . . ."

"Right." If only Violet had given me a specific time. She might be here in the next five minutes or not for another two hours.

Feeling discouraged, I puttered around the lobby, straightening the magazines on the end table, picking up lint off the carpet, and brushing dust off the ficus leaves. At least the rain had stopped, and blue sky was now visible in patches.

Gordon cleared his throat. "All out of marketing work today?"

I offered him a smile. "I want to make sure the place looks its best for the guests."

"I already took care of that," he said stiffly.

"Of course. Just giving you a hand."

"Perhaps Gretchen needs help in the spa," Gordon said.

"I'm sure she has everything under control. Hey, how's the toast coming along?" I crossed my fingers that it didn't include the words *reliable* or *certifiable.*

He twisted his pinkie ring. "Much more challenging than I'd expected, but I believe I've come up with something we can both live with."

Something we could live with? Like mediocre coffee or slightly dinged furniture?

Before I could say more, a car pulled into the parking lot outside. The silver Mercedes looked vaguely familiar, and I wondered if it belonged to Violet, although I wouldn't have pegged her as the luxury car type.

The driver parked next to my car and got out. I blinked in surprise. It was Carter. What was he doing here?

He went around to the passenger side, presumably to open the door, but before he could get there, the door opened and a woman got out on her own. She was tall with curly brown hair. While she wasn't exactly overweight, she's what I would call sturdy. Carter said something to her and she laughed so loud, I could hear it through the glass of the lobby windows. If this was Carter's sickly wife, she hid her illness well.

They crossed the parking lot together and stepped onto the sidewalk. He said something again and pointed toward the lobby. She nodded and waited on the sidewalk while he headed to the door. I was standing in the corner, partly obscured by the ficus, when he walked in.

"Excuse me," he said to Gordon, "I'm looking for—" He broke off when he caught sight of me. With a sharp intake of breath, he marched over to where I stood. "You better watch it," he snarled, "or I'll sue you for harassment."

Criminy. What did I do this time?

Chapter 28

Ever the professional, I stepped out from behind the ficus and faced Carter. "Is there a problem, sir?"

"The problem is that you're following me." He was so close I could smell the wine on his breath. "Are you going to show up everywhere my wife and I go in some pathetic attempt to scare me into paying you? I already told you, Miss Johnson. I won't be blackmailed."

"You need to get over yourself." Wow, that sounded like something Ashlee would say. In fact, she'd said that exact thing to me. More than once. I pointed to the embroidered part of my work shirt that announced the name of Esther's place. "I'm not following you. I work here."

He squinted at my shirt. "What?"

Gordon came around the counter, fiddling with his pinkie ring. Even if he hadn't heard the threat, he must have sensed Carter was angry. He said, "Is there something I can assist with?" at the same moment Carter's wife entered the lobby from outside and said, "Everything all right, honey?"

Carter turned to his wife. "Everything's fine, Patty. I was merely asking for directions to the spa."

Mostly because I felt like being a pill after Carter's little outburst, I said, "I'd be happy to show you where it is."

Carter threw me a sharp glance. I smiled back.

"That's very nice of you," Patty said.

"My pleasure." I stepped around Carter, who had me penned in the corner, and strolled to the door. "If you'll follow me . . ."

I went outside and held the door open for Carter and his wife. Carter continued to cast suspicious glances in my direction, but I pretended not to notice. We started down the sidewalk toward the vegetable garden.

"I'm guessing this is your first time here?" I said.

"Yes," Patty said. "I usually don't pamper myself at spas, but Carter decided to spoil me with a gift certificate for our wedding anniversary."

"How nice," I said, trying not to let my knowledge of his affair color my response. "How long have you two been married?"

"Fifteen years," Patty said with a touch of pride as we turned onto the path that led past the vegetable garden. Carter remained silent. "To this day, my father says Carter married me for my trust fund, but I say you don't stick around that many years only for the money."

Well, maybe not *only* for the money. I snuck a peek at Carter, who was studiously avoiding my gaze while he tugged at his shirt collar.

"Fifteen years is an awfully long time," I agreed. "I'm actually about to get married myself."

Patty slapped me on the back like we were sailor buddies at a bar, and I almost stumbled. Apparently she wasn't that sick.

"Congratulations," Patty said. "I'm sure your marriage will be as good as ours. I know Carter and I have plenty of years ahead of us."

This time, it was me who avoided Carter's eyes. "And I hope those years are full of good times and good health." Hey, that wasn't half bad. Maybe I'd suggest it to Gordon for his wedding toast.

"I'm sure they will be. Carter's too refined to get sick, and I come from hearty Midwest stock." She let out a bellowing laugh as if to prove her vitality. "Isn't that right, honey?"

"Yes, dear," Carter said.

I'd been almost positive he'd been feeding Phoebe a line about his wife being too sick to divorce. If Patty suffered from anything, it was from being too trusting.

She stopped on the path and pointed to a bush. "Is this a Blue Blossom?"

"Um, I think so." I was pretty sure that's what Zennia had told me once.

She turned to Carter, her face alight with excitement. "We'll have to return here in late spring. The plant is beautiful when it's blooming."

"Yes, of course," Carter said. "I'll mark it in my calendar."

It was all I could do not to stare at Carter. I was having a hard time reconciling this meek man with the guy who usually insisted on control in any situation.

"I'm a big flower buff," Patty told me. "I can't get

enough of them." We resumed walking toward the spa, with me leading and Carter and Patty right behind.

"It's unfortunate you weren't with me the other day," Carter said. "I saw the most exotic flower with petals that were yellow at the base and edges, but the rest was a deep red. It almost looked as if the flower was on fire. I've never seen anything quite like it."

Patty put a hand to her chest. "That sounds gorgeous."

"I've seen a flower like that somewhere," I said, trying to remember if it was here at the farm so I could show Patty.

"Hey! Wait up!" I heard a voice call behind me. I turned around and saw Violet hurrying down the path, a cardboard box in her hands.

Beside me, Carter flinched. "You gotta be kidding me," he muttered.

I almost laughed. This must be his worst nightmare. Here was the only other woman, besides Phoebe, of course, who might know about Carter's affair, providing Bethany had shared her secret with Violet.

She caught up to us, slightly out of breath. "The man at the desk said I'd find you out here." She looked at Carter and Patty. "Hi, Mr. Hawking. I didn't mean to interrupt."

Patty raised her eyebrows and turned to Carter.

He nodded at Violet. "This is Violet Lancaster. She runs the Don't Dilly-Dahlia flower shop, after her mother's untimely demise."

Violet set the box on the ground and held out

her hand. Patty gave it a vigorous pump. "Sorry to hear about your mother," Patty said. "I have to tell you that the roses from your shop are absolutely amazing. Receiving a bouquet of those wonderful blooms is the highlight of my week."

"Thank you so much," Violet said, "though my mother deserves all the credit. She ran the shop for twenty years and ferreted out the best flower suppliers in the business. I've simply inherited what she set up with her hard work and determination."

I listened to Violet's impassioned response. If I hadn't known better, I'd have said she loved the flower business.

"I'm glad to hear you'll be carrying on with the shop. I don't know what my husband would do without it."

"He's one of my best customers," Violet said.

Carter tugged at his collar again. "Yes, well, we'd better get to your spa appointment, dear. We don't want to be late."

I nodded toward the spa, which was within easy view on the path. "It's right there. I can escort you if you'd like."

Carter grimaced. "That won't be necessary."

"Fine. Enjoy your afternoon," I said.

Carter and Patty continued up the path, and I turned to Violet, glad to have the chance to talk to her alone. I found her watching the departing couple.

"That's not how I pictured Carter's wife," she said. "I expected her to be more, I don't know, high maintenance, maybe."

"She certainly seems down to earth," I said.

"I never did figure out why he always ordered her two separate bouquets of roses each week. I never asked, because it's none of my business, but that costs a lot of money."

So Violet didn't know about Bethany's blackmailing hobby after all. I wouldn't be the one to tell her either. "Maybe one was for home and one was for her work," I said.

"Maybe. Although he did just cut his order to only one bouquet recently." She shrugged. "I'm not going to worry about it."

I picked up the cardboard box. "Are these the bows?"

Violet nodded. "I found a bunch of different sizes, so I threw them all in."

"I can't tell you how much I appreciate this, Violet."

I started down the path and she fell into step beside me. Up ahead, Carter and his wife had reached the entrance to the spa, but when Violet and I reached the cabins, I headed left, toward the farmhouse and back patio.

"Have you given any more thought to Mitch's offer?" I asked as a way to get the conversation rolling.

"That's all I've been thinking about. Night and day." Violet wrung her hands. "I promised him an answer in the next two days, but I can't make up my mind."

We came to the picnic tables, and I set the box on one of the tables and sat down on a bench. Violet sat across from me and started chewing on a nail. "When I first got the shop, all I could think about was getting rid of it. I was so sick of working there. I wanted to focus on my writing. But then when I hear how happy people are with their flowers, like Mr. Hawking's wife, I can see why my mom loved the shop so much."

"Still, it's a huge commitment, especially if you don't love it as much as your mom did."

Violet groaned. "I know, but I feel so guilty about selling the business she loved."

I wondered about the source of the guilt. Was it simply because Violet knew how much pride her mom had had in building up the shop and making it successful? Or did she feel guilty because she'd killed her mom to get out from under her thumb and now regretted it?

Violet slapped her hands on the table, and I jumped.

"You're a big girl, Violet. You'll figure it out," she said to herself. Then she looked at me. "I guess we should take a look around the place. I see what you mean about the farm providing plenty of natural decorations."

We both stood, and I indicated the herb garden near the kitchen door. "This is our herb garden, although the bushes aren't nearly as vibrant this time of year."

We wandered around the area, with Violet sniffing the occasional plant. After a few minutes, we walked back over to the gazebo, where the ceremony would be taking place in only two days. My stomach did a flip-flop at the thought.

"How exactly will everything be set up?" Violet asked as she eyed the expanse of patio.

I pointed. "Jason and I will stand with the minister near the hedge. We have a lattice archway we'll be putting up. My boss found some ribbon that we'll tie to the posts and weave through the latticework. We're going to shove the two picnic tables out of the way and set up the folding chairs with those bows, thanks to you. A strip of white cloth will run down between the two rows of chairs to create an aisle."

"Sounds lovely," Violet said. "Why don't we look around a little more? I'm sure this place is packed with wildflowers. Maybe I could add some to your bouquets to tie everything together."

Once more, it occurred to me that Violet might not make a bad flower shop owner after all. "Great idea," I said. "Let's go back out to the vegetable garden where you met up with me earlier. I saw some flowers over there."

We went past the guest cabins, hung a right, and stopped to look at a variety of wildflowers growing nearby. Violet walked off the path, muttering to herself. "Hmm . . . I don't know. The colors are too vivid. I was hoping for something with softer tones."

"I see a lot of wildflowers when I'm walking around the back of the property," I said.

Violet came over to me, close enough to make me uncomfortable. "Can we take a look?"

I paused, unease washing through me. For someone who professed to only be hanging on to the flower shop to honor her mother, Violet was awfully enthusiastic all of a sudden. And what kind of florist made house calls anyway? She'd insisted on driving the box of bows out here instead of me picking them up. Was this some sort of trap to get me alone? Why hadn't I wondered about that before?

Violet frowned. "Is something wrong?"

"I'm surprised, is all. You seem so interested in looking at all these flowers, but I didn't think you wanted to be in the family business."

"I'm surprised myself. But this is fun. Hunting down the right blooms, searching for the perfect colors. It's almost like being a detective. A flower detective."

She seemed so sincere, I felt a pang of guilt for questioning her motives. But I wasn't a total idiot.

"You know, now that I think about it, last time I was out that way, all the flowers were gone. But I saw a few plants over by the pigsty." While the pigsty wasn't exactly as busy as someplace like the San Francisco airport, it was a lot better than the isolated woods on the backside of Esther's farm.

"Sure. We can look there."

I led her over to where Wilbur was lolling in the mud with the other pigs, and pointed out a few groupings of wildflowers that I'd noticed when I'd visited the sty earlier in the week. While she looked at the flowers, I leaned over the fence and chatted with Wilbur. He flicked his tail a few times in response but didn't bother to come over and see me. Maybe he knew I was going away and was giving me the cold shoulder. My mom's cat used to do the same thing whenever the family went on vacation.

"I'll only be in Hawaii a few days," I told him. "You won't even have time to miss me."

"What's that?" Violet asked as she joined me at the fence.

I nodded to the cluster of pigs. "I was just talking to Wilbur here." I realized how ridiculous that sounded and felt my face flush. "Never mind."

Violet smiled. "I talk to my goldfish all the time. My mom never did understand why. Guess I don't have to worry about that anymore." She gazed at the pigs, her mind seemingly a million miles away.

I'd been planning to wait until we got back to the farmhouse before I asked her about the day her mom died, but standing here with nothing but the pigs for company and no interruptions, now seemed like the perfect time.

"Violet, I need to talk to you about something."

She tore her focus from the pigs. "What?" she asked slowly.

I took a deep breath. "I could have sworn you said you didn't go to the flower shop the day your mom was killed."

Her head snapped back. "That's because I didn't."

"But someone saw you there that day."

She squeezed her hands into fists. "Who told you that?"

I scrambled around in my mind for a suitable answer, not wanting to put Esther in a potentially awkward position, if she ever bought flowers from Violet. "What difference does it make?"

"I want to know," she said.

She took a deep breath as if getting ready for something, and my whole body tensed. I wasn't sure whether she was about to lunge at me . . . or run.

Chapter 29

"Who told you I was there that day?" Violet repeated. Her eyes darted around, as if the witness might be lurking behind one of the hedges, ready to jump out and point an accusing finger her way.

"It's not important who told me, just that someone saw you there. Is it true?"

Violet's hand flew to her mouth. She started gnawing on her fingernail. "I only stopped in for a minute."

Every nerve in my body lit up. Finally, we were getting somewhere.

"What for?"

"Why do you need to know?" Violet asked, a pleading tone creeping into her voice. "It doesn't make any difference why I stopped by. I didn't kill my mom."

I didn't say anything. From the strained expression on Violet's face, she seemed to be fighting an internal battle with herself.

She released a heavy sigh and dropped her hand.

"I forgot my sunglasses, okay? I stopped by to get them."

My eyebrows shot up. Surely I'd heard her wrong. "That's it? You lied about picking up your sunglasses?"

"Gah! You don't get it." Violet let out a strange grunting noise that made Wilbur's ears perk up.

Rising to his feet, he trotted over to the fence and stuck his nose through the rails. He nudged Violet's hand. She snatched it back, but then looked at Wilbur with his upturned snout and wagging curlicue tail and reached out to pat him.

I leaned against the top rail. "Maybe you could explain it to me."

"I was on my way to meet some actor friends in the park. I told you how I'd been secretly writing at night, but I wanted to see my script in action. Make sure I was getting the emotions right, that the scene would play out like it did in my mind. When I stopped by the shop, I made the mistake of telling my mom where I was going. She immediately got on my case about how I was wasting my time with this writing nonsense, as she liked to call it. Said my place was at the flower shop with her." She paused and patted Wilbur again. "We started arguing. I said some things I shouldn't have. I even told her I was quitting."

Wow. Good for Violet. I'd gotten the impression she never stood up to her mom, but apparently, given the right incentive, she did have a backbone. "What did Bethany say when you told her that?"

Violet scowled. "She laughed at me. Acted like my idea of being a professional writer was some big joke. But when she saw how serious I was, she started in on the guilt. Told me what an ingrate I was. How she'd given me a job when I was down on my luck, and that I owed her. By the end, we were both yelling at each other."

So Nicole at the ice cream shop hadn't overheard me talking to Bethany. She'd heard an honest-to-goodness argument between Violet and her mom. That fight could have been the precursor to Bethany's murder.

Wilbur wandered down to where I stood and waited for me to pet him since Violet had stopped. I obliged, scratching behind one of his ears. "So that's why you didn't admit you were at the shop."

"How could I? Sure, the fight happened hours before my mom was killed, but the detective would probably think I went back later to shoot her."

"You don't have an alibi for when your mom died?" I asked. Maybe the detective had good reason to be suspicious.

She shook her head. "I spent the afternoon at the park, then went home to revise my script. Whenever I had a day off, I usually worked on my writing. I was alone in the house all evening until a neighbor called to tell me about the emergency vehicles at the shop."

Her story made sense. And I could understand why Violet would hesitate to tell the detective about the argument with her mom. Still, wouldn't she want to tell him everything she could to help find her mom's killer? Unless this story was one giant fabrication. She was a writer, after all.

I looked around and licked my lips, noticing how

alone we were out here. Even this close to the house, I hadn't seen another living soul the entire time we'd been talking.

Trying not to be obvious, I sidled away from the pigpen and toward the path. When I felt my shoes touch the smooth dirt, I started walking backward while talking to Violet, casting the occasional glance behind me to keep from tripping. Violet had done nothing to imply she was dangerous, other than chopping off a bunch of flower heads in her shop, but why press my luck?

"Now that you've explained everything, I can understand why you didn't want to talk to the detective. That argument does make it look like you had a reason to hurt your mom—" Wait, should I have said that? "But I'm sure he knows what a nice person you are," I added.

Violet watched me walk backward with a puzzled look on her face. After a moment's hesitation, she followed me. I only needed to lead her to the back patio, where the farmhouse—and Zennia and Gordon—were within easy reach.

"I know I should tell him the truth," Violet said, "but I've waited so long, I'm worried it'll make me look worse."

I reached the redwood tree on the edge of the patio, turned, and stepped through the gap in the bushes. Safe at last.

"Nonsense," I said. "It's better to tell the detective later than not at all."

Violet stepped onto the patio after me and chewed on another nail. "I suppose you're right, but I don't want to get in any trouble."

I heard a noise behind me and glanced over my shoulder. Gordon was coming out one of the French doors from the dining room.

With him so close, I turned to Violet and said all in a rush, "I'm glad you feel that way because I convinced the person who saw you downtown to call Detective Palmer this morning, and you'll want to call him as soon as possible to tell him your side of things."

Violet only had time to say, "What?" and clap a hand over her mouth before Gordon reached us. If he noticed Violet's pale face and startled expression, he showed no reaction.

"Good, I see your friend was able to locate you," he said to me.

"Yes, thanks for pointing her in my direction."

Violet still had her hand covering her mouth, as if trying not to throw up. "I have to go," she mumbled between her fingers, not looking at either of us. She darted off in the direction of the parking lot.

Gordon twisted one of his pinkie rings. "Was it something I said?"

"No, more like something she didn't say." Whoo-hoo, wasn't I the witty one today?

"Okay, whatever. I need to check with Gretchen about her work schedule. Excuse me."

With Gordon on his way to the spa and Violet out of sight, I headed to the back door. In the kitchen, Zennia was pulling a tray out of the oven. She set it on top of the stove and removed her oven mitts.

I caught a whiff of cheesy goodness, and my mouth watered. "What is that?"

She smiled. "I call them golden cheese rounds, for lack of a better name. I put them alongside my salads on occasion when I want a special treat and thought I'd make a small batch for the guests this afternoon. If they like them, I can serve some at your wedding and top them with microgreens or perhaps sour cream and chives."

I reached for one but stopped. "Wait. Are these made with actual cheese? Or some sort of weird healthy version?" Just because I was trying to eat better didn't mean I wanted to do it all the time, especially where cheese was involved.

Zennia swatted me with an oven mitt. "I already told you, for your special day, I won't hold back on the butter or cheese for one or two dishes."

"I'm so glad to hear that." I grabbed a cheese round off the tray and popped it in my mouth. The crispy disc burned my tongue, but the decadent flavor more than made up for the pain. "Delicious. Better than your stuffed mushrooms, even."

Esther came into the kitchen. Her eyes fell on the cookie sheet, and she made a beeline for the stove. "What have you got there?" She tried one and let out a moan of pleasure. "My goodness these are yummy. They'd be a real hit at my Bunco games."

"I can always give you the recipe. There are only three ingredients." Zennia gestured to the tray. "Have another one."

Esther eyed the rounds as if considering it, but then shook her head. "I really shouldn't." She turned to me. "Dana, is there any chance you could clean out the pigsty this afternoon? I have some errands to run, so I'm afraid I won't have time to do it myself."

I suppressed a sigh. From cheese rounds to pigsties. Not quite how I'd envisioned my afternoon, but work was work, after all. "Yes, I can do it. Wilbur was just giving me a hard time about how I'm leaving him for a few days, so maybe this will get me back in his good graces."

Zennia raised her eyebrows. "How exactly does a pig give someone a hard time?"

"I could see it in his eyes. They spoke volumes."

Esther laughed. "It's a good thing you're going on your honeymoon. Sounds like you need some time off."

I wagged my finger at her. "Don't say I didn't warn you when he goes on a food strike."

I resisted the urge to grab another cheese round and went out the back door to the tool shed. I grabbed the broom, rake, and shovel, slipped on the boots that always waited near the sty, and stepped inside the pen. Thanks to the rain, the outside area had already turned muddy, and I had to step carefully to avoid slipping. I'd had more than a few accidents when cleaning out the sty, and I didn't feel like having another one today.

As I shoveled out the old straw and shavings, I thought about my talk with Violet. She'd provided a decent reason for lying to Detective Palmer. I'd been in an absolute panic when the detective had thought I'd been arguing with Bethany, and I barely even knew the woman. Here, Violet was her own daughter, someone who stood to gain from her mother's death. If the fight had been as big and loud as she claimed, no wonder she'd lied.

I finished shoveling and grabbed the hose. Wilbur and the other pigs watched from the sidelines as I continued my musings.

A big argument might also explain why Violet was so conflicted about selling the shop. She'd finally gotten up the guts to tell her mom she quit; then her mom was murdered only hours later. That would definitely make me think twice about selling the store my mother had poured her heart and soul into. But again, she might also hesitate to sell if she'd killed her mom and regretted it. Talking to Violet hadn't cleared up nearly as much as I'd hoped.

I squirted water into the far corner of the pen. The water bounced off the boards, raising a spray of droplets into the air.

Maybe Violet would decide to keep the business after all. She'd certainly seemed excited when she'd been walking around the farm with me. She wouldn't get to work on outdoor weddings every day, but surely enough people got married in Blossom Valley to keep her busy. Then again, she didn't seem that enthused about the flowers themselves, certainly not as much as someone like Carter's wife.

While I had the hose out, I moved over to the water trough. The pigs tended to keep the area clean, but I liked to spray any extra gunk out. I aimed the nozzle and targeted the very bottom of the trough while I continued to think.

Carter's wife had been nothing like I'd expected. I'd pictured a frail, fussy debutante who didn't lift a finger to help herself. Instead, Patty was a strong, vibrant woman who clearly didn't need coddling. After meeting her and seeing how friendly she was, I had to wonder why Carter was cheating on her. But then, why did any guy cheat?

I turned off the hose and rolled it up, then returned to the tool shed to drag over a new bag of shavings. As I backed into the pen, I kept an eye on Wilbur and his pals, but none looked as if they were about to make a break for it, or even stand up for that matter.

I tried to tear open the bag with my hands, but gave up and went back to the tool shed. I found the pair of old scissors Esther kept there and returned to the pen. I cut open the bag, set the scissors on a fence post, and started spreading the shavings around.

One piece stood out among the paler shavings. It was a dark red color, much like the color of the flower Carter had mentioned to his wife. He must have been talking about Bethany's fire lily.

A shiver ran up my spine. How had he even seen the flower? When Bethany had shown it to me, she'd mentioned it had arrived that very day and she was keeping it in the back room away from customers. Had Bethany shown Carter the flower as well, since he was a regular? But I'd seen him pick up his weekly flowers a couple of days later from Violet. If he always picked up his roses on the same day, he wouldn't have needed to stop by the shop the day Bethany died.

I shook my head, dismissing the thought. Seeing a rare flower didn't make a man guilty of murder.

He might have gone to Bethany's shop that day for another reason, perhaps to send flowers to a sick coworker or something. Even so, when I finished up here, maybe I'd call Detective Palmer. Every little bit of information could help his case.

I hurriedly finished my work, anxious to get in the house and to my phone. When I'd dumped out the last of the shavings, I gathered up the empty bags, my mind already on my call to the detective. I turned to head out of the pen and froze, feeling as if my heart might stop.

Carter was waiting for me at the gate, a calculating expression on his face.

I might be in some trouble here.

Chapter 30

My breath caught in my throat. Panic fluttered in my chest. I told myself to calm down. Carter wasn't a mind reader. He couldn't possibly know I was planning to call Detective Palmer about the flower.

I forced myself to speak, in case he wasn't already suspicious of what I knew. "Hi, Carter. Where's Patty? Finishing up at the spa?"

He stared at me, stone-faced. "Yes, I wanted to talk to you privately."

"Me?" I asked, my voice an octave higher than usual. "About what?"

He let himself into the pen. I watched as his shiny black dress shoes sank into the soft mud.

"You'll ruin those shoes," I said.

Carter glanced down, his face still expressionless. "I can buy more."

He stopped a few feet away and leveled his gaze at me once more, causing my stomach to twist into a knot. "I realize you might know more than you should."

"Me?" I said again.

He edged closer, and I shifted back, my mind racing. Was Gordon at the spa with Gretchen? Was Zennia in the house? Was anyone close enough to help me?

"You saw that flower in Bethany's back room," he said.

I felt like a swarm of insects was crawling up my back. I suppressed a shudder. "That's right. I'd forgotten where I'd seen it," I lied.

"Bethany's place is the only flower shop in town. You couldn't have seen it anywhere else. And you know I saw the flower, too."

Carter was way too concerned about the lily. That didn't bode well for his involvement in Bethany's murder. Or for my safety at this very minute.

I tried to placate him. "Bethany showed it to me when I stopped in that day. Just like she must have shown you, too." Maybe he'd seize on my offered excuse and go away. But in case he didn't, I took a step back. I didn't have much space before I bumped up against the water trough, but every inch of distance helped.

"Even though you knew about my relationship with Phoebe, I was willing to let it go," Carter said. His gaze never wavered, increasing my anxiety. "After all, you don't come across as the blackmailing type, so I trusted you not to tell my wife."

I nodded. "I already promised you I wouldn't. You have nothing to worry about." But *I* clearly did.

"I have a very comfortable lifestyle. One I'm not willing to give up, especially after all the years I've had to kiss up to my wife to make sure she kept me around. You know too much, and I can't risk you telling anyone else."

I spread my hands. "I don't know anything." But then I realized I did. Phoebe had complained about how Carter had stood her up for the first time ever on Friday night. I hadn't been paying attention at the time, but Friday was the same night Bethany had been killed. Add to that the fact he'd seen the fire lily in the back room, and there was a good chance Carter didn't show up for his date because he was busy killing Bethany.

While these thoughts swirled around my head, my focus on Carter wavered. Before I could react, he lunged at me. I jumped back, but not before he managed to give me a small shove. My foot hit a patch of mud and slid out from under me. I fell backward, banging my spine on the water trough as I landed on my butt.

I pushed off with my hands in an effort to stand, but Carter crouched down and grabbed my shoulders before I could. He heaved me sideways. I found myself flat on my back, staring up at the gray overcast sky, a grim setting that matched the look on Carter's face as he loomed into view.

He threw himself down in the muck, straddling me. His thighs pressed in from the sides, pinning my arms. He gripped my throat with both hands and squeezed.

In a panic, I managed to wrench out one arm, bringing globs of mud with me. I tried to pull out my other arm, but Carter tightened his hold with his knees. I yanked again and my arm flew free.

I beat at his chest and clawed at his hands. He

shifted his hands for a better grip, and I managed to suck in a tiny bit of air. I tried to scratch at his eyes, but his face was just out of reach. I twisted and arched my back, but he was too heavy. Under his unrelenting weight, my legs were useless.

"I told you to stay out of it," Carter hissed, the pressure on my throat increasing as he readjusted his grip, "but you're as bad as Bethany. Which means I have to kill you, too."

Black dots filled my vision. My lungs screamed for air. How much longer could I hold on?

I heard the pigs squealing behind me. Did they understand what was happening? Did they know I was about to die? That I'd miss the chance to spend my life with Jason?

I felt my strength wane. In a last-ditch effort, I clenched my right hand into a fist and swung it up, hoping to clip Carter's chin. Instead, I connected with his Adam's apple, leaving a streak of mud across it.

He gagged. I felt his grip on my throat ease a fraction. I grabbed a mouthful of air and brought my arm up again, connecting with the same spot, only harder this time. He coughed, and his hands flew to his own throat.

With the pressure gone from my neck, I greedily sucked in breath after breath. I felt like I would never get enough. But I couldn't enjoy the moment. I had to get Carter off of me.

I shook my head to clear my vision as Carter reached for me. I blocked him with my forearms, but he lunged forward again. We grappled, and I was able to lift my shoulders a few inches off the ground. I drove one fist toward his family jewels. I couldn't tell how hard I hit him, but it was enough. Carter let out a grunt and jerked back.

I used the sudden freedom to sit up. I tried to wriggle my legs out from under Carter's body, but he was too heavy. What was I going to do?

"Help!" I screamed. "Somebody help!" I grabbed fistfuls of mud and flung them at Carter's face.

He tried to bat the mud away. His face turned purple with rage. "Shut up!"

He stretched toward me, hands shaped like claws. I shrank back, but I had nowhere to go. As long as my legs were trapped, I was stuck.

I heard a powerful snort from a corner of the pen and then the pounding of hooves. Carter's head whipped toward the sound, and his eyes widened as Wilbur barreled toward him. With his head down and nostrils flaring, the pig butted Carter in the side.

Carter let out a loud "oomph" and fell off of me. In the corner of the sty, the rest of the pigs squealed and grunted.

I drew my legs in, rolled over, and pushed myself into a crouch. I unsteadily rose to my feet as Carter did the same. Patches of his white dress shirt shone through a thick layer of mud. The goop was in his hair and smeared across one cheek. His pants were covered. I didn't need to check to know I looked the exact same.

I glanced at the gate. On the post sat the scissors I'd used to cut open the bag of shavings. I returned my attention to Carter. His shoulders were up, and he held his arms out. He looked like a wrestler about to take down an opponent.

Wilbur sneezed. Carter's attention flew to the pig, no doubt fearing a repeat attack. I used the momentary distraction to run for the gate. Even with the slick mud, the tread on the work boots gave me enough traction.

Behind me, Carter growled. I looked over my shoulder and saw him charge. At the first step, his dress shoes slid out from under him, and he fell straight toward me.

I tried to hop to the side but couldn't lift my feet high enough with the boots on. His hand closed around one ankle, and he pulled.

I went down.

With one hand still gripping my ankle, Carter latched on to my shin with his other hand. He started to pull me toward him. I slid easily in the mud. I dug my fingers into the muck, but it did nothing to slow my progress. A trail of fingermarks formed in my wake as I kept sliding toward Carter.

His hands moved up my leg and closed around my knee. I pulled my other leg toward my waist and then kicked out with all my might.

A tremor shot through me as my foot made solid contact with his face. Carter howled, and I kicked him again.

I staggered to my feet and lumbered over to the post. I snatched up the scissors and whirled around.

Carter stood on his knees in the middle of the pen, one hand on his nose. Blood streamed out from under his fingers.

I pointed the scissors at him. "Don't come any closer."

Over my shoulder, I heard Gordon's voice, clearly agitated. "What's going on? Dana, are you all right?"

Carter swore and dropped back on his heels. He spit in the mud.

"Dana, what's happening?" Gordon asked again.

With Carter clearly defeated, I risked a peek at Gordon and grinned. "Wilbur just saved my life."

Chapter 31

Two days later, I stood before a full-length mirror in Esther's bedroom and smoothed down my wedding dress over my midriff. I leaned in to see how visible the marks on my throat from Carter's attack were, but Brittany had done a phenomenal job covering them with makeup.

"Don't worry. No one can tell that psycho almost strangled you in the pigpen," Ashlee said.

Brittany giggled.

Mom tsked. "Let's not talk about what happened. We only want good thoughts today." She fussed with my veil.

"Dana didn't have the life squeezed out of her," Ashlee said. "That *is* a good thought."

Mom glowered at her. "You know what I mean." She stepped back and clasped her hands together. Pride and fondness were written clearly across her face as she studied me. "My little girl, all grown up. I only wish your father were here to see you walk down the aisle."

My throat instantly narrowed, and my nose burned. "Please don't make me cry. It makes my face blotchy, and I'd hate to get married with a blotchy face." I'd kept my tone light, but I, too, wished my father could be here.

The door to Esther's bedroom inched open, and Esther squeezed inside before hastily shutting it. "Can't let anyone see the bride before your big moment."

"Thanks, Esther." I was fairly sure no one else was upstairs, but I appreciated the thought.

She looked at my reflection in the mirror and pressed her hands to her mouth. "Don't you look beautiful? I'm so thankful you were able to escape from Carter. To think that man murdered Bethany." She shook her head.

So much for not talking about Carter. I tucked in a piece of hair that had escaped the bun. "He told the police it was an accident. Said Bethany demanded more blackmail money, they started to argue, and he grabbed the gun from the shelf on impulse. He was only trying to scare her. He never intended to shoot her."

Ashlee rolled her eyes. "He's probably going to plead temporary insanity, like they do on TV. He is a lawyer after all."

I shrugged. "Possibly. He must have known Bethany could blackmail him for years, with or without Phoebe in the picture, so maybe he saw a way out. We'll probably never know for sure."

In the mirror's reflection, I saw Mom shiver. "I'm

glad he didn't kill you the moment he found out you knew about the affair."

"Good thing I gave him that fake name when we first met. He really had no way to find me."

Mom pointed a finger at me in the mirror, and I turned around to face her. "This is exactly why I don't like you playing detective. It's too dangerous."

I laughed. "Look who's talking. You wanted to take Mitch on a date strictly so you could question him about Bethany's death. If he'd been the killer, you could have really put yourself in harm's way."

Mom laid a hand on my arm and leaned in. "Speaking of Mitch, I forgot to tell you that when I learned Carter was the killer, I called up Mitch and invited him to be my date for today. I hope that's all right. The mother of the bride needs a dance partner."

"Doesn't it bother you that he's been lying to his customers about where his ice cream comes from?" I asked.

"Of course, but we talked about it. He admits he made some poor decisions when his business ran into trouble, but he's promised to start making his own ice cream again. He never felt right about the deception."

"In that case, I'm delighted Mitch will be joining you. He seems like a decent enough guy."

"Yeah, Mom, he's not half bad," Ashlee said. "Plus, I bet he gives you free ice cream. Maybe even your family members." She winked.

Mom ducked her head, as if embarrassed to be talking about her dating life. "I don't know which of us will be happier today. Me, because my oldest daughter is getting married, or Mitch, because Violet has agreed to sell him the flower shop."

I smiled. Finding her mom's killer must have given Violet the closure she needed. "That's wonderful. For both of them. Mitch can expand his shop like he's always wanted, and Violet will have the money to focus on her writing."

"Yes, and Mitch received approval for his business loan, which will help him make all the changes he wants. It's a win-win for everyone," Mom said. She turned to Ashlee. "Who's your date for today?"

"Logan. We've gone out a bunch of times."

I opened my mouth in mock surprise. "Wow, he made it past the third date? That's quite the commitment for you."

Ashlee stuck her tongue out. "Knock it off. He's not even as hot as most of the guys I go out with. But there's something different about him. I can't figure out what."

She looked genuinely confused, and Mom and I exchanged a knowing look. "Sounds like he might be the one," Mom said. I'd swear I heard Esther giggle, followed by Brittany.

Ashlee let out a groan. "I barely know the guy." She tilted her head. "But, you know, if things work out with him, it wouldn't be the end of the world."

Wow. Who was this woman? She couldn't be my sister.

"We should double date," Brittany said. "That's what Lucia and I did one time when some guy asked her out who she didn't know too well. Hey, we could triple date!" She giggled again.

"How is Lucia?" I asked.

Brittany wiggled her hand back and forth to indicate she was so-so. "She told the police about that lady she ran over."

Mom flinched. "What's this?"

"She ran into some lady on her bike and hurt her back or something," Brittany said. "She's working with the public defender. He said that since she's a first-time offender, she might end up with community service rather than jail time. If that happens, she could probably go back to school next semester."

"Good for Lucia," I said. "I hope things work out for her."

A knock sounded on the door. Esther rushed over and opened it a crack. When she saw who it was, she swung the door wider. Gordon stood on the other side of the threshold in a black tuxedo, his combed-back, oiled hair almost as shiny as his wingtip shoes.

I felt tears prick my eyes. With my father gone, Gordon was the perfect replacement to walk me down the aisle. I checked the cow clock on the wall. It was time.

I looked at my reflection once more, touching the corners of my mouth to make sure my lipstick hadn't smeared.

"You look good," Ashlee said. "Don't mess it up."

Gordon cleared his throat, looking decidedly uncomfortable. "I must say, you do look lovely."

"Well, thank you, Gordon." I almost curtsied but

stopped myself in time. "I guess this is it." I gave Mom and Esther a quick hug. Both instantly reached into the sleeves of their dresses and pulled out tissues.

"We'd better get down there," Mom said to Esther. They hurried past Gordon and out the door. Brittany and Ashlee followed.

Gordon held out his arm, and I hooked mine through his. He escorted me down the stairs, through the hall, and across the empty dining room. Ashlee waited near the door, her bouquet at the ready.

Beyond the French doors, I could see friends and family waiting on the patio. After my little run-in with Carter, Esther and Zennia had stepped up and decorated the patio for me, while Violet had added the bows she'd promised. Even through the glass, I could see that everything looked perfect.

Gordon poked his head out the door and spoke quietly to Zennia, who stood nearby. She gave a little tug on the leash in her hand, and Wilbur popped into view.

I had no idea how she'd managed to get a leash on him, let alone the little bow tie he now sported, but after all that had happened, I'd decided Wilbur deserved a spot in my wedding. Since I didn't know any little girls the right age to be the flower girl, I'd given Wilbur the role of flower pig.

The wedding march started to play. Wilbur picked up a basket of flowers with his snout and trotted down the aisle, Zennia by his side. A murmur rose up from the guests. A few pointed at Wilbur, while others laughed.

Ashlee leaned toward me. "Last chance to ditch Jason and keep loving the single life."

"No, thanks. I think I'm going to love the married life way more."

"You could do a lot worse than Jason, that's for sure." She headed out the door.

I felt my stomach do a flip-flop. I gently lifted my own bouquet from a nearby table, held it before me, and walked with Gordon out the door. The guests rose. In true Gordon fashion, the walk down the aisle was brisk and efficient.

Jason waited at the end, looking more handsome in his tux than I'd ever seen him. Gordon released my arm, the two men shook hands, and then Jason took my hands in his. The minister started speaking, but I had trouble following his words. The first part of the ceremony was a blur.

But when he got to the part where he asked if I took Jason as my lawfully wedded husband, I looked straight into Jason's warm green eyes and smiled. "I do."

The minister said a few more words and checked to see if anyone had any objections to Jason and me getting married. I half expected Ashlee to speak up, but when she didn't, the minister nodded to Jason. "You may now kiss the bride."

Jason and I leaned toward each other and engaged in a kiss that brought a round of clapping and one wolf whistle. I felt myself blush as we broke apart, and I glanced at Mom, slightly embarrassed. She smiled at me, dabbing at her eyes with her handkerchief. I smiled back.

Together, Jason and I walked back up the aisle

and into the dining room, managing to steal one more kiss before everyone crowded in behind us. Esther and Zennia immediately made a beeline for the kitchen to retrieve the hors d'oeuvres, while the photographer ushered the wedding party down the hall to the lobby to start the picture-taking.

When my cheeks started aching from all the smiling, I leaned toward Jason. "I think we have enough pictures. Shall we go spend time with our guests?"

"Whatever you say, Mrs. Forrester," he said with a wink.

We thanked the photographer and headed back to the dining room. As soon as Gordon saw us enter, he stood up from his seat at one of the tables. I didn't recognize the woman beside him. She wore a business jacket and had her hair pulled back in a bun so severe that the skin at her temples was stretched taut. She looked like she was attending a conference rather than a wedding. I knew immediately that she must be Gordon's date.

Gordon tapped his wineglass with a spoon, and I focused my attention back on him. He cleared his throat.

"I'd like to propose a toast." He tilted his glass in my direction. "When Dana first asked me to walk her down the aisle, I'd thought I'd misheard her. After all, our working relationship has been rocky at times, what with her tendency to take long lunches, especially when she decides to play amateur detective."

A few people in the crowd laughed nervously.

Good grief. This was his speech?

"But after considering the request, I came to realize that Dana and I have developed a much closer relationship over these past few years. I've come to trust her work ethic and know she can be counted on. I was honored that she considered me an adequate stand-in for her father." Now he tipped his glass toward Jason. "I've been reading Jason's articles in the *Herald* for years, and I already know he's a top-rate reporter. Anyone who takes his job as seriously as this man does will make a world-class husband. I know these two will be happy together for years to come." Gordon raised his glass high. "To the bride and groom."

Everyone in the room raised their own glasses as a chorus of "To the bride and groom" came back. I felt myself choke up a bit and swallowed the lump in my throat. As everyone else took a drink, I whispered into Jason's ear, "I feel like the luckiest person in the world."

He kissed the tip of my nose and whispered back, "Make that the second luckiest."

Then we each took a sip of our champagne, and I silently toasted the first day of the rest of my life.

Tips and Recipes from the O'Connell Organic Farm and Spa

Thanks for joining us once more at the O'Connell Organic Farm and Spa. Here are a few recipes, along with a tip or two, to share with your friends.

Golden Cheese Rounds

Dana has asked me to share my recipe for the golden cheese rounds. While these are not the healthiest appetizers in the world, they're sure to be a crowd-pleaser.

To make the rounds, preheat the oven to 400 degrees and line a cookie sheet with parchment paper. Heat 1/4 cup butter in a microwave-safe bowl at 15-second intervals until the butter has melted. Mix in 1/3 cup flour and 1-1/4 cups of grated sharp cheddar cheese. With your hands, roll the mixture into 1-inch balls and place on the parchment paper. Cook for 10 minutes. Let cool slightly before eating, or you may burn your tongue like poor Dana did!

Mushroom, Spinach, and Mozzarella Panini

While the cheese rounds should be only an occasional treat, these panini are a great healthy lunch choice anytime. Feel free to swap out the vegetables and cheese for any of your favorites. Just make sure to pick a soft cheese that melts well, like Fontina.

To make the panini, heat 1 tablespoon of oil in a large skillet over medium-high heat. Add 8 to 10 ounces of sliced mushrooms and sauté them until they begin to brown. Next, add 3 cups of baby spinach, making sure to remove the thicker stems from the leaves. Once the spinach has started to wilt, add salt and pepper to taste and remove the pan from heat.

Now it's time to assemble the sandwiches. Layer thinly sliced or shredded mozzarella onto a slice of good-quality bread, then add the mushroom and spinach mixture. Top the sandwich with another bread slice and cook in a panini maker according to the manufacturer's directions. If you don't have a panini maker, you can toast the sandwich in a skillet and press another heavy skillet on top of the sandwich, flipping once during cooking to brown both sides. Bon appétit!

Broccoli and Avocado Guacamole

Here is Zennia's go-to guacamole recipe. While avocados contain mostly monounsaturated fats, which are more heart-friendly than other fats, she has swapped some of the avocados for broccoli to lower the overall fat in the guacamole. Plus, the broccoli provides additional vitamins and minerals without sacrificing any of that delicious flavor.

To start, dice up one large ripe avocado and place in a bowl. Add half a cup of raw broccoli florets (no stems) that have been chopped super fine. Add one diced Roma tomato; two tablespoons of red onion, and half a jalapeño, seeded and diced. Next, add two teaspoons of lime juice and two tablespoons of cilantro, chopped. Stir it all together and add salt to taste.

This recipe makes about two cups. Feel free to tinker with the amounts in the recipe. Some of Zennia's friends like spicier guacamole, so they dice up the entire jalapeno, while others like the added punch of more red onion. The sky's the limit!

Cleaning out the Teakettle

Dana here, with my tip for cleaning out the tea kettle. Between the occasional evening cup of tea and the mugs of instant hot chocolate, I use the kettle quite a bit and have noticed floating white bits start to appear in the water after a while and the bottom of the kettle starts to appear dirty. Good news! The kettle could not be easier to clean. Just add a 1:1 ratio of water and white vinegar to the kettle (amounts will vary based on kettle size, but 1-1/2 cups of each usually covers the entire bottom of my kettle) and bring the mixture to a boil. Once it's boiling, turn the burner off and let the liquid sit for twenty minutes. After that, dump out the mixture, rinse the kettle out two or three times with plain water, and the inside of the kettle should be as good as new.

Connect with
Us